ASH·MISTRY
AND THE
WORLD OF DARKNESS

ASH·MISTRY
AND THE
WORLD OF DARKNESS

Sarwat Chadda

HarperCollins *Children's Books*

First published in paperback in Great Britain by HarperCollins Children's Books 2013
HarperCollins *Children's Books* is a division of
HarperCollins*Publishers* Ltd
77-85 Fulham Palace Road, Hammersmith, London W6 8JB

Visit us on the web at
www.harpercollins.co.uk

Visit Sarwat Chadda at
www.sarwatchadda.com

I

ISBN 978-0-00-744735-0

Set in Centaur MT by Palimpsest Book Production Limited,
Falkirk, Stirlingshire
Printed and bound in England by
Clays Ltd, St Ives plc

For my family

Be not entangled in this
world of days and nights;
Thou hast another time
and space as well.

Muhammad Iqbal
poet

Chapter One

Ashoka Mistry tripped over the tree root. A second later he crashed flat on his face, eating leaves as he slid down the muddy slope and landed in a grey, stagnant puddle.

He lay there, in the foul water, groaning.

And this was exactly why he hated cross-country running.

"For heaven's sake, Mistry," said Mr Leach, the PE teacher. "Are you auditioning for the circus or what?" He scampered down the slope, moving with what could only be described as cat-like grace. He finished with a controlled skid that brought him to a perfect stop in front of Ashoka. A few boys clapped.

"Sorry, sir," said Ashoka, slowly sitting up and spitting out leaves.

"Well, get up. Get up."

Ashoka tried to stand, but his shorts were caught on something. "Sir..."

Mr Leach took hold of his arm and pulled.

"Sir!"

The loud, sickening tearing sound made the whole class erupt in laughter.

"Nice underpants," said one of the boys.

"Your mum buy you those, Mistry?" said another.

Ashoka stood ankle-deep in the water, smeared with mud and plastered with leaves, his running shorts bearing a long gash down the back, exposing his limited-edition *Doctor Who* underpants.

Mr Leach sighed then tucked his clipboard under his arm and scrabbled up the slope to where the rest of the class stood waiting. He turned back to Ashoka. "Come on, lad."

Ashoka stared at the steep incline and the long, brown trench he'd left in it. The entire wood was just a sea of mud and here he was, at the bottom. He tried to adjust his shorts but all he got was a longer tear. He clambered up the slope. Or tried to.

The laughter and the snickering and the catcalls he blanked out. They were the same taunts no matter which sport he did. Football, rugby, basketball, gymnastics. If there was a piece of equipment that he could stumble over, he would. But cross-country was a special type of hell. It was bad enough doing laps around the school grounds, but this, out in Dulwich Woods, brought a whole new meaning to the word 'humiliating'. This first run of the year was the worst. The snow had barely melted and the earth was a mixture of freezing puddles, slush and deep, thick mud. Ashoka was not a January sort of person. Now he was going to have to jog

❖

all the way back with his backside hanging out. And that included going past two girls' schools.

"Come on, Ash," urged Josh.

"Ashoka, my name's Ashoka," he muttered under his breath. How many times had he told Josh? He wasn't Ash, not any more.

Gritting his teeth, Ashoka grabbed hold of a fistful of weeds and began hauling himself up. He was going to get to the top, no matter what.

His boots, totally sodden and slick with mud, couldn't get any sort of grip. He slipped to his knees, panting, but still hanging on.

Mr Leach drummed his fingers on his board.

Don't rush. Just get to the top.

His arms ached. His grip weakened. The root was damp with dew. With awful slowness, Ashoka began to slide backwards.

He dug his fingers into the ground, but he was too heavy. Sharp stones scraped his shins and knees, but Ashoka didn't care — he would not fall back. Vainly he tried to find another handhold, but before he knew it he was back at the bottom.

Mr Leach rolled his eyes. "I should have known." He turned to the rest of the class. "What are you lot waiting for? Get back to the school right now." The group of boys began to move off, but not before a few of the wits waved goodbye to Ashoka.

"Don't worry, we'll send a crane for you!"

Mr Leach, hands on hips, gazed down. "Look, Mistry.

Follow the path that way and you'll come to another gate. Go through that and you're back on to Lordship Lane. Got it?"

"Yes, sir."

"Then off you go."

Ashoka stood up and wiped the worst of the mud and leaves and blood off his knees. Jeez, when would this ever end? He was hopeless.

He plodded along towards the gate. The clouds had that fat, grey, swollen look about them and he hoped he'd get back before they finally opened up.

Last. As usual. He was just not built for exercise. Or any sort of physical activity beyond handling a games console.

No, not totally true. He was one of the school's best archers, but then shooting an arrow didn't require much running and jumping. Still, technically it was a sport and he was pretty good at it. So why did they have to torture them with cross-country runs in the middle of winter? There should be a law against it.

He reached the gates and found them locked. Of course. The gods had it *especially* in for him. A heavy chain went around the bars a dozen times and the padlock was about the size of his fist. The gates and fence were almost three metres high and topped with spikes.

Ashoka searched for some convenient gap and found one. Unfortunately it was only wide enough for half of him.

He sat down on a bench. He could only think of one other way out, but that was three miles uphill towards Crystal

Palace, in totally the wrong direction. He'd be lucky to get back before dark.

Could this day get any worse?

Then he saw the boy. In the hoodie.

Magnificent. Now I'm going to be mugged.

The boy didn't move. He sat opposite Ashoka on a tree stump, elbows resting on his knees. He could be looking at him, he could be asleep; the hood hid his face. All Ashoka could tell was that the guy was lean and tough-looking. His stillness was like that of a viper or mantis, about to pounce.

Ashoka gazed through the bars, hoping someone might be passing by, walking their dog or something.

I don't have a mobile, or any money, thought Ashoka. *He can see that. Maybe he'll just let me go.*

The boy got up. He moved with sure, athletic confidence. Black hoodie, pair of dark jeans, and all Ashoka could make out was a pair of glistening dark eyes. Trouble with a capital 'Extreme Bodily Harm'.

"You need some help?" said the boy.

"No. I'm fine. Just resting."

"The gate's locked, in case you hadn't realised."

"Thanks." *Which is exactly why you're here, waiting to trap someone and steal everything they've got.*

"I haven't got anything," said Ashoka.

"Nice underpants."

Oh, Jeez. He wants my underwear.

"They so won't fit you," said Ashoka.

"True. I've lost some weight recently." The boy pointed at them. "Though I do, did, have a pair just like those."

❖

"You a *Doctor Who* fan?"

"David Tennant or nobody."

Ashoka smiled. "Me too. The new guy just doesn't count."

There was a nod. "We have a lot in common."

Ashoka peered at him, not sure whether or not the boy was being funny. He couldn't tell.

The boy went to the padlock and lifted it up. He shook it, head tilted as if he was listening to it.

"You can't open it," said Ashoka.

The boy felt along the lock, probing with his fingertips. "Everything has a weakness. You just need to find it."

He shook the padlock again, then squeezed it between his forefinger and thumb. He jerked it, hard.

The padlock held.

Ashoka tried not to laugh. "Er, well done."

"I used to be better at this," the boy muttered. He punched the padlock.

It snapped apart.

"Wow," said Ashoka. "How d'you do that?"

"Just a trick, nothing special." The boy drew the rattling chain out and pushed the gate open.

"Thanks." Ashoka gazed down the path out of the woods. If he was quick he could be back before dinnertime. "Thanks a lot."

"Anytime, Ash."

Ashoka half opened the gate. "My name's Ashoka. Not Ash. Not any more."

"Since when?"

"Since—" He turned around. No one. He looked towards

the trees. Just trees. The boy had been standing right there. Ashoka glanced up at the branches overhead. The boy must have flown away to vanish like that. Weird. Ah well. At least he was safe.

Ashoka set off, not fast, but steady. This last bit was downhill, thank goodness. He got to the Lordship Lane exit and stopped. Hold on.

"Anytime, Ash."

How did he know my name?

"You heard that the next Doctor Who's going to be a woman?" said Akbar. "Seriously, it's all over the blogs."

Ashoka bounced his dice in his hand. "Never going to happen."

"Oh, and why not?" said Gemma. "I think a female doctor would be great. And about time too."

"Yeah, Ash," said Josh. "Why not a girl Who? You'd still watch it if they had Kermit as the Doctor."

"How many times do I have to tell you, Josh? It's Ashoka. Three syllables. Not complicated."

"Joshua," said Josh.

"What?" said Ashoka.

"If I have to call you Ashoka, you need to call me Joshua."

"Fine. Joshua. Whatever. Can we get back to the game? My paladin aims his magic arrow at the necromancer."

Tuesday night was Dungeons & Dragons night. Ashoka, Josh (sorry, *Joshua*), Akbar and Gemma were in the middle of exploring the 'Caverns of Chaos' and right now they were trying to stop an evil sorcerer from turning the entire

❖

population of the Greyfalcon into zombies. Or vampires. Or miscellaneous undead types.

Gemma picked up her dice. "My thief sneaks around the back of the columns. She'll try and get closer to the Big Bad."

Gemma had only joined a few months ago, right after Guy Fawkes Night. He'd thought she'd play once or twice, then stop and go off and do something cool with the other cool kids like Jack, but, proving that there was a God, she'd turned out to be a closet geek. So Tuesday night, as well as being Dungeons & Dragons, was Gemma night.

They reached over the table and repositioned their miniature figures. Akbar started describing how the evil necromancer was raising a horde of skeletal warriors from the ground, and Josh — Joshua — retaliated with his elvish sorcerer casting a fireball spell.

"Ignore Josh," said Gemma as the battle progressed. "I like 'Ashoka'."

"Thanks." It still took people a bit of getting used to. Most of the teachers remembered and his parents too, but half his mates still slipped up and he reckoned Josh — Joshua — was doing it on purpose. But Ashoka's trip to India last year had changed his outlook on a lot of things. It had been the *best holiday ever*, and after coming home he'd decided to use his proper 'Indian' name from now on.

The battle wrapped, the bad guy dead and the city saved, they began to tidy up. Ten minutes later and Ashoka and Gemma were strolling down South Croxted Road. The wind blew along the path, carrying a vortex of leaves that

❖

swirled in the amber light of the streetlamps. Ashoka adjusted his coat, zipping it up to his chin. The cold went into the bones. Gemma had her hands stuffed in her jacket. They walked in silence.

I should try and hold hands, or something, he thought. *How hard can that be?*

Yeah, Ashoka, and while you're at it you can try leaping that building in a single bound.

"Saw you coming back from cross-country," Gemma said. "I assume it was you: covered in leaves and mud and your shorts all ripped at the back?"

Oh, no. Ashoka pulled his cap down, hoping she couldn't see him blushing.

"Nice underpants, by the way."

"Shut up, Gemma."

She laughed and they got to the corner of Tesco. "This is me," she said, gesturing over her shoulder. "See you tomorrow, Ashoka."

Wow. Ashoka sounded so much better the way she said it.

They waited at the traffic lights. Cars went by.

Go on. Do something. Kiss her. You know you want to.

Ashoka shuffled. "Yeah, tomorrow. G'night."

The traffic lights changed from green to red and Gemma crossed.

You are a total coward.

That was a golden opportunity and he'd blown it. Why didn't he just go for it? What was the absolute worst that could happen?

❖

She'd say no. Face it, that's what she'd say, isn't it? Better not even try than suffer the rejection. Girls like that don't go out with guys like you. Especially once they know you wear Doctor Who *underpants.*

Ashoka adjusted his backpack and took the gap between the shops, his shortcut home. The alleyway wasn't wide and they still hadn't fixed the lights, but he'd done this route a million times and his feet went on autopilot. It was along the estate and the rubbish wasn't collected till the morning so he had to watch his step around the black refuse sacks. Two red-eyed rats watched him pass.

"Gross." He kept away. The things looked evil.

A dog barked nearby, then whimpered and shut up.

Someone chuckled ahead of him.

"Who's there?" said Ashoka.

The chuckle turned into a grotesque howling laugh and a figure appeared at the end of the alleyway. The light from the courtyard behind cast an eerie light over everything.

A woman, dressed in a white suit, stood waiting for him. She leaned against the wall, arms folded, her thick, tawny hair framing her face like a mane. She wore a pair of dark glasses and a hungry grin.

"Ash Mistry?" she asked. Her accent was posh, clipped, with each syllable bitten off.

"Do I know you?" He was tempted to correct her, tell her it was Ashoka, but a large part of his brain was sending signals to his mouth warning him that this was not the sort of woman who liked being corrected or made upset or angry on any level.

"My name's Jackie." She stepped forward and her fingers

❖

flexed. Her long, curved nails shone like daggers. "We've been waiting for you."

A snarl from behind him raised the hairs on the back of his neck. He turned to see two men standing there. They glared at Ashoka, smiling with crooked, jagged teeth in their thin mouths and long, greasy whiskers under their rodent-like noses. Their eyes were malevolent, burning crimson.

Cold terror flooded Ashoka. He held out his bag. "Here, take it."

Jackie tutted. "Oh, Ash, that is not what we want."

"What then? What do you want?" said Ashoka. *How does she know my name?*

She smiled. Even the darkness couldn't hide the brilliance of her fangs. "We want to kill you, dear boy."

Chapter Two

"There must be some mistake, I... I don't know you," stuttered Ashoka. "Please, it's a mistake."

He looked at the woman, hoping to see a glimmer of pity, or compassion. But she just smiled, and there was no humanity in those fangs. "Please," he repeated feebly.

"Begging, Ash? How disappointing," said Jackie. "But then we can't all be heroes."

Without thinking, Ashoka slammed the bag into one of the rat mens' face. He didn't think about it; it just happened. The bag contained three huge hardback books, a large bag of dice, some lead miniatures and his boots. Rat-face Number One squeaked as the bag smashed into his nose. Ashoka then kicked Rat-face Number Two between the legs.

He'd seen it done a million times in movies and the guy always went down. Always.

Rat-face Number Two didn't go down. He just leered.

Ashoka charged. The two tumbled into a pile of rubbish and knocked over a bucket of compost. Ashoka pushed the rat-face down into a bag of rotting, stinking onions as he scrambled to his feet.

Claws, hot and sharper than razors, tore open the back of his coat and sliced his skin. But he was too full of fear and adrenaline to feel the pain, and was up and running a second later, stumbling out of the alleyway.

"Run, Ash, run!" Jackie laughed.

What am I doing? What am I doing?

He'd never been in a fight before and this was for *real* — life and death. His heart was pounding violently in his chest and his boots beat the pavement, the heavy impact echoing like a drum in the night. He was only a few hundred metres from his front door, but suddenly the alleyways through the estate turned into a labyrinth. He ran down one and came out into a small enclosed green, empty but for a pair of swings and a see-saw. He stared at the blank, unlit windows of the apartments that overlooked it.

"Help!" He raced past the swings, throwing them behind him in a desperate attempt to stop Jackie. She moved on all fours and bounded over them. *How is that possible?*

Lights came on in the estate around him, but he didn't dare stop to call for help. One swipe of those claws and she'd have his head for a football. He ran on, down into another narrow gap between the apartment blocks—

—and crashed straight into the rat-faces, who grabbed him. Ashoka wrestled and punched but couldn't get free.

❖

"Hold him," Jackie ordered. She panted and her tongue hung red and loose from her wide jaw. The rat-faces twisted Ashoka's arms behind his back until they felt as if they'd break.

"What do you want? I don't even know you!" Ash shouted. This was insane.

Jackie looked him over, coming so close he could smell her breath. Worse than a dead dog's guts. "No, but I know you." Jackie stroked his face with the back of her nail. "And I'm here to make sure you never do." Then she turned her hand and dragged her fingers through his shirt. The cloth ripped open and she drew three thin, bleeding lines down his chest. She pulled his shirt wide open and peered at his skin. Her nail pressed against his belly. "No scar." She grabbed his left hand and stared at his thumb. "Interesting."

She flexed her fingers and the nails struck like a butcher's blades. "Hold him still. I don't want his blood on my suit."

"Please..." begged Ashoka.

A steel scream rang out right in his ear and Ashoka cried out as blood showered over his head.

The rat-face gripping his right arm wobbled and Ashoka turned towards him to see blood vomiting from his severed neck. The head was still spinning in the air and Ashoka stared at the wide, surprised expression on his face, his mouth a perfect 'O'.

A moment later another figure appeared to the left, a long triangular blade of bright, sharp steel shining in its right fist. The rat-face who still had a head dropped Ashoka and drew out a pistol. It wasn't some cool Desert Eagle or Walther

❖

PPK, it was an ancient gunpowder thing from a hundred years ago. But the barrel was huge, and in the narrow alleyway he couldn't miss. The flint burst a bright flash of powder, and then thunder exploded from the barrel opening, filling the entire alleyway with acrid gun smoke.

The bullet sparked on the steel blade as the figure swatted it aside, the lead ball rebounding to tear a chunk of brick off the wall.

He swatted a bullet, thought Ashoka. *That's not possible.*

The rat-face stared as the shadow rammed his right fist, and the steel triangular blade, into his chest so hard that he came off his feet. A second fountain of blood sprayed out as the tip of gore-coated metal tore through the rat-face's back. He scrabbled, and screamed a scream that should have shattered all the glass nearby, and almost did the same to Ashoka's eardrums. Then the figure, a boy in a hoodie, tossed the dead rat-face aside and stepped past Ashoka, his attention on Jackie alone. The boy's fingers tightened around the steel dagger in his fist.

A katar. *An Indian punch dagger.* Ashoka hadn't seen one since—

"Jackie," said the boy in the hoodie.

"It's true. You're here," Jackie snarled, edging away. She looked from Ashoka to the boy and back again. Then she threw back her head and screamed with demonic laughter and with two bounds vanished into the night.

"Are you all right?" asked the boy, turning to Ashoka.

Ashoka blinked and tried to wipe away the blood that covered his face. He thought he'd swallowed some. He swayed, his legs suddenly as solid as jelly.

❖

"He's going to fall," said the boy.

Someone helped to support Ashoka: a girl of about fifteen or sixteen, dressed in a close-fitting suit of black-green. "I've got you," she said. Despite the darkness she wore shades, so all Ashoka could see was the reflection of his own petrified face.

"Let's get away from here," said the boy. "And bring him."

"I only live—"

"I know where you live," the boy snapped. "Now come on."

The girl steadied Ashoka. Then she picked up a long steel coil off the ground. The weapon had a sword hilt, but instead of a single blade there were four razor-sharp steel strips.

"An *urumi*," said Ashoka. "The serpent sword. That's... cool."

He looked down at the now headless corpse of the first rat-face. She'd done it with the urumi. He could see the open arteries and the spine and neatly sliced muscle of the neck stump.

"Oh, God." Ashoka tried to hold it down, but bile flooded to the top of his throat. Then came straight out over the ground and his shoes. His stomach spasmed and bitter vomit poured out again and again.

The boy in the hoodie sighed. "Pathetic."

The girl was patting Ashoka's back. "Oh, please. You were just the same when I first met you."

"Was not." The boy sounded petulant. "Have you quite finished?"

"Yes. Yes, I have." Then Ashoka saw the second rat-face,

24

torso slick with black blood and white bone jutting from the gaping hole where his chest must once have been.

"No. No, I haven't." He vomited some more.

Once the vomiting was all done and he'd downed a bottle of water, Ashoka was eventually able to walk again, and he followed the boy and girl out of the estate. *I could run*, he thought, but something told him he wouldn't get very far.

"What's going on?" Ashoka demanded. "Has the world gone bat-loony? Why were those people trying to kill me? Who *were* those people?"

The boy hurried Ashoka across the road, his face still hidden in the deep shadow of his hood. "Last question first. Those aren't people. They're *rakshasas*."

Ashoka scoffed. "Indian demons? Yeah, right."

"You don't have to believe me."

"Thanks. I won't."

"But you should."

Ashoka paused. "You were at the woods today, weren't you? Have you been following me?"

"That's right. I knew Jackie would make her move sooner or later."

"Who are you?" Ashoka said, suddenly filled with a dreadful anticipation. A small part of his subconscious didn't want to know. There was something terrible and familiar about the boy.

The girl nodded. "Tell him."

The boy took off his hood. A pair of dark eyes gazed back at Ashoka. Eyes he knew. The boy's face was gaunt, but smooth and brown like his and his hair was the same as Ashoka's, maybe longer than he wore his and more dishevelled than his mum would allow. The boy smiled, and it was a smile Ashoka could mirror, perfectly. He struggled to breathe. "Who are you?" he whispered, even though he knew.

The boy's smile softened. "I am Ash Mistry."

Chapter Three

"Sit down," said the girl.

Ashoka took a seat in his kitchen, his back against the wall, staring at the other boy.

The other Ash Mistry.

Weird did not begin to describe what it felt like to be face to face with himself. The boy had all his mannerisms – the way he pulled his hair from his forehead, the way he stood and tilted his head as he thought. But there were differences. The most obvious was that this other Ash was as sleek as a dagger and the way he moved was almost scary. He had a confidence that Ashoka lacked. Ashoka shuffled through life, a bit wary, a bit timid. This guy wasn't just in charge of the situation – he *owned* it.

"This is too weird," he said, and not for the first time. "How can you be me?"

❖

"Check the house, Parvati," ordered Ash, "and get him some clean clothes." The girl nodded and left the two of them alone.

"There's no one here," said Ashoka. "Mum and Dad have taken Lucky to a gymnastics competition." But he glanced at the clock. They should have been back by now.

"As soon as they return we all leave."

"Leave?"

Ash checked out the window. "He'll come after you. After everyone. We can't stay here."

Ashoka looked down at his torn shirt. He was still shaking. He walked over to the sink and filled his Yoda mug with water. He rinsed the vomit taste out of his mouth, then splashed his face, closing his eyes and letting the cold water refresh him. "Who's after me? Why would anyone be after me?"

"Sit back down. Stay away from the window." Ash's hand twitched on the hilt of his katar.

Ashoka faced him. "Listen, this is my house and—"

"No, you listen," snapped Ash. "There are people out there that want to kill you. I am the only one who can keep you alive, but I can only do that if you do exactly as I say. This is not open to discussion."

Parvati reappeared. "All clear." She had a bundle of clothes under her arm and a bag over her shoulder. She gave it to Ash. "And I found this."

"Hey, that's mine!" Ashoka said.

Ash paused, then held the bag out to Ashoka. "Show me."

Ashoka unzipped the black canvas bag and drew out his bow.

Matt black with a magnesium-alloy main body, composite limbs with pulleys to increase the power. The bowstring was made of coated steel cables. State of the art. Right now the frame was folded in on itself and the bowstrings wound into the pulleys so the entire weapon was less than half a metre in length. He'd been given it as a present on his last day in India.

Ashoka held the central body and gave the bow a sharp flick.

The two limbs snapped out and locked. The pulleys whirred as the bowstring unreeled and quivered, springing into tension. Fully extended, the bow was just shorter than him.

"You any good with it?" asked Ash.

"Is that important right now?" said Ashoka.

"You're right, it isn't." Ash tapped his watch. "Want to get a move on?"

Ashoka looked at the pile. He didn't like getting changed in public. He had enough teasing about his weight in the changing rooms. "Do you mind?"

Ash shook his head, turning away. "This is ridiculous. I am you, Ashoka."

"How can you be? I don't look like you. I can't do what you do."

"I am you, but from a different timeline."

Ashoka stopped. "A different timeline. Right." That was the craziest thing he'd ever heard. The other boy frowned, no doubt seeing Ashoka's disbelief.

"I know it's hard to believe," said the other Ash.

"You're right about that."

A distant cousin he could have believed, given how similar they looked. Maybe, just maybe a long-lost twin, some bizarre mishap at the hospital when he'd been born.

But different timelines?

"But if we are the same, right down to our fingerprints and DNA," said Ashoka, "how come you look like that and I look like this? Which is very different. Shouldn't we be really mega-identical?"

Ash shook his head. "Things happened in my life that never happened in yours. In my world, in my universe, I've a sister called Lucky, I live in this house and my mum and dad are the same as yours. But a month ago my timeline ceased to exist and somehow I ended up in yours."

"What happened?" asked Ashoka, pulling off his bloody, tattered shirt and putting on his Nike T-shirt instead.

"The past was changed. I've spent the last five weeks investigating, and as far as I can tell, it changed ten years ago. A person went back in time by a decade and altered his past. So, from that point on, our existences diverged. Your universe took a different route to mine."

"Just like that?"

Ash nodded. "Just like that. No big flash or bang. I shouldn't exist here – this is your universe – but I do. I'm here with Parvati because we're somehow immune to the effects of the Time Spell."

"Time Spell? Someone cast a spell? This is *truly* weird."

Parvati interrupted. "Your lives are different, but your destinies will be the same."

Ashoka frowned. "Sorry, I don't understand that."

❖

Ash rolled his eyes and, looking around, grabbed pen and paper from the kitchen counter. Ashoka watched over his shoulder as Ash began to draw a line. "This is us. We are the same person. We are born, and then, when we are four, something happens." He drew a thick dot, and two parallel branches emerging from the same line, one above the other, close but separate.

"Year by year we live different lives, me along this top path, Timeline A, you along the bottom one, Timeline B. Then in December I jumped from my timeline to yours." He did a loop from the top line to the bottom. "Instantly. There was no going backwards or forwards in time, but I left my universe and carried on in yours."

"And what's happened to yours?" asked Ashoka.

Ash frowned. "It could be continuing, everyone living their day-to-day lives without me. I simply vanished and the universe continued. Or it could have just..." he bit his lip and Ashoka saw a flicker of anguish "... stopped. Ended. I don't know."

"Amazing," said Ashoka. "Totally amazing. But I don't believe a word of it." He'd calmed down now and was putting it all together. Attacked by demons? It had been a set-up. Clever special effects, plus it had been dark and he'd been scared. Things look different in the dark. Masks might look real, things like that. Any second now Ant and Dec were going to leap through the doorway. This was some new TV series, about freaking people out with stories of time travel and demons and alternate selves. Ashoka inspected the boy before him. It had been dark and he'd been in shock when he'd first seen him. Sure, he did look a lot like him, but there were subtle differences. Stuff that the make-up and whatever prosthetics they used couldn't disguise. The eyes were darker, more haunted. His lips harsh and stiff. Things this boy had seen and done lay under his skin. Shadows of his deeds flickered in his penetrating gaze. Why had they picked an actor like him? Same height but definitely not the same physique. Ash had the body of an Olympian, all hard edges and harder muscles. Though the months of pulling a bow had built the muscles on Ashoka's arms and back, they were still hidden under layers of podginess.

"Any second now," he said. Maybe the presenters were getting their make-up sorted first.

Ash and Parvati looked at each other. "Any second now what?" said Ash.

Even with bad traffic, his parents and Lucky should have been home by now. It was almost ten.

Ashoka smiled. They must be in on the joke.

His mobile rang. It was Dad.

Ashoka sighed with relief. He'd freaked when he'd seen Ash and the girl, Parvati, freaked some more when Ash had told him his bizarre story of gods and monsters, but now normality had returned.

"OK, Dad, where are you? Joke's over."

"This is no joke, boy." It was a man's voice, but not one Ashoka recognised, or liked.

"Who is this?" Ashoka asked.

"Speak to him, child," said the voice.

Ashoka heard sobbing and a sniff. This wasn't some game

32

or TV show. As cold dread crept through his veins, Ashoka realised his world had changed and all the earlier stuff, the easy life, was about to end. Right now.

"Ashoka?" said a young girl's voice.

"Lucks?" Ashoka's fingers tightened around his mobile. "Where are you?"

His sister sobbed again and then she screamed.

"Don't you dare hurt her!" yelled Ashoka. "Don't you dare hurt her!"

"Give us the *Kali-aastra*, boy," said the man. "Do that and your family go free."

Kali-aastra? Wasn't that some sort of magical weapon? A weapon of the gods? What made them think he had it?

"I don't have any Kali-aastra. I've told you already — this is some big mistake. Please, let my family go."

"He was with you tonight."

He? That made even less sense. An *aastra* couldn't be a person. Could it?

Ashoka looked at Ash. He'd seen Ash in action. How he'd taken out the two rat-demons without breaking a sweat. How he'd knocked aside a bullet. If anyone could be a weapon, it was Ash.

Kali's weapon. Kali, the goddess of death and destruction, was the most terrifying of all the gods, more feared than the demons she fought. If Ash was her weapon, then maybe Ashoka should be as afraid of him as of the demons, if not more.

He should give them Ash. No question.

Ashoka put his hand over the mobile. "They want you."

❖

"It's a trap."

"Yeah, and my family are in it and I want them out, right now. You need to turn yourself in."

"That would be a mistake."

"The only mistake is you being here! It's a straightforward swap. You for them."

Ash shook his head slowly. "The moment you do that, they'll have no reason to keep them. They'll be killed."

"No," said Ashoka. "You're just saying that. I can't risk it."

"Give me a chance to save them." Ash's gaze hadn't shifted. He drew a deep breath. "But it's your choice."

Ashoka lifted his hand away.

"Ashoka?" said Lucky. "Are you there?"

"Yes, I'm here." What should he do? He shouldn't be making these sorts of choices! It was as if he'd gone into an alternative universe too, one with demons and death and horror. Ashoka closed his eyes, but no wish was going to change things. He had to act. "He's... gone."

Lucky yelled as the mobile was snatched from her. "Where is he?" the man snarled.

"He didn't tell me. I think he went after that Jackie woman," Ashoka replied. "He said he'd be back tomorrow." He gulped and steadied himself. "Please, as soon as he comes back, I'll call you."

"Do that," said the man. "Or I promise you I will eat your sister's eyes for dinner."

The mobile went dead.

"What have I done?" Ashoka stared at the mobile, tempted

❖

to call right back and tell them the truth. Tell them to come and get Ash right now and give him his family back. That's all he wanted.

Parvati spoke. "They were only taken a few hours ago. They can't be far."

"London's a big place," said Ashoka. "How will we find them?"

"We've some help," said Ash. "Come on."

Ashoka looked around his kitchen. His home. It felt shockingly empty.

Lucky grinned at him from a photo, sitting proudly on her black and white pony, Domino. She'd nagged and nagged, and right after coming back from India, Dad had got her one. She'd almost exploded with happiness and Ashoka had just acted all cool, ignoring her excitement. Now he'd do anything to have her back. "Promise you'll find them."

"They're my family too," said Ash. "You need anything?"

He had a state-of-the-art games system upstairs. He had his books and gear and clothes and trainers and everything. But that was all junk. The only things that mattered were gone.

His gaze fell to his bow and he picked it up.

"You got any arrows for that?" asked Ash.

"No. Dad said they had to stay at the club. He was worried I might put one through a neighbour's window by accident."

Ashoka pressed open the catches and disassembled it in a matter of seconds.

Parvati look across at him intently.

"What?" he asked.

"Nothing," she replied.

"If Jackie's just hired help, then who's she working for?" asked Ashoka as they headed down into Brixton tube station. Ash and Parvati stood either side of him, scanning for trouble.

"Lord Alexander Savage," said Ash.

Ashoka stopped. "Savage? He can't be. Savage is one of the good guys." He looked around until he saw a poster on the wall across the street. "See that? The Savage Foundation. He owns it. It's his charity. It saves millions of lives. Medical supplies, fresh water to villages in Africa, humanitarian aid to war zones. He's an amazing man. And a friend of ours."

Parvati snorted. "No, he's not."

"Savage is just a businessman. He wouldn't get mixed up in demons and kidnappings. Why should he?"

"Savage is much more than a mere businessman," said Parvati. "He's a three-hundred-year-old sorcerer. He's been looking for the secret of immortality and it looks like he's finally found it."

They rushed down the escalator on to the platform, looking around them as they went. Not too many people about, and definitely no rakshasas.

"My uncle works for him," continued Ashoka. "We stayed with him in India last summer. Savage gave me that bow. Why bother if he wants me dead?"

"You're just bait, Ashoka," said Parvati.

"Bait? For what?"

"Save it for later. The train's coming. Look sharp..." Ash forced Ashoka back a step, "...and stay close, all right?"

The train carriages weren't busy at this time of night and they kept Ashoka wedged between them, both Parvati and Ash watching the other passengers, ready for the first hint of trouble. It freaked Ashoka out that Ash had exactly the same greatcoat as him, his Sherlock Special.

But Ash looked really cool in his. Way cool.

How were they the same guy?

They weren't, not in a million years. Ash was the Kali-aastra.

He'd read about aastras. They were super-weapons, made by the gods and carried by the great heroes of Indian mythology. Rama, the prince, had used an aastra to destroy the demon king, Ravana. Ashoka loved that story, the Ramayana. Rama and his brother Lakshmana had spent years searching for Rama's wife, the beautiful Sita, who'd been kidnapped by Ravana and taken to his island fortress of Lanka. The story had climaxed with a massive battle where Rama and Lakshmana had fired aastra after aastra, killing tens of thousands of demons with each shot and destroying Lanka.

And what would an aastra of Kali do? That was a no-brainer. It would be the ultimate weapon, the ultimate killing machine.

Was that what Ash was? Some divine terminator?

They came out at Finsbury Park station and on to the streets again.

"What are we doing here?" said Ashoka.

"Keeping you safe," said Ash. "We've a friend—"

"Acquaintance really," interrupted Parvati.

❖

"... Who knows the situation. We've been staying with her for the last month. She's helping."

Ashoka turned up the collar of his coat to cut out the chill wind. The only place open was a kebab shop and the only people around were tramps loitering under the bus shelters.

Everywhere they looked were boarded-up shops. A man stood guard outside an off-licence, a snarling pit bull tugging at its leash. The car parked opposite had smashed windows and no wheels.

"Nice neighbourhood," said Ashoka.

Ash pointed to a shop on the corner.

Elaine's Bazaar.

It was a junk shop. Steel grilles covered the windows, not that what was in there looked worth stealing. Old dust-covered VCRs, a kid's bike, mannequins wearing last century's clothes, and cheap Formica furniture. The paint on the overhead sign, three golden balls, was turning green and flaky with age. The shop had an apartment above it and lights shone within. Ash got out some keys.

"This is your secret hideout?" asked Ashoka. He peered through the shop window. Was that a stuffed bear inside? "It's not exactly Wayne Manor, is it?"

"And you're not exactly Bruce Wayne," said Ash.

The interior smelt musty. The stuffed bear wore a feather boa and a top hat. Clothes spilled out of battered trunks. A small door behind the counter opened up and a light came on.

An old woman wearing a faded tartan dressing gown

paused to look at them. Her wild grey hair stuck out in all directions and she was scrawny, her skin wrinkled and thick on her bones. A cigarette glowed between her yellow teeth. "Where are the others?" she said.

"Captured," said Ash. He took the cigarette out of the woman's thin fingers. "And I've spoken to you about these already."

Parvati interrupted. "Ashoka, meet Elaine. She'll be your host for the next few days."

Elaine peered at Ashoka. She didn't look impressed, but then neither was Ashoka. Wasn't there somewhere better than this dump? Like a cardboard box under a bridge?

"Were you followed?" asked the old woman.

"Please," said Parvati. "Give us some credit."

Elaine pulled the dressing gown up to her neck and double-locked the door behind them. "I just don't want any unexpected guests, that's all. Not safe for an old woman like me, living all alone."

Ashoka felt exhausted. The last few hours, all the panic and fear and running, were catching up with him. He wasn't used to this. "This is not my life," he muttered.

"It is now," said Ash, not too unkindly. "I'm sorry."

Elaine turned around and started back upstairs. "I've a room for you, boy."

The apartment upstairs wasn't exactly flash, but, unlike the shop below, it was at least neat and tidy. There were some photos on the wall, a frame with Arabic calligraphy and a painting of a scene from the Bible. He spotted a statuette of Ganesha on the mantelpiece and a menorah

❖

beside it. Sticks of incense smouldered in a narrow brass fluted pot, the sweet smell mixing with coffee and nicotine. Ashoka picked the sofa with a Rajasthani cover and fell on it.

He'd never been so beaten in his entire life. Every part of him was on the verge of collapse.

Rakshasas. Time travellers. Kidnappings. And Savage. Was it true? Was Savage behind all this? It was too much to take in.

He put his face in his hands.

Ash pulled off his coat and dropped his katar on the dining table. "You've had a busy day. Get some sleep and we'll go over everything in the morning."

"How can you be so calm?" Ashoka snapped. "They've got my family."

Parvati smiled at him. "Please, Ashoka, we're here to help you. Get some rest."

Elaine came through with a bundle of linen, a pillow and a duvet. "Here you go."

He wasn't happy, but Ashoka took the pile off the old woman. She directed him through a doorway and Ashoka entered a small room with a single brass bed and table. There was a window, but it faced a brick wall. He dropped the duvet over the mattress and dropped himself on to the duvet.

He was asleep before he hit the bed.

Chapter Four

*P*arvati stood at the door, listening. "He's asleep."

Ash turned back to the dining room as Elaine put a mug down. She shook out another cigarette, then caught the look in his eye and put it back with a forlorn sigh. "Well, what next, boss?" she said.

"A shower." Ash sniffed his clothing. "I stink of rat-demon." There were flecks of blood on his sleeves. "Then we talk."

He entered Elaine's bathroom and dumped his clothes on the cold tiles. The pipes rattled as he turned the hot tap full on. The shower head gurgled, then steaming hot water blasted out. He put his head under and let it burn him.

The water turned pink and Ash watched it swirl around the plughole.

Calm? Ashoka thought he was calm? Couldn't he see how terrified he was?

Ash felt along his chest, from the smooth skin, taut across his muscles, to a ridge on his solar plexus. To the scar.

He glanced down at his thumb. There was a small cut. Last summer a sliver of metal had entered, kicking off his transformation from schoolboy to master of the arts of death. Servant of the goddess Kali. Her divine weapon.

The Kali-aastra.

He'd acquired superhuman strength and reflexes and even mastered Marma Adi, the ability to kill with a touch. He'd even gained the ability to glimpse the future, as his patron goddess was also the mistress of Time.

But all that power had gone the moment he'd jumped timelines.

It was as if he was half sleeping. Everything was slow, dull, colourless, compared to how he'd felt as the Kali-aastra. Had the jump to Ashoka's universe drained him of all his power?

He shouldn't be here. It had to be because of the Kali-aastra. Somehow it had protected him from the Time Spell, but in doing so burnt out his powers.

He needed to find a way to awaken them again. He needed a Great Death because that was what Kali craved. By killing for Kali, Ash gained more power.

He'd slain those rat-demons though and nothing had happened. He'd not felt even the slightest trickle of supernatural energy.

Perhaps their deaths weren't great? Perhaps Kali wanted more death before she granted him anything? The last time, he'd had to sacrifice himself. How was he going to top that?

And in the meantime, without the power of Kali, what

was he? Just a normal boy all over again, trying to defeat the greatest evil the universe has ever known.

And Ashoka thought he was calm?

He made a fist, looked at the water run and steam over the hard knuckles. Normal? Maybe that wasn't totally true. He'd seen Kali dance. He still knew all the moves she'd shown him. He could fight better than any man, but once he'd been able to tear down buildings with his hands, move faster than an eye-blink, kill with a touch. That was all gone. Physically he was in perfect condition, perfect *human* condition. But that wasn't going to be enough for what they faced. Not by a million miles.

Calm? He was so scared he wanted to puke.

He should tell Parvati. Why hadn't he? He should have told her the instant he'd realised. Was it because he was afraid she'd think less of him for being 'merely' human? Was it pride?

He had to tell her. And he would.

When the time was right.

Ash spun the tap closed, dried and slipped on fresh clothes. Barefoot, he re-entered the main room and sat down on the sofa, facing Elaine and Parvati at the dining table. He ached everywhere.

Parvati looked up from her tea, frowning. "You all right?"

Ash forced a casual smile. "Fine."

Elaine had her laptop open and a bundle of papers waiting for him on the dining table. She patted them. "All the information I could get on your boy." She gazed at the screen. "Lord Alexander Savage. Multi-millionaire. Philanthropist. One of life's good guys. And very easy on the eye."

❖

Ash looked at the photo. It was Savage with the US president, collecting some humanitarian award. The man was tall, handsome, with that floppy blonde hair common among dashing aristocrats, and wearing a white suit designed in Savile Row and sunglasses, like a Hollywood superstar. Even though the other guy in the photo was the most powerful man on the planet, there was something about Savage that just overshadowed all else. The president looked small and insignificant next to him.

Elaine had been working since December on finding out all she could, and they had built a timeline out of what they knew. Elaine was an occultist, a woman Ash had known in his own world, the only person they could go to who would believe them. The three of them had holed up in her apartment for the last month, scouring through the web, newspapers and Elaine's own private library, digging up and assembling the pieces of the jigsaw. They didn't have it all, but a picture was emerging.

"Savage came on to the scene ten years ago," said Elaine. "He bought the old maharajah's palace down from Varanasi and immediately started excavating the local area."

"He was looking for the Kali-aastra," said Ash. "It had been buried there."

That's where all the trouble had started, back in Ash's timeline. Ash and his sister Lucky had been exploring the excavations. Ash had tumbled down a pit and ended up finding the golden arrowhead of Kali, the Kali-aastra, instead of Savage, a bit of Kali's arrowhead embedding itself in his thumb.

Now that Savage could move through time it made sense

44

❖

that he'd have gone back into the past and made sure that he found the Kali-aastra first.

How can you defeat a guy who can travel in time? In Ash's world Savage had been defeated, all but destroyed. Now he was the most important man on the planet.

Elaine nodded. "Reckon he found it pretty quick as the works didn't last more than a month. He knew exactly where to look. It was at that point that he hired your uncle to oversee the dig, there and in Rajasthan."

Parvati grimaced as she looked through the photos of a vast archaeological dig in the desert. "Where Ravana was imprisoned. Savage knew where he was, and now he had the means to free him."

Elaine gave a low whistle. "Imagine – freeing the demon king himself. Savage plays for the highest stakes, doesn't he?" She turned to Ash. "And in your timeline, you destroyed him?"

Ash nodded. "In my timeline it was me who found the arrow of Kali, not Savage. The one weapon in the universe that could kill the demon king. And it did."

Parvati frowned. "But that was in your timeline. What do you think happened here?"

Ash continued. "Savage told me he never intended to allow Ravana to live. He just wanted to free him long enough to be granted immortality. Judging by the more recent photos, it looks as if he got his wish. Then I think he used the Kali-aastra to kill Ravana himself. Savage could not stand to have a rival."

"Then what?" asked Parvati.

Elaine opened up the top folder. "Then Savage goes shopping. He's spent the last decade turning the Savage Foundation into the biggest provider of medical and humanitarian aid in the world. It's more or less wiped out childhood diseases. The rich countries pay for the medicines and Savage gives them to the poor ones for free. He's got hospitals everywhere, even in the war zones no one else would dare enter. He could be the richest man in the world, but chooses to spend most of it on his charities. The Church wants to make him a saint, the Muslims consider him the Mahdi, the Buddhists say he's a bodhisattva and the Hindus think he's an avatar, a reincarnation of Vishnu. I think I've got a photo somewhere of him blessing the Pope. Or was it the Dalai Lama?"

"What's Savage planning?" asked Ash.

"To make the world a better place?" suggested Elaine.

Parvati scoffed. "That's what they all say. Every tyrant, every dictator in the world. Throughout history. They all promise a better world, but their utopias are always built with bones." She drummed her fingertips and her long green nails clicked upon the wood. "I've seen men perish building the Great Wall. Watched children crushed under the marble they used to clad Rome. Slaves working in the Russian gulags, digging for diamonds in Africa, gold in the Americas. It's all paid for in blood, Elaine. Every bit of it."

"Your family, I mean *Ashoka's* family, seem to have done pretty well out of it." Elaine handed over a collection of cuttings. "Your uncle heads up the Savage Foundation's Archaeological Institute, and your father's business is booming, thanks to construction contracts from Savage. Why?"

Ash had thought long and hard about that. Savage had been like a fairy godfather to Ashoka's family for the last decade. "He wanted them close. What better way to keep an eye on them? He must be worried Ashoka might somehow become the Eternal Warrior. He probably never expected me to turn up here."

"It all changed on 12th December," said Parvati. "That was the day Savage, in our universe, cast the Time Spell. It sent him back ten years to change the past. And Ash and I woke up in a different timeline — we just jumped sideways. I'd felt... *something* was happening a few days before. So I came straight over from India to here. I was on my way to Ash's house when the Time Spell was cast. By the time I reached West Dulwich station the past had changed. I felt it happen."

"Savage must have felt it too. He must have sensed our presence," said Ash, "which is why he didn't make a move against Ashoka and his family any earlier — because we hadn't arrived yet. It's only since we turned up on 12th December that he feels threatened."

"So he sets his rakshasas on Ashoka to draw you out of hiding?" said Elaine.

"Exactly."

"If the rest of this world changed, then why not you two?"

Parvati answered. "I had my father's scrolls on sorcery for many centuries. I have studied some, though none to any great depth. I think, subconsciously, I knew enough about the magic of Time to make myself immune to the change. Ash is the Kali-aastra; Kali is the goddess of death and destruction, and Time. I believe she protected him."

❖

Ash shifted in his seat. "It's only a theory." He picked through the newspaper cuttings, trying to work out what changes Savage had made in the last ten years. Governments were different, the prime minister was an old friend of Savage's, a board director at the Savage Foundation. He owed his entire career to Savage. No one would say a bad word against the aristocrat. Why should they? He had done only good.

But Ash knew Savage. There had to be more. "What's he planning?"

The scale of his organisation was vast, global. The business papers joked about it.

The Savage Empire.

But Ash didn't find it funny. "They think he's the Messiah."

Parvati sat down beside him. "He's not the Messiah, he's a very naughty boy."

Elaine turned the laptop around to face them. "I found this clip on YouTube. It's Savage being interviewed by Letterman last year."

The frozen image had captured Savage close up. Eyes hidden behind his shades, he was smiling, the easy smile of a man who knew it all. His skin shone with an inhuman purity, too perfect to be real, as if he was shining from within. He relaxed into an armchair, left heel of his boot up on his right knee, dressed immaculately, of course. The interviewer leaned over his desk, captivated.

Ash pressed play.

"So, Lord Savage—"

"Please, David, it's Alex. I know how you Americans feel about us aristocrats."

❖

"We love you Brits!"

The audience cheered and clapped.

Savage smiled. "You weren't so keen on us in 1776."

The interviewer shook his head. "Alex, if you'd have been in charge, maybe we wouldn't have been so desperate to rebel."

Ash noticed the change as Savage's radiant smile darkened for just a second, then switched back. "Well, you can't fix the past."

"But you can fix the future, right? Is that what you're about?"

Savage nodded solemnly. "I've seen the future, David. It's not good. Unless someone does something, then we're on the path to destruction. Mankind has all these gifts and we don't know how to use them. If it's not war, it'll be pollution, overpopulation. No one country is to blame. You're all at it. Grabbing what you can without caring what you leave. Expecting your children, their children, to sort out your mess."

"Alex Savage, saving the world. All by yourself?"

Savage's smile broadened. "No. I've got some friends on their way."

Ash shivered.

"You've come a long way in a short time, Alex. You're the number-one pharmaceutical company in the world and your donations to charities run into the billions. What's the secret of your success?"

Savage laughed. "I learned from my past mistakes."

"Come on, there must be more. Your vaccines will save millions of lives. Some say your genetically modified crops that can grow in barren deserts will end global hunger. And you've done this all for free. Why?"

❖

"I own the Savage Foundation. I have a lot of money. How rich does one man need to be?" said Savage.

"So, any ambitions still left unfulfilled?"

Savage smiled. "Oh, just one."

The interviewer leaned closer. "And what's that?"

"I want it to be a surprise."

The audience howled with disappointment, and the clip ended.

"You can't argue with the facts," said Elaine. "Savage has helped improve the lives of millions of people."

"He wants to keep the sheep happy," said Parvati. "It makes them easier to handle when you take them to the slaughterhouse."

"Maybe he's changed." Elaine put a cigarette between her lips. "People do that, y'know."

Ash took it out of her mouth and squashed it. "But for most, old habits die hard."

He stared at the frozen image of Savage on the small screen. His ruthless smile, his casual air of superiority. It was all there, but no one else seemed to see it. Savage hadn't changed. He was planning something and Ash had no doubt it was something terrible and on a massive scale.

But what?

Chapter Five

When Ash awoke the next morning, the others were already up and in the kitchen having breakfast. Elaine was keeping herself busy while Parvati was trying to talk to Ashoka about something.

Ash pulled up a chair and looked at the boy sitting opposite him. Ashoka had his arms crossed in front of him and a look of disbelief on his face.

"I don't get it," said Ashoka.

Ash and Parvati looked at each other. Parvati shrugged. Ash met Ashoka's gaze. "What don't you get?"

"Like, *how* are you the Kali-aastra?"

Ash took a deep breath. "Last summer I went to India with my sister, Lucky. We were visiting Uncle Vik and Aunt Anita in Varanasi."

"And that's when you found the golden arrowhead of Kali, right?"

"That's right, and a sliver of it entered my thumb. What I didn't realise at the time was this meant I became the Kali-aastra."

"A superhero then."

"I wouldn't go quite that far."

"But you have superpowers, right?"

Ash frowned.

"A superhero. With or without the cape." Ashoka was clearly smirking. "What does being the Kali-aastra allow you to do? Heat vision? A spot of leaping tall buildings?"

"Depends," Ash said, ignoring the smirk. *Don't rise to it. He's trying to wind you up.* "When a person dies, I absorb some of their life force. When I killed Ravana—"

"Ravana, as in the demon king?" The smirk widened.

"Yes. Him. When I killed him I gained superhuman strength, speed, endless endurance, all of that."

"OK," said Ashoka. "I don't want you to take this as an insult or anything, but you three are clearly insane. You've obviously escaped from some loony bin, and that Jackie is another escapee from the asylum, and she was after you, not me. You all have major issues that need resolving, either in group therapy or with medication. My family have got mixed up in all your craziness and you need to call whoever has them right now and tell them to free them. Whatever drama you have going on is none of my business."

"I give up," said Ash. He'd tried to be reasonable, but now it was time to hand it over. "All yours, Parvati."

❖

Ashoka smirked. "What is this? The good-cop, bad-cop routine?"

Ash picked up his tea. It was cold. Typical. "Don't say I didn't warn you."

Parvati smiled. "So, you've got it all sorted, have you, Ashoka? No such things as rakshasas?"

Ashoka nodded. "No. Such. Thing. Fairy tales."

Parvati took off her sunglasses and leaned towards Ashoka so they were nose to nose. "Then these must be some... genetic defect?" Her eyes were pure serpent; green with a pair of black slits for pupils.

Ashoka leaped out of his seat. "Bloody hell!"

Parvati had him flat against the wall. Ashoka's face had turned sheet white. Ash almost felt sorry for him.

Almost. Actually, he didn't feel sorry at all. He was enjoying this. Maybe it was bad of him, not warning Ashoka about Parvati in advance. But he'd had enough of that smirk. Ash leaned back and watched, smiling to himself. How can you explain a girl like Parvati? She might look like a teenager, but she was more than four and a half thousand years old. Her mother had been a human princess and her father was Ravana, the demon king. Her early years had not been particularly stable. She had a deep psychotic streak and was a one-girl weapon of mass destruction.

But when she laughed, nothing else seemed to matter.

Ashoka tried to slide sideways towards the door, but Parvati extended her fangs, pausing a few centimetres from his throat. Sweat ran down his pallid face. "And this must just be poor dental work." Each one was slick with venom.

She shivered, and scales, shiny green scales, rose through her skin, clustering like a collar around her neck at first, then extending to her jaw, her cheekbones. Her hair sank into the skull as it widened, swelling either side into a cobra's hood. "And this? Do you think some dermatologist might be able to fix this?"

Ashoka's breath had deteriorated into short, desperate pants.

Ash was impressed. He'd thought Ashoka would wet his pants. Still, Parvati's shock tactics seemed to have done the job.

"Enough, Parvati," said Ash. He didn't want Ashoka having a heart attack.

She dropped on to the table and the transformation was complete. A cobra now rose up before the terrified Ashoka. Its tongue flickered, it hissed, and Ash could tell Parvati was laughing.

Ashoka stared. Jaw moved. No words came out.

"I said enough," said Ash. "You've made your point."

The snake curled up, wound itself together and then unfurled back into a young woman. Scales still covered her like armour, taking a moment or two to recede back under her skin. She winked at Ash, took up her sunglasses and left the room.

Ash smiled and looked back at his doppelgänger. "Are you all right?"

Ashoka stared after her. "Rakshasas, they're for real?"

"Very. But she's on our side."

"I'm glad to hear it," Ashoka replied, his voice still

quivering. He picked up a glass of water and tried to hold it steady enough to drink. Eventually he gulped it down. "My God."

"Well, what do you think?" Maybe they'd overdone it. They'd just planned to frighten him, not break his fragile little mind.

Ashoka huffed. "A rakshasa." Then he smiled. He grinned. "That is bloody awesome."

"Do we have any leads yet?" asked Ashoka, looking anxiously at the clock. "We're running out of time. You said you'd rescue my family and it's already five. They'll be expecting our call soon, and then what?"

"Pacing up and down will not help," said Parvati. "Just sit."

Elaine was still on the phone, as she had been all day. The woman knew almost everyone. Ash wasn't sure, but he thought he'd heard her speaking to an archbishop earlier. She was in the hallway, turning an unlit cigarette in her fingers.

Ashoka hurled himself back into the sofa. "This is hopeless."

"That's the attitude," snapped Ash.

"We wouldn't be in this mess if it wasn't for you."

"Don't forget who saved your life."

"Yeah, only to get my family killed instead."

Ash sprang up, tossing the chair aside. That was it. He grabbed Ashoka's shirt, hauled him off the sofa and stared hard into the boy's eyes. "You have no idea—"

Elaine cleared her throat. "Finished?"

❖

Reluctantly, most reluctantly, Ash let Ashoka go. "Please tell me you have something."

Elaine flicked through her notepad. "Your dad drives a Range Rover? Licence plate MISTRY 1?"

Ashoka straightened his shirt, smoothed down his crumpled collar. "Yes. It's grey."

"Well, a friend of mine in the police has just found it. Abandoned in Docklands, Jardin Street. Just around the corner from—"

"East India Dock," interrupted Ashoka.

"You know it?" asked Ash.

Ashoka nodded. "Savage owns a house there. Actually a converted warehouse, overlooking the dock. The dock itself is where he moors his yacht whenever he's in town. Place was done from top to bottom. Dad was the project director, at Savage's request. The guy had the works: new floors, windows, upgraded the IT systems, the security, the whole audio-visual thing, home cinema. Major, major money was spent."

"When was this?" Ash asked.

"About a year ago."

"This security, what's it like?" asked Parvati.

"Top notch. Presence detectors on the roof. Thermal and motion sensors on all floors. Six-digit PIN on entry. CCTV as standard with remote recording. Alarms hard-wired to both the local police station and a private security firm with a two-minute response-time guarantee."

Ash looked at Parvati. "What do you think?"

Parvati frowned. "Thermals I could bypass. My body temperature is the local ambient."

Of course Parvati, like all reptiles, was cold-blooded. "And the rest?"

"If there was a vent or drain, I could get in without worrying about the door alarm system."

"I've a suggestion," said Ashoka.

"Yeah, in a minute," replied Ash. "So the problem's the motion sensors, right?"

"Ahem," said Ashoka.

"In a minute. But they would be deactivated if the house was occupied. Stands to reason."

Parvati shook her head. "The building would be zoned. All the unoccupied spaces would still be alarmed. If Savage has any sense."

"Look, I've an idea—"

Ash turned around. "Will you just be quiet and let the grown-ups talk?"

"So you don't want to hear how I can bypass the security system?" Ashoka shrugged. "Fine. Carry on. Ignore me."

"What? Seriously?" said Ash, trying his best to hold back his irritation. "Why didn't you just say? Oh, never mind. How?"

Ashoka looked at Elaine. "Your laptop still on?"

"All yours."

Ashoka took the chair. A few seconds later the screen went to the webpage of Mistry and Partners.

"Dad runs his own company?" said Ash.

"Yours doesn't?"

"No way. He's not even an assistant director."

"All perks of being on the Savage payroll," said Ashoka.

❖

"Anyway, Dad designed the security system. And, like all software, it needs upgrading on a regular basis." He skimmed over another page and logged in. "You'd think Dad would have a better password than—"

"AshandLucky?" said Ash.

"AshokaandLucky," corrected Ashoka. "And... open sesame."

A 3D wire diagram of a large four-storey townhouse appeared. Ashoka spun it around using the mouse so they could see the outline of every room. It was drawn in immense detail. Zooming in, Ash could inspect the doors, the windows and even the chimneys which were, sadly, blocked. "That's pretty cool."

"I helped design it," said Ashoka. "The model, that is. Got me the science prize at school last year."

"All very lovely," said Parvati, "but what about the security?"

Ashoka scrolled down to a series of reference numbers. "These are temporary PINs. If we needed to upgrade the system, we'd need to disable it first. These numbers here give us access. Then the PIN returns to whatever code Savage has been using. It's just a manufacturer's reset really, like on most electronic items. A security system's not much different."

Parvati grinned at them both. "Then what are we waiting for?"

While Ashoka went to get ready, Ash and Parvati stacked the plates and bowls in the kitchen sink. Ash got the tap running and the sink filling with steaming water. He glanced over his shoulder. "Ashoka is such a smart-arse."

"Ha!" replied Parvati as she passed him dirty cutlery.

"What do you mean, 'ha'?"

"He's so like you it's just bizarre."

Ash frowned. "I am nothing like Ashoka. His mouth is on constant overdrive and he thinks he knows everything."

"*Sooo* different from you."

"Y'know, Parvati, sarcasm is the lowest form of wit."

Parvati glanced slyly sideways at him. "What was that you said about being a smart-arse?"

The mobile on the table rang. Ashoka must have left it. Where was he? Ash picked it up. Then he saw the name on the display.

Gemma.

"Ashoka?" Ash heard Gemma's voice coming from the phone. He hadn't even realised he'd answered it.

"... Yes?"

"It's me, Gemma."

Ash could only listen. In his timeline Gemma had died in his arms. Just a few months ago he'd watched her eyes fade and heard her last sigh.

Ash had been friends with Gemma since primary school. They had played together every day as kids, but had gone their separate ways at secondary school. Gemma had gone off to join the cool kids while he'd become a founding member of the Nerd Herd. It was only after he'd become the Kali-aastra and defeated Ravana that he had found the courage to ask her out. Funny that he wasn't afraid of a demon king, but was terrified to ask a girl out on a date.

❖

He hadn't realised that when he came back from India his troubles would follow him to his front door and the people he cared about would suffer, would die, because of him.

He'd wanted things to get back to normal. But they would never be normal again.

This was a second chance. His heart quickened. In this timeline Gemma was alive! Like Savage's, his mistakes had been fixed.

"Say something, Ashoka."

"It's good to hear your voice again, Gemma." She had no idea how good.

"You weren't at school today. What's up?"

"Family emergency. Sorry."

"Oh... all right. Everything OK?" asked Gemma, sounding concerned.

"Fine, fine," said Ash, wishing it was.

"Anyway..." she paused, "... last night was great, wasn't it?"

The world was too weird. In this timeline Gemma hung out with Ashoka! Unbelievable.

Parvati was looking at him with a funny expression that Ash couldn't read. But it could have been her 'Are you totally and utterly mental?' face. He turned away and tried to ignore her.

"There's something I wanted to say to you, Gemma." He couldn't help it. "I think about you a lot, as a matter of fact."

"Oh yes...?" He could almost see the dimples in her cheeks as she smiled.

"You mean a lot to me, Gemma. I just want you to know that. There've been so many times I wanted to tell you that, but I always chickened out. Stupid really."

"Ashoka, are you all right?" Gemma said. "This isn't like you."

"It is, but you just don't know it. Sometimes I don't know what I am either."

"Maybe we can talk tomorrow. I'd like to."

"Really?"

"Of course. Why do you think I come to Josh's to play Dungeons & Dragons every Tuesday?"

"Er... because you're a geek?"

Gemma laughed. "That too."

Gemma was interested in Ashoka? The world had gone officially loony.

"You'll call me?" she asked. "So we can meet up? Just you and me?"

Totally loony. "That would be great. I've got some family business to sort out first. Might take a few days. But, yeah, I'll call you."

"All right. Listen, the bell's about to go. Take care of yourself, Ashoka."

"You too."

He clicked off the phone just as Ashoka came back in. They looked at each other. "Was that for me?"

Ash gave him his most casual look. "Oh, just someone checking up. On stuff. You know. And, you know, Gemma."

"You spoke to Gemma?"

Parvati sighed. "He asked her out. As you."

❖

Ashoka's mouth dropped open. "A date? Why? What? Seriously? What did she say?"

"She said yes," said Ash, grinning. "As unbelievable as it might seem."

"She said yes?" echoed Ashoka. "Aw, excellent! Thanks!"

"This is too, too insane," said Parvati, shaking her head.

Chapter Six

Ash couldn't get it out of his mind. Gemma was alive. Of course he'd known she would be, but it was different actually speaking to her.

She lived. His uncle and aunt lived. All the trauma he'd been through had never happened to Ashoka.

Was that why he found his other self so irritating?

Admit it, you're jealous.

Ash was the Kali-aastra. He'd saved the world a couple of times. He was the Eternal Warrior, the reincarnation of some of the greatest heroes the world had ever known, and he was jealous of a podgy, lazy kid who'd achieved absolutely zero with his life.

And he was still going to get the girl.

"Get with the programme," snapped Parvati. She handed him his punch dagger.

"What? I didn't say anything."

"It's all over your face. Life not being fair and all that."

"Well, it's not." Ash glanced towards the sofa. Ashoka was bending over to do up his shoelaces. "Look at him. He can't even touch his toes and yet he gets it all."

"You're such an idiot," fumed Parvati.

"What's up with you, anyway?" said Ash, looking at her.

Elaine came in jangling a bunch of keys. "I reckon if you're heading into the lion's den you might need some hardware."

"What have you got?" Ash asked.

"More's the question, what haven't I got? Come downstairs. You too, fat boy. And bring that bow of yours."

Ashoka flushed. And tried to hold his stomach in. "I'm not fat," he muttered. "It's water retention."

Elaine smirked. "It looks like cake retention to me."

There was a small door behind the counter that led to the basement. Elaine shuffled through her keys, shaking them off a cumbersome steel ring, inspecting one after another. "If you wait a month or so, I could get you some reinforcements."

"Who do you have in mind? The SAS?" asked Ashoka.

Elaine tried another thick iron key in the door. "Better than that. But they're all out in Russia right now."

"We haven't got a month," said Ash. "Savage will catch up with us well before then. We need to take the initiative."

"Ah, here we go." Elaine pushed a key into the lock and twisted.

She flipped on a switch and a lone light bulb illuminated

a narrow set of stairs leading into the basement. "This is where I keep the toys for the boys." She gave Parvati a mock bow. "And the demon princesses."

Ash followed Parvati down and then gazed about him. And grinned. Ashoka stepped in after him.

"Wow," said Ashoka. "You really are ready for the zombie apocalypse."

The wooden rack to his left was stacked with *katanas* — samurai swords — each wrapped in a silk cloth. Axes stood up against the wall opposite, their blades bright as mirrors. Spears, maces, even suits of armour ranging from stiffened leather to chain mail to plate helmets. Ash picked up a curved *tulwar*, slowly rolling his wrist in loose figures of eight.

Parvati picked up a flat steel ring, slightly bigger than palm size. "A *chakram*. It's been a while since I saw one of these."

Ashoka collected a pair of *nunchakus* and adopted a Bruce Lee pose. "I'll take these."

Parvati raised an eyebrow. "You know how to use one?"

"I've seen *Enter the Dragon* a billion times."

She took it from him. "You're more likely to knock yourself out."

Ash picked up an arrow. The tip was needle sharp. "I don't want you getting close enough for a punch-up. You leave that to Parvati and me." He handed the arrow over. "You stay at the back and use these with your bow, if you think you can handle it."

"I can handle it."

"Actually, you don't have to come," Ash offered. Maybe it would be easier if just he and Parvati went? That way he wouldn't have to spend half the time looking out for Ashoka.

Ashoka inspected the arrow and ran his fingers through the fletching. "No. I want to do this. I have to." He chose a collection of barbed arrows, broad leaf-shaped heads and some narrow, needle-pointed bodkins. The first two were designed for maximum damage, while the bodkins were for armour penetration. Ash would have picked the same.

Maybe we aren't so different after all.

Elaine pushed open a wonky cupboard and lifted out a Kevlar jacket. "What about body armour?"

Ash peered at the rest. She had ancient mail shirts and even a knight's helmet. "Why do you have this stuff?"

"You don't want to know."

Ash inspected the jacket. "Too heavy."

Ashoka notched the arrow against the bowstring.

He knows how to handle a bow, that's for sure. Maybe he wouldn't be totally useless.

Ashoka turned to Elaine, arrow pointed safely down, but the bowstrings seemed to hum. "Care to put an apple on your head?"

Elaine grunted. "I'll get the van warmed up."

Ash inspected the rest of the weapons while Ashoka followed Elaine out to the van. Parvati watched him go, her long fingers on her chin, her green eyes glowing. "Interesting, don't you think?"

"What?" said Ash. "Ashoka notched an arrow and didn't shoot his own foot?"

"It's not crossed your mind why he's picked a bow?"

❖

"Involves minimum running around? What's your point, Parvati?"

Parvati tapped his forehead. "He's the Eternal Warrior. Just like you. He just doesn't know it yet."

Ash stopped and looked at her. "You're sure?"

She nodded. "It might manifest itself differently, but the bow, his handling of it, I've seen it before, a long, long time ago. He didn't learn that in archery class."

Could it be true? thought Ash. Why not? They were the same person. They would have had the same past lives. Ash had had visions of his own past existences. They'd come to him in his dreams, with subtle messages as to what he'd be facing, offering coded clues and advice. The problem was, they were always obscure. "You think he's accessing the talent of one of his past lives? I've never been able to do that."

"Ashoka might be different, though. I don't know for sure, but, at least at a subconscious level, he's tapping their knowledge."

Ash heard the engine start somewhere above them. He picked up his punch dagger. It was all he really needed. "Do you think we should tell him?"

"No. He'll find out soon enough."

Chapter Seven

Ash sat in the back of the van with Ashoka. Parvati was up front with Elaine.

It was good to be doing something. Now they knew where Savage lived there was a buzz in the air, a crackle of anticipation.

He'd been here before, at the eve of a battle.

Then why are my hands so sweaty?

Ashoka strummed his bowstrings nervously. He had an arrow clip fixed to the bow, and six arrows, double-stacked, ready and waiting.

How would Ashoka do in battle? Was he really the Eternal Warrior, just like him?

"How much further?" Ash asked. He just wanted to get started now. Then the nerves would go.

"We're almost there," said Elaine.

✲

The Docklands in east London were a mixture of old and ultra-modern. Their route took them through Canary Wharf and past the headquarters of Barclays Bank, Credit Suisse, HSBC and all the other global financial houses. In the dark the skyscrapers shone as if covered in crystal.

Beyond the bastions of super-wealth came endless, squalid council estates, low and mean and hidden in the gloom, shadowed by the glass titans and circled by busy ring roads.

"Not surprising Savage would set up here," said Elaine as she drove. "This was where it all started."

She was right. Savage had begun as a soldier of the East India Company back in the eighteenth century. From there he'd built his fortune through slavery and drug smuggling and conquest. He'd marched with the likes of Napier and Clive, carving up India, creating what would be the heart of the British Empire. Spice ships had docked here, bringing pepper, once more valuable than gold, but there had been gold aplenty too. Gold, silver, diamonds, ivory, and tea and cotton and countless other treasures of the East.

But the old warehouses had all been turned into offices or fashionable apartments for the merchant bankers, now trading electronically and growing just as rich as the nabobs of the Honourable East India Company.

Snow had just started to fall. The clouds were a deep orange from the city. It never truly became dark in London, and small flurries of snowflakes swirled in the pool of amber from the sodium streetlights.

❖

Elaine slowed down and came to a halt at the corner of the road. "There it is."

The warehouse took up an entire block. Four storeys tall with a multi-pitched roof with plenty of nooks and crannies among the chimney stacks. As it stood alone they could see the building backed on to a dock: a square, artificial bay with a few designer barges and yachts moored, quiet and idle. Two hundred years ago the basin would have been filled with high-masted clippers and men heaving the fortunes of nations off the boats and into the warehouse.

The windows were dark. A white Humvee stood outside the front door.

Ash slid the side panel open and stepped out of the back of the van. He shivered as the wind whipped along the street, but pulled off his coat and threw it back in. He didn't want it getting in the way. He touched his katar handle, strapped to the back of his belt. "You ready for this, Ashoka?"

"No, but I'm coming anyway." He slung his bow across his back.

Parvati smiled at him as she stepped out, hand on her urumi.

Elaine leaned out of the driver's window. "I'm going to hide over the other side of the dock. Good luck and don't be long."

They made their way towards the warehouse. Ashoka was pale, eyes darting everywhere.

Ash flexed his fingers, trying to keep the cold out. This wasn't how he'd wanted to take on Savage. They were on the back foot, going into unknown territory without all their powers.

But that was just the way it had to be.

What and who was in there? Ashoka's family? Jackie?

Savage even? Ash wished he was more ready; that they all were. The only one who looked at ease was Parvati. Nothing ever phased her. Always cool, always in control.

She peered through the letter box in the front door. "What's the PIN?"

Ashoka inspected his palm. "040776."

Parvati shrugged off her coat. "I'll just be a minute." Then she reached through the letter box, sliding into her cobra form as she did so. Her tale flicked before vanishing through the slot.

Ashoka glanced up and down the street. "I've never done anything illegal, and now I'm breaking and entering."

"How are you finding it?"

"I feel half sick and half excited, you know?"

"Yes," said Ash. "I do know."

A minute later the door opened and Parvati, back in human form, smiled at them. "Come in."

Savage hadn't stinted on the decorations. It was an elegant mix of old and modern. The walls were original bare red brick, but full-height portraits lined the hallway, each lit by a discreet spotlight hidden among the old wooden beams across the ceiling. A long, dark red Persian rug ran all the way to a wrought-iron staircase, and the doors leading off the hallway were antique wood, their colour glossy and dark from the varnish.

Ashoka stood facing a life-sized portrait. "It's Savage."

Ash had seen it before, back in India. "At the beginning of his career."

Savage wore the red jacket of an officer of the East India Company. He gazed down at them with half-lidded eyes that were cold blue chips of ice. They burned with all the greed, hunger for power, the sense of destiny, and of superiority that would define his three-hundred-year existence. All present in this first portrait of him as a mortal man in his mid-twenties. He held a tiger-headed cane, and the beast's own gaze was pure red, two small rubies glistening from the silver face, snarling at the painter. Behind Savage lay a pair of manacles and a bundle of dried poppies, the source of his wealth. Further along the hallway was a portrait of him as an old man, then nearest to the stairs the most recent — just him sitting on a stool, dressed in his customary white suit, wearing his black shades. His skin was pearly white, almost luminescent. Behind him was desert and the faint outline of a vast archaeological excavation. His cane rested across his knees.

"That's the dig in Rajasthan," said Ash, "where we found Ravana."

Parvati stood by a small electrical panel beside the door. A schematic of the building showed all the alarm locations, now all green. She double-checked and sighed. "The entire building is alarmed."

"Which means no one's at home," said Ashoka. "What are we going to do?"

Ash knew Ashoka was gutted, and he was too. But then did he really believe it would have been that easy? This was Savage they were dealing with. The Englishman would have backup plans to his backup plans.

But they were here. In his house. Who knew what they might find?

"We need to have a good look around," he said. "Maybe

we'll find a clue as to where they've gone. We know they were here recently."

Parvati didn't look happy. "It's a big house."

"We should split up."

Ashoka shook his head. "Nope. No way. I've seen too many movies where that happens and the loser in the party..." he looked to Parvati, then Ash, "... which, under these circumstances, would be me, comes to a bloody and awful end."

"Which is why you'll be staying with Parvati," said Ash.

"How come I get stuck with him?" replied Parvati.

"Hey!" said Ashoka.

"You have him," she continued.

"No. Hanging out with him, it's just too... freaky." Ash smiled. "And look, you dealt with me when I was young and useless, so—"

"Who says I'm useless?"

Parvati put up a finger. "Shh." She turned to Ash. "OK, then what are we looking for?"

"The house is huge, and I don't want to stay here a moment longer than necessary, but we need to try to find out where they've gone, and we need to work fast, and that means splitting. I don't like it any more than you do, Ashoka, but otherwise we have no leads. I'll start at the top, you two start down here, and we'll meet in the middle. All right?" Ash turned to Ashoka. Yes, it was still odd, staring at himself. "You do exactly as she says. Got it?"

"I am not useless."

"Whatever." Ash checked his watch. "We'll meet in fifteen minutes."

❖

Parvati nodded, then took the left corridor, Ashoka close behind her.

Ash went directly to the wrought-iron staircase and climbed, moving quickly and keeping to the shadows. A clock chimed somewhere in the house, but all else was silence. He paused at the first floor to listen, gazing down the corridor. There was no one around. He continued on up.

Clues. I'm looking for clues. Now which door leads to clues?

He was at the top of the house. A skylight illuminated a large square patch of the corridor in a silvery blue. The space was mean compared to the rest of the house. The ceiling was low and the doors were plain, without the ornate panelling of the floors below. It smelled musty and a cold breeze sank through the old frame around the skylight.

He peered into the first room, opening the door slowly to minimise the squeak of the hinges. Linen sat in neat white stacks upon a row of shelves and there was the stuffy odour of mothballs. Ash moved on.

He went quickly from room to room, finding nothing of interest. He saw the stairs at the opposite end. One more room to check, then he'd make his way down to the floor below and search there.

The door was oak and the handle a brass curl, different from the rest. Ash opened it and entered.

Chapter Eight

$\mathcal{A}$ study. Savage's home from home. It had to be. Small, cramped and with a row of windows overlooking the street, but there was a tiger skin on the floor and a large desk by a window. The desk was bare but for an old-fashioned telephone. Most of the wall was covered with shelves overstuffed with books, mainly old, worn and leather-bound. Alongside these were some glass cabinets, each filled with archaeological artefacts from around the world. There were ancient bronze arrowheads, clay statues, feather headdresses and gold coins, rusty swords and urns. Animal heads decorated the walls, everything from tigers to boars with massive tusks.

A chill breeze caressed Ash's nape.

He'd been in a room a lot like this once, in the Savage Fortress. It had been the night he'd learned his world was stranger than he'd imagined, when he'd discovered monsters – demons – were very real.

A photograph caught his attention. Age had turned it yellow and the black had given way to a metallic sheen.

Savage wore an officer's uniform. His legs were in puttees, long strips of cloth wound round for protection, and he had an old-fashioned tin hat, a Brodie, on his lap. The soldiers around him looked at the camera, cigarettes or pipes loose in their mouths, weary, with muddy shovels and picks lying around a half-dug trench. One man rested his arm across a large machine gun.

The First World War.

It had to be. The style of the uniforms and the weapons were consistent with the Great War. Ash had studied it and read about the terrible slaughters of the first mechanical war and how thousands of men would march across no-man's-land to be decimated by machine-gun fire and poison gas.

Only Savage looked relaxed. He knew that he was going to get out of this alive. He knew the bullets and the gas and the bombs couldn't hurt him.

One of the men was gazing across at Savage. Ash looked at his face – just some nameless private. Forgotten in history. Was there anyone alive now who knew his name? What sort of life he'd led? What sort of death he'd had? Whether or not he'd made it out of the Normandy mud alive?

If only I could slip into the picture, thought Ash. Stop Savage then, before he became too powerful.

But that might only make it worse. He'd be changing Time

❖

himself then, and who knew what the effects would be? The further back you went, the bigger the ripples.

He came to the desk and checked the drawers. Then he grinned.

Got it.

A notebook, the electronic variety. He ran his palm over it. There might be some useful info on it, and if Ashoka could bypass all this security then surely he'd have no problem hacking something like this. He put it in its plastic case and zipped it closed. Too big for his pocket, he tucked it inside his shirt. Ash closed the drawer, had a last look around to see if there was anything else of use — nope. He had what he wanted.

He was out a moment later, the door clicking as he closed it behind him.

He jumped as Parvati appeared in front of him. She was just a silhouette at the top of the stairs, but he knew it was her by her stance and her shape. Even in the darkness he could see the faint shimmer of her scales.

"I've got Savage's notebook." He patted his chest as he approached her. "It could be useful. You find anything?"

Parvati hissed and Ash stopped.

"Parvati? What's up?"

Her front foot slid forward and her fingers flexed.

Now, as his eyes adjusted to the gloom, Ash noticed something different about the rakshasa princess. "What happened to your hair?"

Her hair was always long, down to her waist and as glossy black as oil on water. Now it was cropped short and spiky.

❖

"Parvati?" Ash stepped nearer and reached out. "What's wrong?"

Her fist rammed into his jaw, propelling Ash into the wall. Stars blazed in his eyes. He blinked and dived as her boot swung towards his head. Her heel smashed the wall lamp, sprinkling Ash with glass.

He blocked the next kick, but couldn't stop the flurry of punches that came from all directions. It was as if Parvati had six arms. One blow rattled the teeth in his mouth and suddenly he was spitting blood.

"Parvati!" he shouted. "Stop!" What the hell was going on? She had gone mad. But there wasn't a chance to ask. Parvati reached over her shoulders and there was the ominous sound of steel against steel. Two curved blades shone in the darkness.

He needed to level the battleground. Darkness was Parvati's element. He stumbled backwards towards the patch of light in the corridor.

"Parvati..."

She swung the twin tulwar blades with mastery. A wall of lightning, blazing silver blurred about him and Ash ripped free his katar, barely deflecting one of the swords before it decapitated him. Sparks jumped as metal struck metal. Ash struck back, a feint to try to wrong-foot her, but Parvati saw through it and he received a cut along his arm for his pains.

"Parvati, please..."

Parvati stepped into the square of light. "My name is Rani."

Three crooked grooves crossed her face. Her left eye was

blind and white, the tip of the upper lip raised in a sneer by the scar that ran from her temple down her cheek. Steel barbs chimed in her hair, tied to the brutal short locks. Her armour was a mixture of ancient and modern, her arms coiled with serpentine tattoos. A pair of daggers had been rammed into the white sash she wore around her slim waist, each with a cobra-styled hilt, matching the designs on her swords, their eyes glistening with emerald stones. She glared at Ash, her forked tongue flicking between her long fangs. Her face was framed by scales, giving her a greenish hue. This wasn't the Parvati he knew.

"Ash!"

Parvati ran up the stairs. *His* Parvati. She stared at Ash and the girl he was fighting. Ashoka, huffing and puffing, clambered up behind her, carrying a satchel. His mouth dropped open.

Two Parvatis. And Ash was obviously fighting the evil-twin version.

That explains a lot. None of it good.

Two Ashes. Two Parvatis. Two of everyone.

Parvati flicked free her urumi. The four steel ribbons danced and lashed, eager tongues wanting blood.

"Wait!" shouted Ash. This was Parvati, of this world. Maybe she could help them.

But Parvati wasn't listening. She pounced.

Rani transformed. She spun between the steel whips, any one of them capable of slicing off a limb, one moment taking the form of a cobra, twisting in the air, then, as the four blades recoiled, landing on the ground, human again.

Parvati couldn't change that fast, nor with such precision.

Rani spun her swords and came at Parvati. She sheared off one of her locks and Parvati flinched as the tip entered her shoulder. The urumi skated across Rani's armour but did nothing more than scratch the black-lacquered steel.

They weren't going to stop. One would kill the other.

Ash wasn't going to let that happen. He charged in.

He jabbed low with the katar, following with kicks and punches as Parvati swept her urumi blades in all directions.

But Rani wove through their assault. Ever changing, often in the blink of an eye, she twisted and spun and struck, one second human, another cobra, sometimes a creature melding both. Her spine did things that should be impossible without crippling herself and her limbs were quadruple-jointed so attacks came from unbelievable angles and she could slip through even the strongest, bone-breaking locks and holds.

But she couldn't defeat them. She stepped back as Parvati and Ash merged their fighting into a single, seamless, blazing *blitzkrieg*.

Ash, panting and sweaty, stood beside Parvati as she shook the urumi, ready for another attack.

"You can't win," Ash said. "Put down your weapon and let's just talk. That's all." He bent down, opening his hand. "Look, I'll go first." He rested the katar on the floor. "See?"

Rani smiled crookedly. "Stupid."

The tulwar flashed at Ash's unprotected neck. She transformed, her arm stretching out an extra metre. Ash didn't even flinch before Parvati barged him out of the way. The blade sliced along her back and Ash heard the skin and muscle rip open. Blood splashed the wall. She was hurt.

The front door crashed open downstairs.

Then Ash heard the cackling howl. Jackie had come to the party.

"Get Parvati out of here," he said to Ashoka. "Now."

How many were there? Did it matter? He could barely hold Rani at bay. She smiled and it was an ugly thing; the moon-shadow made her look gaunt and turned her face into a death mask.

The house echoed with the beat of boots. They were going to be trapped. Ashoka helped Parvati up while Ash stood between them and Rani. But the cobra girl wasn't interested in attacking, she was just waiting for reinforcements.

Ashoka's gaze darted from one end of the corridor to the other. "They're coming up the staircase. There's no way out."

Ash nudged them back, his attention never wavering from Rani or her two swords, which she twirled in slow, supple circles. "The skylight."

"How am I going to get up there?" asked Ashoka in a panic.

"Just think!" He really was useless. "Climb on that table."

Ashoka muttered something and knocked a vase off a small coffee table. He dragged it into the spot right under the skylight.

The howling rose in pitch and the air quivered with Jackie's giggling delight, accompanied by a chorus of other snarling beasts and who knew what else.

The glass shattered. He dared not take his eyes off Rani,

but heard Ashoka huff and puff as he clambered up on the table, which creaked ominously. What a bloody farce. The lump of lard was going to break the table. Ash would have been out and gone by now. "Any time today would be good."

"I'm doing my best!"

Ash grunted again and then the roof creaked as a weight rested upon it. Ashoka was up.

Just at that moment Jackie appeared. Her mane shook with excitement and her face was a hideous amalgam of human and jackal, a long snout dominating it and each fang dripping with spittle. Her amber eyes shone hungrily.

Parvati groaned as she slithered up on to the roof, Ashoka pulling her from above. "Come on, Ash."

"You get going. I'll catch up once I've dealt with this lot." Wow, that sounded almost confident.

Four more men ran up behind Jackie, pausing on the stairs. A couple of heavy-shouldered dog-demons — thick necks and blunt noses and small feral eyes. Two more rats, each carrying a pistol, those old-fashioned flintlock things with wide barrels.

"Come on, Ash," urged Parvati.

He glanced up.

She stretched out towards him, sweat covering her face and her scales shimmering nervously. A trickle of blood ran down her arm, dripping from her fingers. "Come on!"

Ash looked up at her, then, reaching into his shirt, he slapped the notebook into her hand. "Go!"

And then she was gone, and Ash charged.

His attack took Rani by surprise. She ducked his swipe

82

but not his knee as it slammed into her belly. Ash tripped over her foot, but rolled past and then was swamped by the musky stench of Jackie's fur. The jackal rakshasa screamed as she sank her claws into his shoulder.

Ash tried to heave his katar into the monster's face, but someone grabbed his arm. He roared and kicked as bodies flew at him, weighing him down by sheer numbers. A bullet whistled and more glass smashed.

Once he'd have carved through this lot in seconds. Once, when he'd been a master of death. Now he took punches and blows and couldn't see for the blood in his eyes.

Winning didn't matter. Ash headbutted one of the beasts. He just needed to keep them busy.

Feet scurried above him, one light and graceful, the other lumbering and uneven. Parvati and Ashoka were getting away.

A fist came out of the bundle and almost took his head off. Ash braced himself, wobbled, then one more dog charged him and they all – Ash, Jackie, the rest – collapsed into a scrum. With Ash at the bottom.

Blood dripped from his cut lip and his shoulder ached from Jackie's claws digging into the meat.

Buried under a pile of demons, Ash couldn't move. His face was pressed against the floor and all he could see were feet.

A dainty toe pushed against his cheek. "So you're the Kali-aastra?" said Rani.

"At your service."

The toe dug hard into the soft flesh under his eye. "I was expecting more – given the way Savage talks about you."

❖

"Yeah, Savage is my number-one fan."

"Get him up."

They held him by the arms, legs and waist. They weren't taking any risks. Jackie gripped his neck from behind, controlling him like a puppet so he had to face Rani.

She looked so much like Parvati. The scars and the white, blind left eye had surprised him, but these details were superficial, meaningless. This was Parvati. How could they be enemies?

Rani slapped him hard. "Don't look at me like that."

He wasn't going to have any teeth left soon. "Just being friendly."

"We are not friends. Savage told me all about you. How you want to destroy the rakshasa nation."

"Some of my best friends are rakshasas."

Rani glanced at the skylight, then spat. "That girl, Parvati? A traitor to her people. Can she do what I do? Not any more. She has allowed her human side to make her weak. She refuses to acknowledge what she is. A demon. The daughter of Ravana."

Was that it? Rani had embraced her supernatural heritage. All these things she could do, change in an eye-blink, fight so far beyond human ability, all because she had full access to her demonic powers, powers Parvati had been denying herself.

Now it seemed obvious. Parvati held back. She'd done it for so long it had become natural.

What other sacrifices had Parvati made to try to be human?

❖

Ash followed Rani's gaze to the broken skylight. "At least they got away."

Rani laughed. The sound could have cut stone. This was how a demon queen should laugh: without pity or joy. It was as cruel as winter. "There is an English saying about out of a frying pan and into a fire, yes? I prefer from the fangs of a cobra into the jaws of a crocodile."

Crocodile? What did she mean?

There had been a crocodile. Along with Jackie and a vulture demon he'd been one of Savage's henchmen. But he'd died. Ash had killed him.

In another timeline.

Oh no. Ash remembered.

Jackie sniggered and her breath was rank on his skin. "You killed my closest friend, but that was in another world, boy." Her claws dug into his neck. "He's been *dying* to meet you."

Chapter Nine

Ashoka hauled Parvati up through the hole in the roof. He heard Ash's roars and thumps and cries. Maybe his double could win, but they couldn't risk hanging about. He looked across the snow-layered roof. There was a flattish path between the chimneys. "Come on, Parvati." He took her hand.

"We need to help him!" cried Parvati.

"Come on!" The roof creaked as he pulled her along.

Parvati hesitated and it looked as if she was going to jump back down into the fray.

Ashoka understood. He'd do anything for the people he loved too. That was why he was here. But Parvati was in no state to fight. And he couldn't rescue his family alone. "You don't stand a chance down there with that injury. And I need you, Parvati."

❖

She didn't say anything, but her lips tightened grimly and she joined him, hardly leaving footprints in the snow.

They weaved their way between the chimneys, and as the snow fell Ashoka couldn't tell which way they were going. He wiped the flakes off his face and tried to penetrate the white wall ahead of him.

Streetlights glowed below, reflecting off the water in the basin. The quay sat alongside the rear of the warehouse, where the ships must once have docked and offloaded their spices and cottons from the East. The deep bay had canals branching off it and modern apartment blocks overlooked the shimmering waters. A flotilla of barges was moored up along the quayside.

They were more than twenty metres above the ground and Ashoka walked, ever so carefully, to look down the side of the warehouse for a ladder or outside stairs. His legs turned to jelly as he saw the drop to the waters of the dock below.

The wind picked up and the flakes swirled about him.

"We need another way down," he said.

"Can't we jump?" Parvati asked, joining him at the edge. "The water looks deep enough."

A flock of birds squawked and clustered above them, circling and swooping this way and that. Ashoka waved his arms. "Shoo!"

Their wings were everywhere, and Ashoka wobbled as his heel went up against the low parapet wall. What was wrong with them?

They broke away and flew off, still cawing angrily as they

vanished into the sky. Ashoka spat out some feathers. "Yuck yuck yuck."

A deafening shriek shattered the night. The wind whooshed, hurling up a wave of snowflakes, and a black shape swooped down. Ashoka screamed as he glimpsed razor-sharp talons cutting through the air and the wings, the massive wings, beating and creating spinning eddies in the snow. A man's face, dominated by a large hooked beak, glared at him. He was bald and a tuft of feathers encircled his scrawny neck. He shrieked again and dived towards Ashoka.

It was impossible. Ashoka stared, a moment too long. He should have ducked, leaped aside, but he was transfixed. The man was like a vulture, a great big ugly one. The demon's greedy pink eyes locked with his.

The talons came straight for Ashoka, tearing at his chest, straight through his coat and jacket and shirt and skin. Ashoka stumbled back and his heel caught the very edge of the parapet. He flailed and reached for Parvati, but she was a hand's breath too far away. Her eyes widened with horror and he tilted backwards.

The demon vulture's wing brushed his face.

Ashoka grabbed it.

Chapter Ten

*V*ulture man cartwheeled as Ashoka held on to one wing. The demon screamed so loudly Ashoka thought his ears would bleed, and the world turned over and over. Talons swished at his face, then dug into his arm. Ashoka let go.

He smashed into the black, freezing water. Straight down he went, the cold clutching his lungs. Arms and legs flapped, as bubbles rose all around him. Faintly he heard another splash and, in the dim light cast by the streetlights he saw Parvati's slim figure pierce the water. She turned to him, gestured to the far side, and kicked off.

At least down here he was safe from the vulture guy. That was the freakiest thing he'd ever seen.

Ashoka broke the surface and began to swim towards the other side. His clothing weighed him down, but the dock wasn't that big. Still, he was panting in no time. He paused, treading water, took several big, deep breaths, and looked around.

"Parvati?"

She was already halfway across. In spite of her wound she cut through the water with smooth, easy strokes. It wouldn't take her long to reach the ladder on the opposite side.

Ash started off. Not easy doing the front crawl wearing winter woollies with a bow across his back, but each stroke took him another metre from vulture man and Jackie and Rani and danger. A horn sounded ahead and he saw Elaine's van. She waved at him.

Parvati was climbing out.

Almost there.

His arms felt as if they were made of lead. His stroke barely broke the surface. The dock wasn't as small as he'd first thought.

Parvati was shouting at him.

What was she saying? Elaine now stood beside her and they were both signalling frantically.

Was it Rani? Jackie? He looked around, but there was no one there.

The water rippled behind him. A gull, sleeping on the surface, bobbed up and down. Looking startled, it raised a wing, squawked and vanished under the water, leaving a small puff of feathers.

That's not good.

"Ashoka! Swim! Swim!" Parvati screamed.

"Put your back into it, boy!" added Elaine.

The water surged and a deep roar shook from under him.

Ashoka pounded the water, splashing wildly. He had to get out. Parvati's eyes were wide with terror. "FASTER!"

The water peaked and troughed now as the huge submerged mass accelerated towards him.

Ashoka gasped with each stroke. He beat the water with his arms and legs, every muscle burning with effort and fear. He had to get out!

The growl broke the surface and he heard a huge splash of something heavy and long hitting the water.

What was it? He dared not look. He just focused on the two women ahead. Parvati had clambered back down and was reaching for him. Elaine just stared past him, hand covering her mouth, her face utterly pale.

Ashoka dragged up all his strength and heaved his way forward.

There was another splash and then the water swelled under him. Something had dived back down. It was coming.

"Ashoka! Take my hand!" Parvati leaned as far as she could, one arm hooked around a ladder rung, the other stretched out.

Just a few more metres!

The submerged roar shook his very bones. A long, huge black shape began to appear below him. Big, thick scales of dark, knobbly green caught the undulating light. Huge yellow reptilian eyes shone, and beneath them stretched a mouth filled with jagged fangs. Wider and wider it opened, enough to swallow a cow whole. A tail, thick as a tree truck, whipped the water behind it and it surged upwards.

Ashoka thrashed forward.

❖

His hand caught Parvati's. She pulled.

Ashoka slapped against her as a creature erupted out of the water, showering them both. Its cry turned his blood to ice and all he could do was cling to Parvati, paralysed by terror. The air rushed around him as the monster rose and he was blinded as its shadow loomed over them both.

This is it. Death.

But if he was dead, he wanted to see what had killed him. He turned his head.

A crocodile, tall as a house, climbed and climbed, water cascading from its open mouth and down its gigantic body. It smashed the water with its tail and towered over them, even over Elaine and her van. The scales looked thicker than his hand and the teeth would crush his skull with ease. A few feathers clung to its jaw.

It looked down at him. The yellow eyes hungered, shining with pure, immortal hate.

"Move!" screamed Parvati.

He did. His hands slipped on the rungs, but he managed to scramble up. Ashoka threw himself off across the ground as the giant crocodile crashed down, tearing the ladder out of the wall. The steel crumbled like wire.

Elaine was already revving the van.

Parvati pulled him upwards and Ashoka stumbled on to the tarmac. Oh God, he'd never been so pleased to be on land. He wanted to kiss it.

The giant monster fell back into the water, throwing up a wave over them all. The tail stood out for a second before it too disappeared.

❖

In the distance, in front of Savage's warehouse, was Rani. She stood there surrounded by her rakshasas. Ash was nowhere to be seen. *What have they done to him?* wondered Ashoka.

Rani raised her sword. A salute? A threat? Who knew?

Ashoka fell into the rear of the van. Gears shrieked and a sudden cloud of black fumes coughed out of the exhaust. Parvati slammed the doors and collapsed beside him. They'd escaped.

"Oh God," gasped Ashoka. "What *was* that?"

It took Parvati a few seconds to get enough breath back to reply. "The vulture was Jat, the crocodile Mayar."

"He really doesn't like me, does he?"

"You killed them both, back in my timeline. Mayar's death was spectacularly unpleasant." She groaned as she got up, then looked him over. "Are you all right? Did they hurt you?"

"No, I don't think so." Ashoka coughed out some Thames water. He wasn't wounded, but was too exhausted to move. He lay there, soaked through and shivering. "But I have wet myself."

Chapter Eleven

"Just patch me up and let me go," snapped Parvati as she lay on the lounge floor, Elaine kneeling over her stitching up the long cut down her back.

"Stop fussing. It's not my fault you can't lie still," said the old woman.

"Ash needs me."

"Ash can look after himself."

Parvati winced as the needle went back in.

Ashoka tried not to watch. It was pretty gross. Blood oozed over the scales shivering across her skin.

He turned back to his own job – drying out the notebook Ash had nicked from Savage's house. Despite its protective casing it had still had a dip in the water and so he'd removed the cover and stood with a hairdryer, gently passing it over the exposed circuit boards.

"At last," said Parvati as Elaine snipped the end off the thread.

The old woman sucked her teeth. "Just let me put a bandage over it."

"Forget it. We've wasted enough time already." Parvati pulled a shirt off the sofa and began buttoning up. "I lost my urumi. Got any?"

"I'll look." Elaine rocked on her heels. "You need to take it easy. Not that you're going to listen to a word I say."

"That's right, I'm not." Parvati glanced over to Ashoka. "You'll stay with her."

"What about my family?" said Ashoka. "We had a deal."

"You had a deal with Ash, not with me," Parvati replied. "I'm going to find him."

"Parvati, you can't leave."

"Never presume to tell me what I can and cannot do, mortal." She stood up, but only got three steps before she wobbled and Ashoka grabbed her. Their gaze met and she snatched her arm free. "I don't need any help."

"You've lost a lot of blood and you're injured. How do you think you can take on that crazy other you and all her demons? That's assuming you can even find them."

Parvati scowled. "So I should waste my efforts on a fool's errand, looking for your family?"

"Ash thought so, yes."

"Ash has a sentimental streak. It's got him into trouble before." She sighed. "And your family were just bait for Ash. Now Savage has him, they're just baggage. And Savage doesn't hang on to baggage."

Ashoka froze. "What are you saying?"

"They're dead."

"No." He shook his head. "No, they're not." He couldn't believe that, not for a second.

"Ashoka—"

"They are not dead," he insisted. "Not even Savage would allow that. He *knows* them."

"You have no idea what Savage is capable of. I'm sorry."

Ashoka threw down the hairdryer and switched on the notebook. It was the only clue they had. There could be something in there about Lucks and his parents.

"What are you hoping to find?" asked Parvati.

The notebook hummed. Thank God. The dip in the dock hadn't damaged it.

"Information. Emails. Anything." The screen glowed to life. It turned blue and a password request popped up.

Ashoka felt Parvati put her hand on his shoulder as she leaned in to look at the screen. "You have a way around that?"

"Yeah." He took a data cable from the table and slid Elaine's laptop up against it. The screen still showed his dad's security site and he connected the two computers together. "Now, this is really illegal, but you can't create a security system without knowing how to test it to breaking point."

"Hacking, right?"

Ashoka activated the burglar icon on the laptop and suddenly the screen rolled into an endless series of letters and numbers. "Right."

"How come Ash doesn't think like you?" said Parvati. She sounded almost impressed.

"Too busy fighting bad guys, I suppose."

A Microsoft Outlook window opened up. Ashoka grinned as he scanned the emails. "We are in."

Parvati dragged up a chair beside him. Both stared intently at the screen as Ashoka opened up email after email.

The correspondence was mostly between Rani and Savage. Suddenly a lot of things made more sense. Savage had discovered Ash and Parvati were here on 13 December, the day after he'd cast the spell back in his original timeline. Jackie's ambush of Ashoka and the kidnapping of his family had been a two-pronged attack. Savage had guessed, rightly, that Ash would be watching one or the other.

But most exciting of all, the emails confirmed that Ashoka's family were alive. At least they had been this morning. An email from Savage ordered Rani to have them delivered to a private airfield in Kent and flown out. It didn't say to where.

"We need to find them, right now."

Parvati gritted her teeth. "We should have stayed and rescued him."

"How? We were totally outnumbered and you were hurt. At least we can do something good; we have a lead. Ash would want us to do this. They're his family too. Anyway, he's the Kali-aastra. That's like being Superman and Spider-Man and Batman combined, isn't it? He's a one-man superhero team. He doesn't need us."

"Perhaps, perhaps not." She looked worried. "He's changed. He's been trying to hide it, but he's not the way he was. We should have beaten Rani."

"How could you beat someone like her?"

"I saw Ash go face to face with Ravana himself. Believe me, we should have won. But he's slower, weaker than he used to be. His powers are fading. But I don't know why, and he's too proud to tell me."

"Oh, this is just great. I was kind of counting on him swooping in and saving the day!"

"The Kali-aastra's not feeding him the power it should do," said Parvati. "It's not awakened."

Ashoka shook his head. He wasn't getting any of this. "Awakened?"

"All aastras need to be awakened before they are of any real use. Each aastra requires a special spell or sacrifice to activate it. Once activated, it can be used to its full capacity. Think about it this way — what use is a Lamborghini without fuel? It has the potential to travel over two hundred miles per hour, but you can't get it out of the garage without some petrol, can you? An aastra's like that."

"So why didn't Ash just awaken the Kali-aastra?"

"It needs a death — a Great Death. You need to kill someone significant to you. Either a great enemy or great friend. That's what Kali wants, before she'll pass her powers into the aastra."

"Who did Ash kill last time?" The idea was horrible.

"Himself. He allowed himself to die. He gave himself wholly to Kali. What greater sacrifice can there be?"

"Wow. That's pretty desperate."

Parvati nodded. "He did it to save his sister." She looked at him. "You'd do the same."

He'd like to think he would. He would have said he'd do

anything to protect Lucky. But to die? Could he go that far? "I'm not that sort of hero."

"Ash said the same thing to me once. Turns out he was."

"You've got us this far, boy, so you must be doing something right," said Elaine, walking back into the room with an armful of weapons. "You got this airfield's number?"

Ashoka maximised the email. It was addressed to a Captain Lee, double-checking that he was on standby to fly the plane at short notice. The response from the pilot had the contact number below it. Elaine picked up her phone. "Is that Biggin Hill? I'm looking for Captain Lee. There's a family emergency. His wife's gone into labour." Elaine nodded. "I know, but she's in the operating ward and I can't find her mobile. I've called the Hilton because he normally stays there, but they don't have him..." Elaine made a writing motion. "Not the Hilton? Oh, of course. I forgot. The Metropole. The number? That would be most kind."

Ashoka quickly handed her a pencil and she scribbled down a phone number.

Elaine smiled and winked at him. "You've been so kind. No, I'll call him immediately. Thank you. Yes, it's his first. He'll be so annoyed to miss the birth — the baby wasn't due for another week. Bye."

She flourished the sheet of paper. "They took your family to Hong Kong."

A glimmer of hope. Savage wouldn't bother flying them to Hong Kong if he was planning to kill them. "Why Hong Kong? Seems a lot of effort."

"Savage spent years there," said Parvati. "He was one of

the major players in the Opium Wars in the nineteenth century. Hong Kong was their base. It's also one of the key ports in and out of the Far East, and the Savage Foundation does a lot of work out there."

Ashoka looked over to Parvati. "I have to save them." Even if she wouldn't come with him, that's where he was headed.

"I would expect nothing less." She inspected the weapons Elaine had brought up with her and picked up an arrow. "Elaine, can you get us a flight?"

"Us?" asked Ashoka.

Parvati smiled. "Us."

Chapter Twelve

He never thought it would be like this. They'd said it would be easy. That the Hun would roll over and they'd all be back for Christmas. His father had been a soldier. It was an honourable profession, a glorious one. How many stories had he heard, around the village fire at night, of swordsmen and bandits and wolves? So when the call had gone out, he and his brothers had gone with the recruiting sergeant and put their marks on the paper. Though he was born and raised in India, Britain was the heart of the empire and he was a son of the empire.

This is not honourable. This is not glorious.

This is war.

Private Reginald Bose sits deep in the mud, clutching his rifle. Blood pools in the murky water and the only sounds are the cries of dying men, lost in the fog and smoke. He should try to find them. But Reggie can't move.

He is alive. Not like Captain Clarke, who's had a hole blown straight

❖

through him, or like Thompson, who danced like a mad marionette when the machine gun perforated him.

He is uninjured. Unlike Corporal Jack, who crawls in the carnage, dragging himself along with no legs. Men lie among the craters and bodies and churned-up landscape wondering where their bits have gone.

Yet Reggie can't move. How can he? If he leaves this hole then death will swoop down and snatch him up.

He shouldn't be afraid of death, but he is. This is his one life. He is only sixteen and has only just come to the table, and the meal, the feast, is being taken away. He feels as if he is clawing for it with his fingertips.

It is as if God has swept His hand over the land and men have fallen like toys. Their bodies are everywhere, abandoned. Did their lives mean anything? What did they achieve? This piece of mud?

The glorious dead. That's what the memorials will say. But Reggie sniffs and wipes tears from his smoke-blackened face. He doesn't want glory if this is the price.

His life means nothing to the majors and generals who send thousands of men to be torn apart by bombs and bullets and to be strung out on barbed wire, their skins ragged and red like sheets.

His is a little life. But Reggie has a mother and a father and a little sister and other brothers and friends and the villagers that waved him farewell and gave him sweets for the journey from India to here, France and the battlefields of the First World War. His little life sends ripples far beyond the horizon. Are his parents thinking of him this very moment? What prayers are they offering?

Who decides the value of his life? Why is it worth so little here, so much there?

Reggie gazes at the face of his best friend, Paul. He still holds his

❖

hand, though it is cold now and Paul's fingers are stiff. A small red hole decorates the centre of his chest and the blood around it has dried.

This was their first battle. Paul had taken a dozen steps before he'd fallen. His life had been worth a spent bullet and a few muddy footprints.

Paul had got married just before joining the army. His wife, Mary, is a maid at a country house in Dorset. Paul had been a stable hand. His master was a colonel and the male staff had all volunteered to accompany him. The colonel died two weeks ago. There will be a plaque in a church, a memorial service and grand funeral for him. Paul will get a blank spot in the earth and a few flowers from his widow. They both died the same way, but one's death has been deemed great and the other's very small.

There is a splash. Voices whisper. Reggie hears a bolt being drawn. Shadows groan within the gently rolling fog.

Death comes.

His bullets are spent and all he has is the bayonet jutting from his rifle. Reggie should fight. He should kill these men. He should give them their own deaths, be they great or small. Is a German's life worth less than his? It has to be, otherwise there would be no point to war. If a man's life was worth the same as any other's then there would be no killing. And all this would have been for nothing.

Reggie releases Paul. He locks his fingers as tightly as possible around his rifle and stands.

I want my death to mean something.

He wants to believe it. He needs to believe it.

He sees three German soldiers.

They see him.

Reggie splashes through the mud, yelling. He charges, rifle thrust ahead of him, aimed at the central soldier.

❖

His boot catches on something. Reggie slips. The rifle drops from his hands and as he falls he sees a hand, the hand of a dead man, the fingers snagged on his shoelaces.

Sprawled in the gore and mud, Reggie struggles to move. A German kicks him, and stars and blinding flashes burst behind his eyes. They slam their rifles into him, beating him. His death will not be worth even a bullet.

A shot rings out. A man cries and falls on top of Reggie.

A fierce, warrior's roar breaks the fog.

Reggie heaves the cumbersome body off, but he's sunk too deep in the mud to free himself. He can only watch.

The remaining two Germans, back to back, shoot wildly. There, a shadow! Then it vanishes.

There is a flash of fire from the grey gloom. Then another German tumbles backwards, a burst of red flowering on his forehead.

A man seems to grow from the smoke, coalescing from nothing, insubstantial one moment, then fully flesh and blood the next, a pistol in one hand and a cane in the other.

The remaining German fires. The man brushes the rifle aside and beats the pistol butt into the man's face. Bones crunch. He drops his pistol and his hand flashes to the silver cane top, a tiger's head. Bright steel flashes free and a narrow blade passes through the German's neck.

The man twists the blade, opening the wound wider as blood sprays from the holes either side of the throat.

The German drops to his knees, then keels over as the blade is pulled out.

"There, all done," says the man. He wipes the blade clean and looks down at Reggie. "Need a hand, fella?"

"You killed them. All of them."

The man helps Reggie up. "It's what they deserved." He brushes his blonde hair from his face. "Just sport, really."

Reggie stares at the carnage. "How?"

"Practice. I've had a lot."

"But he was standing right next to you when he fired. How did he miss? It's not..."

Reggie stops. The German fired when the man was right in front of him.

There is a gaping, bleeding hole in the man's chest. Blood dribbles down his jacket, black and thick in the semi-darkness.

Bewildered, Reggie can only stare at the hole. "How?"

The man's blue eyes shimmer and he puts his finger to his lips. "Shh, let this be our little secret."

Chapter Thirteen

When Ash woke, he wasn't sure at first where he was. Then he felt the steel manacles around his wrists and fetters around his ankles, and remembered.

Rani hadn't taken any chances. She and Jackie had hauled him into the back of the Humvee, then driven for what seemed like hours.

They'd arrived at some airfield just as the sun was rising in a grey sky to see a plane waiting for them. A sleek, dagger-like Learjet, one of three, each with the Savage logo on the tail. He'd been half dragged, half carried up the steps, then dropped into a seat. Minutes later the plane was in the sky and they were heading into the sun, flying east. Ash closed his eyes.

So he'd slept, and dreamed. Dreamed of being a soldier back in the First World War.

❖

No one famous. No one out of the history books. That was odd. Ash's previous visions had been of legendary heroes like Rama and the first emperor of India, the first Ashoka. So why some nobody of a private in the trenches? The memories didn't come by chance; they came for a reason. He'd been thousands of different people, so why was this one coming forward now? This Reggie was trying to tell him something.

There was a vividness to these dreamed memories of his past lives that was utterly different from his conventional dreams, or even his nightmares. By now he knew the difference. What he'd remembered, he could count on being real, and true.

So, he'd met Savage before. There was no doubt in his mind that the man who'd saved his life in this vision, his life when he'd been Reggie, was Alexander Savage. He was in his late thirties, wore a moustache and a captain's uniform, but there was no mistaking him.

Ash shifted again in his seat, and peered out of the window. Ten hours flying east and they'd re-entered the night.

The moon shone high over a vast landscape of deep shadow and brilliant crystalline snow, sparkling faintly blue under the lunar light. As Ash leaned up against the window, he knew it could be only one mountain range. The Himalayas.

Ash's belly grumbled. The plane juddered and banked to the right. It swept through a thin mattress of clouds, and Ash spotted lights below, a narrow strip of red eyes laid out upon the snow. It was wedged between two sheer cliff faces and beyond the landing strip fell away to nothing.

❖

The jet shook, the vibrations passing through the floor and up Ash's toes. It jerked from side to side as the winds accelerated through the mountain pass, buffeting the small craft.

"Scared?" asked Rani. She sat facing him, buckled up and wearing a heavy fur-lined coat, the collar done up to her cheeks.

The mountain walls seemed to almost touch the wing tips. Ash smiled. "Are you? You can hold my hand if you are."

Rani ignored him.

Jackie stumbled to her seat and she didn't look good at all. Her tawny mane shivered as she watched the rocks blur past and her nails dug deep into the armrests.

They were flying low over a collection of huts. Plainly built from stone and roofed with tiles, they were simple farmers' huts with corrals where long-haired yaks huddled together for warmth. Then the nose of the Learjet rose and the engines screeched as it hit the tarmac. Ash jerked forward as the brakes slammed on. The jet raced along the runway, the scenery whizzing past until, not as soon as he would have liked, the plane slowed.

Jackie gave out a huge sigh.

They had barely come to a stop before Rani was up and pushing open the door. Freezing wind threw in a flurry of snow and she sank her chin deeper into her furs. "Bring him."

Jackie grabbed Ash under the arm and pushed him forward.

Jeez, he was going to be an icicle. The snow was knee-deep and the wind howled between the mountains, bringing

❖

swirling clouds. His skin stung as if thousands of tiny ice crystals were attacking him. And the air was so thin. Ash gulped big lungfuls and even then was panting as he came down the dozen or so steps.

Headlights dazzled him. Four white Humvees faced them, engines running, their tyres half submerged. People moved about, but they were just silhouettes against the glaring headlights. Ash clenched his jaw to stop his teeth chattering.

"Ash, you look positively frozen," a man shouted over the roar of the winds and the noise of the jet engines. He stepped forward, taking off his own coat. "Here, boy. We can't have you catching pneumonia."

Of course. Why else bring him here? "Savage."

The man held out his coat. His face wasn't made of human flesh, it looked more like porcelain, or marble — perfect, unblemished by any mark or wrinkle or colour. He was dressed in white and his eyes were hidden behind black shades. Tucked under his arm was a tiger-headed cane, the handle a snarling beast with ruby eyes. His blonde hair was almost as pale as his skin and it shimmered as it blew loose around his face. He put the coat around Ash's shoulders.

"And I hardly think we need these. Please, Rani. Young Ash is our guest."

Rani said nothing, but undid the cuffs and manacles and tossed them aside into the snow.

Savage, arm still around Ash's shoulder, directed him to the nearest vehicle. "You ride with me. We've so much catching up to do."

Ash gazed at the man. The last time he'd seen him he'd

been a grotesque, deformed monster with barely a spark of life left in him. This version was little short of a god. In spite of himself, Ash struggled to control the sense of... awe that threatened to overwhelm him. It was like a heatwave radiating off Savage.

"Where am I?" Ash asked.

Savage paused as he reached the Humvee and turned to face Ash, taking off his glasses.

Ash stiffened. A pair of black eyes gazed at him. They were black upon black, and inside the pupils swirled the darkness of the abyss. A thin border of fiery red circled the edges of the irises and there was nothing good or human in the blank gaze. These were the eyes of someone who'd stared into hell. Savage's smiled broadened. "Welcome to Tibet."

Jackie and Rani travelled separately, leaving Ash alone with Savage and the driver. The going was tough; the roads were narrow tracks with a sheer drop to one side and ten-metre-high piles of snow on the other. Savage lit a cigarette as he made himself comfortable on the seat opposite Ash. He waved the first cloud of smoke away and peered at Ash, that superior smile never fading from his bloodless lips. "You do not look well, Ash."

"Looking at you makes me sick."

"No, it's more than that." Savage laughed. "Kali has abandoned you."

There was no point denying it. "How can you tell?"

"My magic gives me enhanced perceptions. You no longer radiate the way you used to. That divine light's gone out, leaving you a dull, dull mortal." Savage scrutinised him. "The Kali-aastra must have used all its remaining power to transport you across timelines. The charge has depleted down to nothing."

"So you brought me here just to gloat?"

"Hardly, Ash. I brought you here to celebrate." He flicked ash off the burning stub. "If it hadn't been for you, I'd never have cast the Time Spell."

"It's not over yet, Savage," said Ash, with a confidence he really didn't feel.

"You know, I knew most of the Time Spell already. It was written on Parvati's scrolls, the ones I took from her back in Lahore."

"So why didn't you cast it then?"

Savage sucked a deep breath and shook his head slowly. "No, that would have been a disaster. Magic's a dodgy business. Even with small, minor spells, the risks are huge. You saw what I'd become with two centuries of spell casting."

"A deformed monstrosity."

"Exactly. Fortunately I had Ravana himself to guide me. But his scrolls were not complete. So when we went to Lanka..."

Ash understood. "The Black Mandala."

The Black Mandala had been created by Ravana. It had all his magic inscribed upon it and last year he and Savage had ended up in the demon king's capital city to find it. Ash had destroyed it, but clearly not soon enough.

Savage tapped his temple. "I'd only studied it for a few minutes before you tore it up, but all the patterns, all Ravana's symbols, were in here, locked in my subconscious. The mind's a remarkable thing, Ash. Everything you see and hear gets stored in here. Vast libraries of knowledge. We don't forget anything, we merely lose the ability to access it."

"So what did you do? Hypnotise yourself into remembering?"

"Something very much like that. I put myself in a trance, pictured the Black Mandala before me, and drew the rest of the Time Spell out. I didn't need to remember it all, just the sections missing from Parvati's scrolls."

"No mistakes at all?"

"I wouldn't be here if there'd been even a single syllable out of place."

"Congratulations," said Ash. "So why are you here, in Tibet? Found your retirement home?"

The vehicle turned off the mountain road and Ash breathed a sigh of relief. The endless zigzagging up the mountain edges had been steep and grim. And the altitude sickness wasn't helping. A powerful headache throbbed within his skull and he could only take in half as much oxygen as he needed so was constantly gasping. How could Savage be wasting breath on smoking?

Now the landscape was levelling out. They passed by a *stupa*, a white-painted religious tower, wreathed with fluttering prayer flags. Piles of stones lay around it, each a token of some long-ago pilgrim. The road was tarmacked, and the houses they passed, traditionally built, were in good condition. A farmer was loading his horse cart and stopped to give a solemn bow as they rolled past.

Savage put out his cigarette and lit a second. "I love Tibet.

I come here when I want to get away from it all. The first time was in the 1950s, with the Chinese invasion. The military conquest was very straightforward. The Tibetans were armed with bows and arrows, and the Chinese rolled in with tanks. But the Tibetans had powerful sorcerers. I was hired by the Chinese to deal with them."

"I would have thought China had its own magicians."

Savage's lips parted slyly. "It has more than mere magicians."

A mountain loomed up ahead. Its top was lost in the clouds, but the sun, just appearing over the jagged mountain range, lit the east-facing side with a soft pinkish hue. Lights shone upon its sheer walls, and as they drew closer Ash saw buildings and terraces and towers. Birds, mere black specks, circled above the many golden roofs and gardens that jutted out from the rock.

"Bukrong monastery," said Savage. "The Chinese gave it to me after we'd cleared out the monks."

As they approached Ash strained his neck gazing up and up at it. It seemed to have been built out of the mountainside. The walls were ochre, red, blue and white, vibrant and fresh against the austere grey of the stone. Vast glaciers surrounded the monastery, brilliant and shimmering as the sun rose.

The gates opened up and they entered a courtyard. Servants, local Tibetans in long red coats, rushed to open the door the moment the car stopped. Behind them came in the other two vehicles and soon Savage was accepting tea from his bowing staff. A cup was offered to Ash and he took it, glad of the hot fluid warming him.

The gates closed with an ominous dull thud.

❖

"Rooms have been prepared for you, Ash, so eat, rest and make yourself comfortable." Savage started up the wide staircase into the main building. "Now, if you'll excuse me, I have work to do."

Jackie growled in Ash's ear, "Let me take you to your rooms."

He followed her.

"You have this floor to yourself," she said when they arrived at his quarters. "There is a servant outside if you need anything."

Ash glanced at the door. "No locks?"

"Where can you possibly go?" said Jackie, closing the door behind her as she left.

Chapter Fourteen

Daylight woke Ash. Bright shards of light illuminated the bedroom, cut into uneven angles by the old wooden window shutters.

Blimey, he was stiff. Ash forced himself up, aching and groaning like an old man. So this was what it felt like to be human. He'd forgotten.

His rumbling belly reminded him that he hadn't eaten in over twenty-four hours. Beside the bed was a brass bowl of fruit. He devoured an apple and set to munching his way through a couple of bananas. A mug of Chinese tea waited on a table and he sipped it as he pushed and stretched himself, roughly knocking the ache out of his muscles. There was a pile of magazines stacked on a table. Ash flicked through a few as he ate.

They all had Savage on the front.

❖

Time's Man of the Year. The *Economist*. *Newsweek*. He was even on the cover of *Rolling Stone* with a bunch of rock stars. There he stood, white-suited, black-framed and gold-skinned, a god among mortals.

It felt as if Savage had already won.

Ash turned the magazines over so he wouldn't have to look at Savage's smug, victorious face.

A bath filled with steaming water waited, with fresh clothing piled on stools beside. Ash dragged his bruised body into the hot water and let the pain soak out.

Now what are you gonna do?

Time to review the situation.

The cons. Trapped somewhere in the highest mountain range in the world. Captive of an immortal sorcerer who can travel through Time. Guarded by a demon princess who wants to kill me really, really badly. Not friends with a jackal-demon who wants the same, if not more.

What else?

Oh yes, total and permanent loss of all superhuman abilities. Which sucks. Big time.

So, those were the cons. What about the pros?

Ash frowned. There had to be some. Hmm...

I'm still alive. That counts.

Refreshed, belly filled, and wearing clean clothes, Ash looked around his room. All over the walls were indistinct images of gods and monsters and legendary heroes that could be seen as faded outlines on the worn plaster. The beams had once been painted, but now they too were bowed with age and rotten. Thin, moth-eaten carpets covered the uneven wooden floor, and the wind blew in around the ill-fitting window frames. Coals burned in tall bronze braziers, but it wasn't enough to keep him warm. Ash found a long Tibetan coat in a wardrobe. The inner lining was fur, maybe goat or yak, and the outer dark red Chinese silk embroidered with dragons. He slung it on over his woollen outfit and leather boots, also lined with fur. His breath steamed in the cold air.

The door swung open and there was Savage. "Rested?" he asked.

"What do you want with me? Why all this?"

Savage stepped aside. "Let me show you, Ash."

Reluctantly Ash stepped out. Savage led the way and they passed along corridors deep into the mountain. The lighting came from small oil lamps and the walls danced with sinister shadows.

"This is something only the Eternal Warrior would understand. That is why I want you here. To be witness to my legacy," said Savage as he tapped his cane along the flagstones.

Legacy? Ash didn't like the sound of that.

"Here, my sanctuary," said Savage, stopping before a pair of doors. Each was encased in bronze and ornately carved with mythological animals. They seemed to stir as Ash approached, but that was probably just a trick of the light. Probably.

Savage pulled the bronze doors open and a sigh of air escaped, gently stirring torch-lit motes into a dance about them. Beyond the doors was a gloomy chamber of bare, crudely chiselled stone, inhabited by vague shapes.

"This is all I have been, Ash," said Savage as he lit a heavy iron candelabrum from an oil lamp and held it ahead of him. "Not many have ever been down here, but you, of all people, should see this."

Ash followed him in.

Savage put the candelabrum down and let its light swell.

It shone upon barrels of muskets, upon the keen edges of swords and on moth-eaten fabrics of old uniforms. There were flags, smoke-stained and bullet-ridden, hanging from banner poles above them. The chamber reached upwards ten or fifteen metres, and was perhaps the same in diameter, a roughly hewn circle with dusty carpets and faded drapes upon the walls. A stool, ornately carved from some dark wood, sat in the centre and Savage offered it to Ash. Ash refused.

He lifted down a long-barrelled musket with a curved stock, inlaid with a vine design in mother-of-pearl. The barrel must have measured almost two metres.

"An Afghan *jezail*," said Savage. "I got that when we stormed Kabul back in 1842."

Ash breathed deep. Despite the thin air he collected the scent of oil, of wood and steel, and of blood and gun smoke. Sweat stained the leather sword hilts black and the edges of the bindings were wrinkled with wear. One mannequin wore a grey uniform; its buttons still shone bright gold, but the shoulder braid was frayed. Ash put his finger in one of the holes in the cloth. "That must have hurt."

"Gettysburg. I was a colonel. Now that was a battle. A slaughter."

Ash wasn't much up on American history, but he knew Gettysburg had been the bloodiest battle of the Civil War. "You fought for the South? Why am I not surprised?"

Savage picked up a pair of iron manacles, shaking the chains. Each link was at least three centimetres thick. "You think slavery is wrong, is that it?"

"You even need to ask?"

"I owned slaves. I spent years involved in that 'peculiar institution'. I shipped them from Africa to the cotton fields of the South and the sugar plantations of the West Indies. Slaves drove the economy, Ash. I even had a farm in Kentucky for a while. Me, a farmer. Can you imagine?"

He dropped the manacles upon the stone with a clang that echoed around them. "Utterly boring for the most part. But I do remember one evening. I'd been riding and stopped at the crest of a hill. The sun was on the horizon and the sky was a beautiful darkening red, the clouds soft pink and the upper tops of the trees just tipped with shimmering purple leaves. Quite, quite beautiful." Savage sighed and his eyes were distant, as if he was still looking at that sunset.

"Down the slope and all the way to that horizon were cotton fields with line upon line, endless regiments, of slaves. Men, women, children. All collecting the white tufts with their dark, nimble fingers. My overseers rested under a tree and their horses grazed by a large pond. There was a perfect peacefulness about it. But how they sang, Ash. No choir of angels could have matched it. It was a tribal song from their home in Africa, mixed in with a hymn they had been taught, so it was both familiar and exotic. Hundreds of voices, in perfect, simple harmony. The children wouldn't have been old enough to have learned it in Africa; it was a uniquely American creation, this song. No free man would have sung it with equal passion. Do you know why?"

"Do tell me."

"Slaves are free in a way no one else is. They have no responsibilities. They worry about nothing. Their needs are simple: food and shelter. Their duties are simple: to work and ask no questions. They know where they will be this year, the next, the year after that and for ever. If they do what they're told, they will be taken care of. That is why childhood is such a blessed state. Deep down, people can't deal with their lives. They want to be taken care of. That evening was the most perfect moment of my long, long life. They were content and untroubled. Happy, Ash. As close to happy as a person can be. On my farm we needed no manacles. No whips, no threats."

"You really believe that?"

"Look at what happens when you give people freedom, choice. Invariably they make a mess of things. What is democracy but rule of the mob?"

"Let me guess — this is where you suggest it would all be better if you were in charge?"

Savage's eyes darkened. "I've seen the future, and humanity will leave only ashes." He spoke with cold conviction. "Time mastery isn't just backwards, it's forward as well. I've glimpsed the future... futures. It's in a state of flux, but one thing they all have in common is that mankind destroys itself. It may be war, it may be overpopulation, pollution, global warming...

All dangers we can see right now, but no one with the will or ambition to do what is necessary."

"And what's that?"

"Be happy with less. It really is that simple. Food, shelter. And life. But people pursue unsustainable goals. More cars. More luxuries. More food. More this. More that. Like parasites you only consume, and sooner than you think you will devour your host. Then what? You cannot eat money, nor drink oil."

"So you want us to be happy with a bowl of rice?"

"In a few years there will be catastrophic climate change. Drought for some countries, torrential rain for others. Crops globally will be destroyed. Wars will erupt as nations fight to control resources. Then, Ash, when you see cities filled with starving populations, where they will eat the wallpaper and their shoes and finally each other, you will be very happy for some rice. I would save the world such pain."

"And how are you going to do that?"

Savage smiled. "With shock and awe."

Chapter Fifteen

Savage led Ash out of the sanctuary and gestured to a staircase. "You'll see better what I mean from outside."

Ash hesitated. Should he let Savage just gloat? That was why he was showing Ash all this. It was typical arrogance. But he'd come this far. He had to know what Savage was planning. For better or for worse.

They climbed up and up and up. Ash was panting after the first flight, his lungs struggling with the lack of oxygen. By the second flight his legs were shaking. But up and up they continued. He forced himself to keep pace with Savage, not wanting the Englishman to see how weak he was, stubborn pride keeping him going while his strength failed.

The stairs were of dark polished wood, and lanterns lit each landing. The servants bowed as Savage passed, never meeting his gaze. They worked in silence, heads down, not

❖

one even looking in Ash's direction. There were no manacles and they looked well taken care of, but they were surely bound by something – fear, perhaps. Each trembled slightly as Savage walked by.

That's how he keeps them under control. They're too terrified to do or say anything.

A strong, freezing breeze descended the staircase, carrying with it a swirl of snowflakes. Sunlight intruded above and they reached the top flight, Ash dripping with sweat and breathing heavily.

"What a view, eh?" said Savage.

It was true. They walked out on to a tiled, elevated landing. The monastery had been partly carved into the mountainside and a natural plateau had been converted into an elegant garden terrace with trees, a narrow iced-over stream and shrubs sitting in large ceramic pots. There was no barrier and Savage walked to the edge. The drop was sheer – more than three hundred metres to bare rock, jagged and shadowy, like the maw of some gigantic beast.

Clouds brooded overhead and a light flurry danced about them. The world was pristine white, the snow below patterned with the shadows of passing clouds, so it felt as if the landscape moved beneath them. Far, far away to the south were the peaks of the Himalayas, barely visible through the snow, but a line that lay between Savage's palace and the rest of the world. Geography wasn't Ash's strong suit, but he knew that beyond those peaks lay Nepal, and beyond Nepal lay India... but a long way beyond the horizon. Ash had never felt so utterly alone.

❖

Rani waited beside a wrought-iron table with a bottle of champagne and three long-stemmed flutes on it. Next to the drinks were some chunky military binoculars and an old-fashioned telescope made of wood and brass.

Her chin was sunk into the thick wool of her long green coat and her eyes were only half open. Her movements were slow and overly deliberate. Her face, deformed by the scars, was drawn and her cheeks jutted hard against the scale-flecked skin.

It's the cold, Ash thought. *Rani's a snake. It's slowing her down.*

"My lord, all is prepared," said Rani.

Savage handed Ash the telescope. "See that building down there?"

Ash slid open the telescope and gazed down where he pointed. The lens distorted the sight, warping the edges, but he did see a large building with a walled courtyard. Children, wrapped up so they looked like colourful snowmen, ran and had snowball fights, while a few elderly monks tried to keep some sort of order.

"One of my charities — an orphanage. The headmaster's an Old Etonian friend of mine."

"Why are you showing me this?"

Savage moved over to the edge. Ash went to join him. *One push and—*

"Don't bother, Ash. I can fly," said Savage. "Please pay attention. This is rather important."

"What is? So you run an orphanage. Lessens your guilt, does it?"

"I have nothing to feel guilty about. Those children down

there are well looked after. They have the best education and the best... medical treatments. Not one has had even a runny nose since they joined. You won't find a healthier bunch of kids this side of, well, anywhere." He nodded to Rani and the rakshasa princess drew out a small radio from her sleeve.

"Now," she said, speaking into it.

Ash turned to the sound of a motor running behind him. The palace continued up, getting narrower and smaller, like a stepped pyramid, and on the level above them one of the larger doors opened.

A missile launcher rolled forward on its tracks and stopped when its head was jutting out of the building. The targeting mechanism turned and clicked, locking into place. Nestled in a tube was a single missile.

The weapon was about three metres long, the nose and the front half made of clear glass, a long tube filled with a green liquid that bubbled and frothed. The tube was painted with symbols: Harappan pictograms, from the ancient language of India.

"I call it the Ravan-aastra," said Savage.

"Only gods can make aastras." But dread filled Ash's heart.

Savage smiled. "Did Parvati ever tell you about her early life? How when she was born she was human? Or thought she was?"

"Yes. The rakshasa soul awakens over time. She said she used to have bad dreams, but they were actually old memories resurfacing."

"That's right. The actual change comes around puberty. That's when the rakshasa takes over. The first transforming

❖

is rather dramatic. They call it the Harrowing. The child has no control over what's happening and they assume their true form. Their monstrous form. Do you know what Parvati did when it happened to her?" asked Savage, quite casually.

"She left her family. She realised what she was and thought it safer for them if she wasn't around."

"Is that what she told you?"

Rani snorted with derision. "We killed them. Killed them all. We lived with parents, grandparents and six other siblings. We tore them to pieces. We ate their flesh and drank their blood."

"No. Parvati would never do that."

Rani looked at him with cold, deadly hatred. "That's what I did, and she is me."

Savage laughed. "Poor, naive boy. When the demon soul awakens it's mad with rage, rage at its imprisonment, and bloodthirsty. Some, a few, hang on to a small human part and perhaps flee before they can do too much harm, but most were raised within families, have homes and people around them, and that first transformation of a reborn rakshasa bodes ill for anyone caught in the vicinity."

The missile hummed as guidance fins adjusted themselves along its sleek, deadly body.

"I intend to take over the world," said Savage. "It's a dirty job, but someone's got to do it. Otherwise you mortals are going to destroy it."

"You and whose army, Savage?" Ash looked around. "How many rakshasas have you got? A hundred? A thousand? Ten thousand, tops?"

"Many, many more. It's just that they don't yet know it." Savage searched the landscape with his binoculars. "I've spent millions in the last decade researching DNA. How to repair it, how to strengthen it. I've discovered there's one ingredient that does the job better than most. DNA from rakshasas. I've cured most of the world's ills by adding just a touch of demon into everything. It is, literally, the magic ingredient, and why I now own the biggest pharmaceutical company on the planet."

Ash felt a bilious lump bubbling up his throat.

Savage continued. "I'm going to save the world, Ash, whether it likes it or not. But one of the problems has been humans. They've overrun. They're top of the food chain with no predator to keep them in line."

"Rakshasas."

"Yes, Ash, rakshasas. But since their near extinction by Rama thousands of years ago, there have never been enough to keep the human population in check. Only a handful are born every decade. A trickle. I'm going to turn that trickle into a tidal wave. I've found a way to activate the Harrowing."

Ash looked at the missiles. "What's in them?"

"My new miracle drug. Retro-Anti-Virus Number One." RAVN-I.

Ash gazed down at the orphanage with creeping terror.

"The results might vary depending on the child." A sly, cruel grin spread over Savage's pale face. "An entire generation of children, transformed into demons. Throughout the world. There will of course be a period of readjustment, but you can't make an omelette without breaking eggs. And tell me, how will you fight them? They will be *children*, people's sons and daughters. What soldier would raise his rifle against his own child? Your humanity, your compassion, will be your downfall."

He gestured to Rani. "Let's show Ash what I mean."

Rani pressed the button on the radio.

The missile launched.

Chapter Sixteen

The missile screamed and flames burst from the exhaust, filling the plateau with smoke and the stench of burning petrol. The flames turned from red to blue to white, the noise rising in pitch as the colours transformed and the missile shook, trapped within the launch mechanism. Ash covered his ears, but it made no difference; the hellish wail pierced him.

Then it was free.

It roared overhead, dipping a moment before locking into its flight path, rising high over the snow-clad landscape in a trail of black smoke, the sun glinting on its glass body.

"Now this is the exciting bit," said Savage, his attention focused through the binoculars.

The missile reached its zenith, then began a slow dive. Even as it fell it altered direction, shifting from side to side with added bursts of speed as it swooped towards the orphanage.

And Ash could do nothing.

Then, still high over the building, it exploded.

Ash's heart swelled. It had failed! He wanted to laugh. All that talk of Savage's—

A green cloud spread out above the orphanage and began to descend over the walled playground and the surrounding area.

"The burst radius is a mile," said Savage. "But depending on prevailing winds the contaminants could cover another ten miles easily."

The orphanage vanished within the green fog.

Savage pointed at the telescope, limp in Ash's hand. "You won't want to miss this."

Reluctantly Ash raised the telescope.

At first all he could see was the green smoke. Dark silhouettes moved within it, flailing around, stumbling and lost within this thick cloud. He caught a glimpse of someone tall, one of the monks, trying to guide the kids indoors, but they were too scared and panicked to pay attention. A few collapsed.

Ash's fingers tightened around the telescope, but he continued to watch.

A wind blew the clouds apart, revealing the playground. A handful of children, all younger than Ash, stumbled or lay in the snow, coughing and crying and choking.

One boy shook. He was curled up, head buried between his knees, his entire body spasming violently. He beat his head with his fists as if trying to smash out what was within. Then he threw back his head and screamed.

❖

His black hair thickened and spread over his face. He tore at his clothes with long claws, and then got to his feet, swaying and writhing.

A monk ran out of the thinning cloud, his scarlet robe covering his mouth and nose. He ran to the boy and held him.

The other children began to shriek and scream. Ash couldn't hear them, he was too far away, but their wide-open silent mouths made him shake.

Scales spread over the face of a girl. One boy, only five or six, stared in horror as extra arms burst out of his chest — long, spindly and covered in black hairs. A group of children ran around on all fours with tails swishing and whiskered snouts twitching. The monks looked about them in bewilderment, horrified. Four of the kids, the youngest, were unchanged; they gathered around the monks, staring and sobbing at what was happening to their friends. One monk fell down, tripping over a boy transformed into a black-pelted wolf. He tumbled in the snow, landing on his back. The wolf sniffed him.

It growled and bared its yellow fangs.

The monk raised his hands, saying something as the wolf shook off the last of its torn and tattered clothes. It put its forepaws on the old man's chest and the other rakshasas crowded around the fallen monk.

The wolf paused. Did some human part of it make it hesitate? It shook its head ferociously and howled.

The monk, ever so slowly, tried to stand.

"Now that's a mistake," said Savage.

❖

The wolf sprang. It hit the monk and both crashed into the snow, throwing up a big cloud of white. The jet of blood shot out and arced over the other demons. They charged in and attacked.

"Run," urged Ash. "Run." He turned away from the frenzy to the monk trying to shield the youngest, still human, kids. "Run!"

It was all in vain.

A huge bear lumbered towards the small group. A trio of snarling wild dogs blocked the doorway. Huge spiders with human faces crept over the snow on their stalking legs. The monk stood in front of the four petrified children, trying to protect them. Ash watched him speaking to them. They closed their eyes.

Ash lowered the telescope. He couldn't watch.

"Oh, Ash," said Savage. "You're missing the best bit."

Ash couldn't breathe and he grabbed the table as his legs gave away. The bottle tottered, but the glasses fell, one smashing on the frosty tiles.

"Careful, that's a '53." Savage took up the champagne. "I think this calls for a celebration, don't you?"

Ash's head swam and the ground lurched as he fell to his knees. Bile fermented in his guts, choking him as it climbed up his throat. He closed his eyes, but all that did was bring the images flashing back. The monk torn apart. The little kids closing their eyes as the demons prepared to devour them. The old man trying in vain to protect them with his feeble body.

Savage's laugh.

❖

Tears blinded him and his stomach clenched. He fell to his knees as the pain doubled, the knots twisting tighter and tighter.

Once, in a fortress far to the south, Savage had told him how jackals prey on the weak, how he'd set his demons on Lucky unless Ash did what he said. Ash had imagined the horror of such a feeding frenzy, but had never thought to actually see it. And this was just a fraction of what lay ahead.

He clawed at the ground, despairing for those kids he had been helpless to save.

"The drug's being delivered to key locations throughout the world," said Savage. "It's not been easy to infect the entire planet, but I've had the time and money to do it."

"I'll stop you," said Ash.

Savage didn't appear to be listening. The cork popped. "Ah, only two glasses. You'll have to go without, I'm afraid."

Feeling along the ground, Ash's hands touched something sharp. Through eyes blurred with tears he spotted something narrow and crystalline — the broken stem of the champagne glass. The tip was as sharp as a dagger. Instinctively his fingers wrapped around it.

Ash wiped his face and struggled to his feet. He had one shot.

"There'll be a period of anarchy, but that will help separate the weak from the strong," said Savage, his back to Ash as he poured the champagne. "Eventually the newly reborn rakshasas will rally to me and then we'll start our work in earnest. With Ravana gone, I now rule the demon nations."

"People will fight against you," said Ash.

"And destroy their own populations? I don't think so. No, society will collapse and region by region, country by country, I will come and establish my rule. Humanity will have to live more simply, but under the dominion of my rakshasas they'll keep in line. It might take a hundred years, but that's not a problem for me any more."

Ash glared at Savage's back. Every ounce of concentration was focused on his mission. He felt a tremor run through him.

Savage turned to Rani, holding two drinks, and passed one to her. "Cheers. Here's to a reign of a thousand years. At least." They clinked glasses.

Ash tightened his grip, his thumb testing the jagged tip of the glass. "A thousand?" he whispered. He stepped closer. "Not if I can help it."

Savage turned. "I'm sorry?"

"You should be."

Ash thrust the shard upwards, a perfect killing blow. Straight and fast. It tore into Savage's neck just below the jaw and went in all the way to the base. Savage grabbed Ash's wrist, but it was too late.

Ash pulled away as Savage stumbled. He still tried to hold on to his glass and the champagne sloshed over him.

Rani smashed into Ash, knocking him against the wall, and she was hissing at him, her fangs just centimetres from his neck.

But Ash didn't care. He just watched Savage slump to the floor, blood pouring from the fresh wound. It came in a torrent, covering his shirt, his sleeve, pooling on the frosty flagstones. With slippery hands Savage got his nails around the base of the glass and pulled it out. Big mistake, as now there was nothing plugging the wound. Blood spurted in time with his heartbeat.

Savage gasped as pink foam filled his mouth, staining his perfect teeth grotesquely. There was a final gurgle. His hands fell to his sides and the champagne glass rolled away.

Ash didn't need *Marma Adi* or any special power to know the blow had been fatal.

Savage was dead.

Chapter Seventeen

Elaine's contacts at the airport hadn't stretched to an upgrade, and after fourteen hours packed into Economy, wedged between a snoring businessman and a kid who played his Game Boy from take-off to touchdown, Ashoka looked and felt like a zombie. He'd not slept at all and was now paying the price.

At night Hong Kong looked as if it was made of jewels. The amber-lit streets shone like rivers of gold and the skyscrapers sparkled like a dragon's hoard, emerald and sapphire, diamond and onyx and ruby. Spires soared, shining citadels of glowing colours and dazzling patterns. It made London look like some provincial village.

Massive tankers and freighters crossed the harbour to and from ports in the New Territories and the world beyond. These ships had sailed ever since Britain had seized the islands from the Chinese in the nineteenth century, and though the age of pirates and the Opium Wars were long over, trade still flourished, but where once it had been tea, silver, silk and opium, now it was electrical goods, mobile phones, cars and the machines of comfort – all the toys the West couldn't do without.

Ashoka yawned as they entered the vast Lantau Airport and wound their way through its labyrinthine glass corridors. Through the windows he saw the forest of skyscrapers of Hong Kong Island.

Parvati straightened her sunglasses as they made their way through customs. "It's changed since I was here last."

"When was that?"

"Late nineteenth century."

"Business or pleasure?"

"The British had established Hong Kong as their colony and it was the base of their opium trade. Savage was one of the main players behind it, and I had hoped to track him down. I didn't get him, but I did make a few friends and am owed a couple of favours."

"What sort of friends? Triads? Tongs? Chinese mafia types? I've watched practically every John Woo movie ever made."

"Dragons." Parvati headed for the exit.

Ashoka shook his head. "Sorry, I must have misheard. I thought you said 'dragons'."

"That's right."

Ashoka stood there, struggling to understand what he'd just been told. "Dragons?" he said again, following Parvati out of the airport.

*

❖

Minutes later they were in a taxi. If Hong Kong was awesome from above, it was mind-blowing at street level. The skyscrapers gathered over the sky like an army of cyber-titans, clad in glass, steel and beams of light. People jostled and crowded out every pavement; there were shops, stalls and outside tables with diners queuing, and all around huge billboards shone with a million dazzling lights. Signs were in Chinese and English and were everywhere. Ashoka peered out of the window as they crossed over a bridge and watched a helicopter landing on a cruiser, which drifted among the sampans and ferries like a vast white whale among minnows.

Parvati directed the driver in Cantonese as he came off the bridge on to a slip road. Suddenly the scenery changed to shambolic, rundown blocks with steel bars on the windows, mountains of rubbish piled outside the doors and dimly lit teahouses and restaurants. The dazzling wealth of Hong Kong still shone above them, but there were deep shadows too, all the darker by contrast with the lights above. Here a vast, winding under-city existed beneath the flyovers and bridges.

How had he ended up here? Just a few days ago the biggest problem Ashoka had ever had in his life was asking Gemma out on a date. Which he'd utterly failed to do. One thing was for sure — if he got through this, he was totally going to ask her out. Somehow all the school stuff, all the 'who's cool and who's not' stuff seemed so not important any more. Not when his family's lives were at stake and there were rakshasas and dragons roaming the world. *Dragons*. Insane. Insanely insane.

❖

"Where are we going?" asked Ashoka. "Guess it's not the Hilton?"

"Nathan Road. It's the home of the Indian population in Hong Kong. Somewhere for us to hide out, and the only place east of Singapore you'll get a decent curry."

Ashoka looked in the rear-view mirror. "Is that Mercedes following us? It's been with us since the airport."

"You sure?"

"Pretty sure. Recognise the model. Dad wanted one just like it. Mum vetoed it, said it was a mid-life crisis thing." They turned into a tunnel.

"Turn around," ordered Parvati. "Now!"

The driver slammed on the brakes.

A car blocked the road ahead. Its headlights glared through their car's windscreen and Ashoka could just make out the men inside. Men with guns.

The Mercedes stopped behind them, pressing its bumper up against theirs.

"I thought you said you'd made friends when you were here?" said Ashoka.

"I thought I had," muttered Parvati. "Maybe they just want to say hello."

"They don't look very friendly."

Ashoka and Parvati opened their doors and stepped out slowly.

The driver ran for it, and they didn't stop him.

Ashoka surveyed the scene. Seven men, four emerging from the big black SUV in front and three from the Merc behind. Smart black suits and slick hairstyles and shades that just screamed 'gangsta' right down to the tattoos that peeked from beneath the double cuffs and collars of their ghost-white shirts.

"I bet they're packing some serious gats," whispered Ashoka.

"What?"

"Gats," he repeated with a trigger motion.

Even through her dark glasses, Ashoka could feel Parvati rolling her eyes.

The SUV tilted as its final passenger got out. He had to squeeze out of the door and the ground shook as he dropped to the tarmac.

This guy looked like he ate sumo wrestlers. His huge jowls wobbled with each step, his stubby fat arms stuck out from his almost spherical body. His skin had an unhealthy, oily yellow-greenish tinge and warts covered his face. His eyes were a pair of ping-pong balls stuck under a heavy brow, swollen and ready to pop. Ugly veins pulsed along his temples and along his forehead.

He glanced at Ashoka and dismissed him with a click of his tongue. He stopped before Parvati. Gold-plated teeth gleamed. "I am Toad, chamberlain to the Court of Dragons. You are not welcome here, princess."

"I want to talk to Ti Fun," Parvati insisted. "It's important."

"That's not possible."

Parvati took off her glasses and the tip of her forked tongue touched her lips. "I don't want any trouble."

Ashoka backed away a step or two. Parvati looked as if she was about to unleash a whole galaxy of trouble right now. Much of it bone-splintering. If this Toad guy was smart, he would give her what she wanted, now.

❖

But he wasn't, and didn't. He snapped his fingers. "Escort the princess and the mortal somewhere discreet. Do them extreme harm, then put what remains on a plane back to India."

Pistols came out. One man held his sideways, and Ashoka wondered if he wasn't the only John Woo fan here. Then he forced a reality check. People. Pointing guns. At him. Super-bad thing. One of the gangsters took Ashoka's arm. He didn't resist. Another two stood behind Parvati. One pushed her, his pistol wedged between her shoulder blades. She did resist.

"I really wouldn't do that if I were you," said Ashoka.

The man pushed her again.

Parvati twisted, spinning almost a full circle and sweeping her arms like whips. The man's shades flew off as her fist shattered his jaw and she used his body to deliver a kick that lifted the second guy two metres off the ground. She caught a pistol as it whirled out of his hand.

Ashoka ducked behind the taxi before bullet time started.

Instead there was a heavy thud and a long, evil hiss.

Ashoka waited. And waited. Where was the gunfire? Wasn't there meant to be screaming, the sound of shattering glass and bodies flying spinning through the air perforated with bullets and such? Instead there was a tense silence. Like a storm waiting to break.

"Drop your guns," said Parvati. "I won't ask twice."

A dozen or so weapons clattered on to the ground.

Ashoka slowly stood up.

Toad lay on his side. Parvati crouched behind him, using

❖

him as cover. She jammed her pistol barrel behind his earlobe.

"Are you all right, Ashoka?" she asked. "You haven't fainted again?"

"No!" he snapped. Right now? Feeling about five centimetres tall. Still, at least he still had his pants up, metaphorically, unlike these guys. Their brains were still trying to work out how they'd just lost.

"Pick up a pistol. Take the Beretta — it's lighter and you should be able to handle it," she said, still not moving from behind Toad.

"Are you saying I should take the girls' gun?"

"Just get it, and put a bullet in each of the Mercedes tyres. Then the same with the taxi. Then collect all the other firearms and put them in the back of the SUV. Understand?"

It was heavier than he'd thought it would be. Ashoka had never fired anything more than an air pistol. The metal was cold and the grip hard and cumbersome. Ashoka carefully pointed it at the first tyre.

What did you do? Line the rear sight up with the front? He held the pistol with both hands and squeezed the trigger.

The gunshot boomed and bounded a dozen times between the tunnel walls, the echo taking its time to die. Ashoka's ears rang. Smoke unfurled from the barrel and the tyre had a fat hole in it. "Cool," he said. "Let's do that again."

Seven bullets later and Ashoka had done it. He gathered up the rest of the weapons and chucked them in the back of the SUV. "Now what?"

❖

"Get in the passenger seat. You..." she gestured at the gangster nearest the SUV, "... drive."

Ashoka got in and a minute later the vehicle dipped as Toad clambered into the back.

Parvati joined him, squashed into the seat as Toad filled most of it. "Tell the driver to get a move on," she said.

Toad sneered, but only until Parvati shoved the barrel up his nostril. "Take us to the Hurricane."

Chapter Eighteen

They drove into the heart of Hong Kong Central. Bars heaved; shops with screens twenty metres high threw colours over the crowds. It was 2am, but busier than London during rush hour. Black was the new black and the men wore tailored suits and the women... well, the women made Ashoka blush in strange ways. Were those skirts or belts they were wearing? Didn't they feel cold?

Parvati kicked the back of his chair. "Did you hear any of that?"

"Er, course I did. Actually no. What?"

"We're getting out. Focus."

The car turned a corner and entered the underground garage to one of the skyscrapers. There weren't many cars down here, but those that there were counted for more than most. Ashoka gazed at Ferraris, two Lamborghinis, a couple of Porsches, a McLaren, an Aston Martin and a Bentley. A few he didn't recognise looked like they were out of a science magazine, one-of-a-kind concept cars, too expensive, too far out ever to make production lines.

The SUV stopped and Parvati jabbed Toad. "Out you hop."

He grimaced, but did as she said. Parvati followed, the pistol left on the seat. She saw Ashoka reach for it. "Leave it."

"But we might need it."

She glanced towards the steel doors of the lift. "We're going to see one of the four dragons, Ashoka. Leave it."

Toad typed in the PIN and a few seconds later the lift doors opened. Ashoka and Parvati peered in. It was compact. She turned to Toad. "You'd better take the stairs."

Ashoka's heart was beating hard as the numbers on the display pinged. The lift accelerated past the thirtieth floor and kept on climbing. "Tell me about this Ti Fun."

"He's one of the four elementals. Lord of the skies and winds. The others are lords of the earth, fire and water. Ti Fun rules southern China. The rest of the Middle Kingdom is divided between the other three."

"Dragons. Wow." Ashoka couldn't get past that. The counter flickered past fifty and the lift wasn't slowing. "I mean, wow." He leaned against the glass. "I can't breathe." He adjusted his collar. Didn't help. "I think it's the altitude."

"No. It's fear. Don't be surprised if you soil yourself. Most humans do when they first meet a dragon. You might faint." She looked at him, slightly worried. "Or have a heart attack. Try not to die."

❖

"Maybe I should wait downstairs and keep an eye on Toad?" His legs were shaking.

The lift slowed. They approached the two-hundredth floor. It stopped at 201.

"Too late for that," said Parvati as the doors slid open.

It could have been an art gallery. Spotlit marble pedestals stood like soldiers over a floor of dark granite. There were statues, vases, ancient Chinese pottery, and Ashoka recognised a trio of life-size terracotta warriors from the famous dig at Xi'an. Uncle Vik had promised to take him there one day, to see the tomb of the first Chinese emperor. Columns rose up into the high ceiling, inlaid with mosaic dragons of gold, sapphire, emerald and ruby, swooping through glimmering mother-of-pearl clouds. Incense burned, thin weaves of smoke unwinding from sticks sitting in small vases and pots. Something fluttered overhead and Ashoka glimpsed a leathery wing darting among the darkened column heads. Eyes blinked down at him. Floor-to-ceiling windows gave a vertiginous view over the city. The streets lay far below in the canyons between the towers, and humanity seemed very small and insignificant from up here.

The heat was overwhelming. The thermostat had been set at sauna level and steam hissed from bronze floor vents, clouds obscuring the furthest corners of the gallery.

Ashoka's stomach tightened until he could barely stand, the blood pounding in his temples. His heart hammered and, yeah, he thought he just might have a cardiac. Parvati took his hand. Hers was cool, dry and firm. How could she stand it? He gulped, tried to wet his mouth, but it was stone dry. He tried to laugh it off. "Oh, I get it. There'll be this fiery head, but it'll turn out to be some old git hiding behind a curtain, right?"

"You're not in Oz," said Parvati.

"*Parvati.*" The steam ahead trembled and a massive black silhouette stood on the other side. "*Welcome.*"

How big was it? It refused to settle into a single shape, or at least not one Ashoka understood. It could be humanoid, and maybe four or five metres tall, or it could be long and serpentine, as great as the mountains.

Yeah, there was definitely a pain in his chest. Breathing hurt, as if his ribs were being crushed. He stood, hand in hand with Parvati, drenched in sweat and fear.

"Stop it, Ti Fun. Come out and talk."

Oh God, no. He could barely stand it here already. Ashoka backed away, wanting to run back into the lift, but Parvati held him.

"*Very well.*"

"No," whimpered Ashoka. "Stay where you are. Please."

The vents stopped. The distant humming of the fans faded to silence and the clouds dispersed. The shadows coalesced into a single, distinct shape.

The pain clenched around Ashoka's heart.

The last of the clouds parted and there stood Ti Fun, the dragon of the skies.

But instead of a massive fire-breathing dragon covered in scales, there was a ten-year-old Chinese boy wearing a *Kung Fu Panda* T-shirt. He pushed a pair of round spectacles up a stub of a nose. Then he pointed one finger imperiously to the floor. "Kneel before me and tremble, mortal."

❖

Ashoka stood there, gobsmacked. He'd been so frightened he'd thought he was going to faint. Or die.

"Were you just winding me up?" Ashoka stared at Parvati. "That's not funny."

She burst out laughing. "Your face!"

Chapter Nineteen

Ashoka knew his mythology; after all, he'd been playing Dungeons and Dragons for years. It was a well-known fact that dragons could change shape, could adopt any form.

But considering Ti Fun was one of the elementals, shouldn't his human form be some jade-armoured warrior? Or some kung-fu *sifu* type? At the very least, an inscrutable mandarin in flowing silk robes.

He should definitely not be some snot-nosed kid who barely came up to Ashoka's elbow.

Ti Fun sipped at his vanilla milkshake. "I know what you want, Parvati, but my hands are tied. Savage has made a deal with the Court. I cannot interfere."

"After all the trouble he caused you in the Opium Wars and you're just going to let him off?" She was angry, but holding it in. "The man grew rich through the misery he brought upon your people."

Ti Fun frowned. "I didn't say I liked it, but firstly, it was a long time ago, and secondly, he's much, much more powerful now. We can't risk a war with him."

"I don't believe it. You're scared of him!"

"Remember you are my guest, Parvati," said the boy coolly. "Why don't you stay here? Out of the way. I can protect you. Let Savage make his mischief. He can't hurt China."

"Was that the deal? He gets the rest of the world, and you four keep China?"

"What is there outside that we could possibly want? This is the Middle Kingdom, the land between heaven and hell. It is all that matters."

Ashoka listened to them argue, feeling very much a third wheel, but taking in as much as he could. He gathered that Toad worked for the Court and had strict instructions to stop Parvati from coming to Hong Kong. This was all part of the deal Savage had struck with them.

"Why doesn't Savage want us here?" asked Ashoka.

Ti Fun didn't reply. He sucked on his straw, pushing it around the cup.

Parvati leaned closer. "Yes. Why is that?"

"He didn't want you interfering with his... business."

Ashoka leaned forward. "What business?"

"This is not something I discuss with mortals." Ti Fun glanced over at Parvati. "Really, you are too indulgent with them."

❖

Ashoka stood up. "Has this got anything to do with my family?"

Ti Fun just shrugged. "Why would I care for the fate of a few humans?"

Ashoka saw red and, marching up to Ti Fun, slapped the cup out of his hand.

A blast of wind swept him off his feet and hurled him across the room. He whacked against a few of the pedestals, knocking them over. Priceless porcelain vases shattered and statues crashed to the floor. Ashoka jumped up, dizzy, but with a heavy iron statue in his hand. He glared at Ti Fun.

Blue scales shone upon Ti Fun's body, now transformed into a tall, sinuous being four metres tall, still humanoid, but with a wild shimmering mane of white, a halo of lightning crackling around it, a towering hybrid of human and dragon. The claws were transparent glass and each a metre long. It drew one across the centre of a marble table and it fell into two equal pieces. *"Imagine what these could do to you, mortal."*

Yes, he should be scared; he should be petrified. But this was about his family, and Ashoka wasn't going to back down. "Where are my parents? Where's my sister?"

Parvati helped Ashoka up and stood beside him. She took the statue out of his hands, though. "Tell him, Ti Fun."

The boy was back. It took less time than an eye-blink. But even in human form the power still shone about him, an aura of unimaginable strength. He kicked one of the

❖

shards of pottery. "All right. For old time's sake I'll tell you where Savage is keeping the mortals, but after this we are quits. I can't have this getting back to me."

"Tell us now," insisted Parvati.

Ti Fun sighed. "Lamma. It's one of the outlying islands. Savage has a large research facility there. That's where you'll find your family."

Chapter Twenty

"*T*here's a huge fence," said Ashoka, peering through the night-scope.

"Let's hope it's not electrified," said Parvati.

"There are dogs. Massive ones."

"Let's hope they're not hungry."

"And guards. Loads and loads of guards. With guns."

"Let's hope they're bad shots."

"Bad shots? They're probably all ex-SAS marksmen." Ashoka lowered the scope; this was too depressing.

"I told you to stay behind and leave this to me," said Parvati.

"They're my family." If Lucks and his mum and dad were on that island, past the fence, dogs and guards, he was going to get over there and find them. He'd been up for twenty-four hours, more, but every nerve was on overdrive. Ashoka couldn't rest until this was done.

❖

Parvati and Ti Fun had struck a deal. The dragon would get them to Lamma and have a boat waiting to collect them afterwards and take them somewhere safe, but that was it.

So here he and Parvati were, at the docks on the south side of Hong Kong Island, climbing into a sampan.

The boat rocked as Ashoka stepped in. It wasn't much bigger than a rowboat, but had a covered deck and a side paddle, manned by a wrinkled old lady. For a secret mission to break into a high-security super-villain's headquarters, it was not scoring high on the James Bond-o-meter. Unless the old woman was a ninja.

One of Ti Fun's men in black passed down a heavy canvas bag. It rattled, and Ashoka didn't need X-ray vision to know there was some serious weaponry inside. The gangster gave him a gold-plated grin, then joined his brothers in the waiting Mercedes.

Ashoka tried to get comfortable in his wetsuit. Not happening. "And this is going to succeed... how?"

Parvati wound her braid into a bun and pinned it in place. "Cos we're the good guys?"

"Easy for you to say; at least you look the part," he said. Jeez, the suit was tight in all the wrong places.

"And what part is that?" She buckled a sheath to her leg and flipped a Fairbairn-Sykes commando knife into it. Then she straightened and stretched. The effect was very different from his own.

"You look like an angel of death." The black neoprene covered Parvati from ankle to throat and she was as sleek as a missile. "Look at me. I look like a blown-up bin bag."

"Hardly. And you know what they say – chunky is hunky."

"Blimey, Parvati, was that a compliment?"

Her eyebrow arched. "A small one. Get over it."

"Given the choice, they'll shoot at me. I'm twice your size."

"Suits me fine." Parvati picked up a mask with a snorkel attached and tried it on. "But you know what they also say – the bigger the gun, the worse the shot. Spray and pray. Just pull the trigger and hope to hit something."

"That's the most stupid thing I've ever heard."

"Be careful of the man who has just the one shot. He's the one who'll make it count."

The old woman handed Ashoka a Chinese-made AK-47 from the canvas bag. He took it and almost fell overboard. It weighed a ton. He'd go straight to the bottom if he tried swimming with that. "Haven't you got anything smaller?"

She gave him a Walther PPK. "Oh, yes," said Ashoka.

"Oh, no," said Parvati, taking it off him. "You've got your weapon." She tapped on the watertight case with his bow and four arrows.

"A gun would be better, don't you think?"

"Leave the rough stuff to me, OK?"

Ashoka sighed, but took it. "I'm such a Ron."

"A what?"

Didn't Parvati know anything? Ashoka pointed to himself. "Well, it's obvious Ash is Harry, you're Hermione, and I'm Ron Weasley. The crappy sidekick."

Parvati frowned. "I thought you were Robin or something."

"I wish. Robin's really cool. The original, Dick Grayson,

155

well, he's grown-up now, and as badass as Batman. And the new Robin is Damian, trained from birth by the League of Shadows to be the greatest assassin of all time. Nope, I'm the Ron in this trio."

"Well, if you have fantasies of any romantic developments between the two of us, you'd better quash them right now."

"Obviously. You're in love with Harry. I mean Ash."

Parvati dropped her own backpack. She snatched it back up and put it on, clearly flustered. "We are so not having this conversation. Ever."

"I never really understood why Hermione fancied Ron in the first place. I mean, who ever goes as Ron to a Halloween party? Nobody."

"Let's focus on the problem at hand, shall we?"

"Sorry, I babble when I'm nervous."

"I've noticed." Parvati tossed over a mask and fins.

The old woman handed Ashoka a spear-gun. He looked at Parvati. She shook her head. He handed it back.

The island of Lamma lay about a mile away over calm, dark green water. The chemical plant dominated the island. Two steel towers rose a hundred metres into the air, their silver skins ringed with red aircraft-warning lights. Floodlights lined the beach and there were cameras all along the fence. The complex had roads, endless elevated walkways and huge pipes running for miles, crisscrossing between laboratories. There were huge tanks and cylinders some forty metres tall, filled with who knew what chemicals. Guards patrolled with dogs and the staff wore white protective suits with full-face visors. There was a helicopter landing pad and a dock where four ships were moored. The nearest floated low in the water and Ashoka watched a trio of cranes load a mountain of metal crates on to its steel decks. The ship had seen better days, better decades, with a patchwork of rusty panels along its hull and black smoke belching from its funnel. The name painted on the prow was 'Pandora'.

"That doesn't bode well," said Ashoka. "Pandora unleashed all the evils on mankind."

Parvati sat on the edge of their small boat. "You ready?"

Ashoka joined her and the boat tilted dangerously low. He smiled weakly. "The backpack's heavier than it looks."

"Sure it is." Parvati put her palm against her mask and rolled backwards into the water.

Ashoka took a few deep breaths as he sat hunched on the side. Then he went over.

Bubbles surrounded him as he hit the water and he clamped his mouth tight as he flailed about. The bubbles shone like silver balloons as they rose and popped upon the moonlit surface. He kicked with his fins. They pushed him up and a second later he was blowing seawater out of his snorkel.

Parvati bobbed a few metres from him. She pointed to a cluster of rocks. "We're going there first." She adjusted her snorkel and kicked off.

The backpack had air trapped within it and was buoyant, making the swim easier than he'd expected. Still, it was weird just kicking with his feet rather than using his arms. Ashoka kept them tucked under him, cradling his elbows as he followed Parvati. The sea below was utterly black, endless and frightening. Who knew what was down there? He knew it couldn't be that deep as they were close to an island, but it was so mysterious. He decided to keep his eyes on Parvati, her fins languidly stroking the water with barely a splash.

Ten minutes later they crawled on to the seaweed-covered rock. Barnacles dented his kneecaps as he struggled up. Parvati reached into his backpack and took out the binoculars. She scanned the beach and then handed them to him. "See over there? By the sand dunes?"

Ashoka looked and saw. "A drainpipe. Looks about a metre in diameter. Our way in?"

"Yup. Notice the discoloured rocks? The foam in the water? That's not rainwater it's pouring out but chemicals. It'll probably melt our faces off, but I don't think we've got much choice."

Parvati slid back into the water. "Come on."

The drainpipe ran all the way down into the water and along the sea floor for about fifty metres. The drain opening was ten metres down. "That's where we're headed, into the underwater opening, and we'll crawl our way up."

"I can't hold my breath that long," said Ashoka. "We should have brought scuba gear."

"Do you even know how to use it?"

"Nope."

They both bobbed in the dark sea. The shore, every grain of sand floodlit, was temptingly near. But the fences looked a lot taller this close up and they were topped with razor wire. Ashoka had spent enough time with his dad to recognise a junction box. The fence was electrified. So no way in there.

"You need to hyperventilate," said Parvati. "Take a few quick deep breaths, then head down and bum up. Kick for all you're worth and you'll feel pressure in your ears the deeper you go. Just wiggle your jaw. It's called equalising. OK?"

"What?"

"Just hold your breath as long as possible." Then she was gone. Her flashlight came on and Ashoka watched a small spot of white light descend into the black.

"If I die, this is totally your fault," he said. Then he took five deep breaths and thrust his head down and bum up. And kicked.

And kicked. Ashoka chased after the spot. It shone on green, algae-covered metal. The drainpipe. The sleek black figure of Parvati waved at him. She was so small and so far away. Ashoka kicked harder, but it felt like he wasn't moving. The only thing he could see was the spot of light.

Air bubbled from between his lips. His chest and lungs ached. He kicked harder. Why wasn't he getting any closer?

He kicked and kicked and his legs burned. He pulled at the water with his hands, trying to claw his way to the bottom.

Something slapped him in his face and he dragged through the tendrils of some aquatic creature, catching his fingers in its trailing strands. Water seeped into his mask, blurring his vision until he could see three separate lights ahead of him. It sloshed back and forth across the glass.

A sharp pain dug into his ears and he wiggled his jaw,

❖

releasing the air pressure trapped in his eardrums. The weight of water squeezed his chest and he let out more precious breath.

How much further? He'd told her he couldn't do it!

Oh God, should he turn around? Head back up before it was too late?

Ashoka turned and faced upwards. It was as dark above as it was below. Which way to the sky? He couldn't tell. Panic beat within him. He turned around, searching for the flashlight. Where was it? Seawater flooded his mask and stung his eyes.

Ashoka locked his teeth together. His lungs were on fire and he needed to breathe. His hand scraped across metal and light blasted his face.

Parvati grabbed his backpack straps and pulled him in. Ashoka bent low, but still knocked his head as he entered the drain.

They swam through opaque muck. It was green and brown and slimy and sticky, and red lumps of who-knew-what floated within it. It smeared his lens and Ashoka dug his nails into the rough steel and crawled upwards, pulling with his fingers and kicking simultaneously. His skin stung and he had a hideous mental image of it melting off, burning and bubbling away and the bones underneath crumbling like charcoal sticks. He'd turn into a blob of human fat and blood, washed out to sea and gobbled up by the local fish.

That was if he didn't drown first.

How much further now? He needed to breathe...

Ashoka banged his knee against stone. The mask was torn off his face.

❖

He blinked and saw steps. He was kneeling on them. He gasped and air flooded back into his lungs. It was foul with the stink of chemicals, bitter and sharp and stinging, but he didn't care. It was air. Parvati had her arms around him and hoisted him up on to a steel gantry, where he collapsed.

She dropped down beside him, pulling off her own mask and throwing it aside. She lay there, staring upwards and breathing deeply herself. "That was further than I thought." She narrowed her gaze and shone the flashlight around the walls and steps. "Where are we?"

They'd come out at the bottom of a shaft, five metres in diameter and about twelve high. The walls were slick concrete and four big outlets were spilling all sorts of foaming foulness into it from holes in the wall. "An interceptor pit — a big one." Ashoka groaned as he got up. Wow, he'd never complain about school sports day ever again. The winter cross-country run was a piece of cake compared to what he'd just done. He took out his own flashlight. "See those smaller holes? Those are drains from the rest of the factory. They all spill into here and get redirected out to sea via the main drain, the one we've just crawled up. There should be a maintenance hatch right..." he pointed the light at a ladder fixed to the wall and followed it straight up to a circular metal panel in the concrete ceiling, "... here."

Parvati laughed. It was a light, carefree sound and chimed softly in the pit. Her green eyes brightened. "How do you know all this stuff?"

"From Dad. He's designed pretty much everything from offices to banks to prisons, and more than a couple of

❖

factories. He once told me how to disable a bank's security system. Easier than you'd think. Though you'd need a crane and a ten-ton truck and a week drilling outside the bank to do it."

"Ash doesn't know these things, and you're the same."

"No, we're not." Ashoka peered around him. "He was busy doing all that important stuff while I was at home with Dad."

"Being with your family is important too. More important than you think. It's the reason we want to save the world." Parvati turned her back. "Unzip me, please."

Wow.

He'd thought he'd have to wait till university before he got requests like that.

Parvati sighed. "I can hear your hormones boiling from here. Get a grip, Ashoka."

"Er... right."

He closed his eyes and unzipped her. She did the same and, back to back, with no peeking, they slipped out of their wetsuits, now slimy with chemicals, and into clean clothes from the backpacks. Loose black trousers and T-shirt, for Ashoka with a pair of black rubber-soled plimsolls, while Parvati dressed in a similar T-shirt, but with shorts and barefoot, easier for her transformations.

The knife went back on her calf sheath and they transferred their equipment to utility belts along with a walkie-talkie they'd use to call Ti Fun's people when they needed picking up. Ashoka took out his bow and snapped it open. There was an arrow clip fixed to the main body and he pushed his four arrows into it. It went over his shoulder.

Parvati nodded approvingly. "Suits you."

"Another compliment?" Ashoka looked up at the ladder leading into the hatch and grabbed the first rung. "I'll get big-headed."

Parvati followed him, smiling.

They emerged through a manhole into an unlit side alley between two large steel-clad warehouses.

"Which way?" said Ashoka, pulling himself out.

"It's your family we're rescuing; you tell me."

Ashoka crept to one end of the alleyway. He looked around him at the vast complex, with its buildings and stores and pipes. Huge clouds bellowed out of two immense chimneys and Ashoka put out his hand to catch what fell. "Ash..." he said, rubbing the dry powder in his fingers and letting it be carried away with a puff. "Whatever they're cooking, they're doing it on overtime."

It covered the ground like snow.

Parvati hissed. Never a good sign.

"What is it?" he asked. Her gaze was on the cloud rising from the chimneys.

"Nothing. Let's get a move on."

Now if I was a criminal super-villain, where would I hide my hostages? thought Ashoka.

Nothing here looked like a prison where you'd hide people away. Would he lock them in one of the tool sheds? No, too simple for Savage; he wouldn't rely on a few barred windows and a padlock. Which building had the most security?

"The medical laboratories," said Ashoka aloud. "They'd

be the most protected for two reasons: industrial espionage and risk of contamination."

"How will we find them?"

"Follow the white coats," said Ashoka. "Like those two."

They wore more than just white coats. The two people crossing from one building to another were in full head-to-toe lab suits. Their hoods were down and they were finishing off their sandwiches as they approached a steel door. The building itself was windowless and the walls white-painted concrete. A field of exhaust ducts stood up from the flat roof and a stream of pipes and cables ran from the building as if it was the heart of the complex and they were its arteries and veins, supplying life to the rest of the industrial machine.

One of the scientists unclipped his badge and swiped it over the lock. The door hummed as the electronic locking mechanism disabled itself. Light escaped.

"Quick," said Parvati, and she sprinted towards them.

The first scientist brushed the crumbs off his hands and went in.

Ashoka looked around — all clear — and ran after Parvati.

The second scientist was still pushing the sandwich into his cheeks when Parvati came upon him.

She sprang into the air and flew the last four or five metres, knees tucked up to her chin, and was about to land on him when she kicked out, her heels rocketing into his back and hurling him against the door. He slammed into it and Parvati sailed past and through the door before he hit the ground.

By the time Ashoka reached the door, a few seconds later, it was all over.

❖

"Drag him in," Parvati ordered, crouching over the second unconscious lab worker. "Before the door shuts."

Ashoka hooked his arms under the man's armpits and pulled him into the corridor. The door closed just as his heels cleared the door frame.

Parvati drew her knife.

Ashoka grabbed her arm. "You can't kill them."

"Do I look like a psychopath?"

"Er..."

Parvati's fangs were extended and her huge brilliant green eyes were sliced by vertical pupils. Scales clustered at her neck. Psychopath would be a polite way of putting it.

"Never mind." She licked the blade. "My venom causes paralysis and organ failure, among other things. In very, very small doses it'll keep these two out for a few hours. No permanent harm. Trust me." She nicked each man on the neck, less than a shaving cut. "Now let's get them out of sight."

The nearest room turned out to be an empty office with lockers and tools and shelves of technical books. The lights were off and it didn't look like anyone would be here before morning. They bundled both men under the desks and tied them up with cables to be doubly sure. Parvati found some tape in a drawer and stuck it over their mouths to make triply sure.

"Look at this," said Ashoka. There was a piping schematic on the wall. "It tells you what's running in and out of this block."

"And that helps us how?"

❖

Ashoka traced his fingers along a line. "These are medical gas supplies. And they disappear here. That floor's not marked."

"They want to keep it private?"

"Exactly. Look at the electrical diagram. The size of the distribution board is huge. There's a floor eating up a lot of juice."

"Let's try that lift." Parvati pointed at the end of the corridor. "That must be where these two were headed."

"Whatever's happening down there is serious business." The seals were fresh and the metal highly polished. "They're taking no chances with leaks."

Parvati hesitated. "Perhaps you should wait here, Ashoka. I'll go down and find your family and bring them to you."

"Why? What's the matter?"

She brushed grey ash from his shoulder. "I'd rather not say, in case I'm wrong. Just stay here. I shouldn't be long."

"Forget it. I'm coming." Ashoka met her gaze, even though his heart was beating with fear. "It's what Ash would do."

"Yes, but Ash has done some incredibly stupid things."

"Then let's get moving before my common sense kicks in."

Parvati hesitated again, and for a second Ashoka thought she was going to say something, but then she opened the door and the two of them walked to the lift. Ashoka swiped one of the lab worker's cards over the sensor and a moment later the doors opened. "This is it," he said, getting in quickly before he changed his mind.

Down they went and Ashoka's heart clenched. What was down there? Parvati bit her lip and tensed and untensed her fists. He could tell that she was afraid, and if she was afraid

❖

then he should be terrified. But his sister and his parents might be down here, so down he had to go.

Eventually the lift stopped. Parvati readied her blade. The door opened. Her eyes widened. "Oh my God..."

And Ashoka entered hell.

Chapter Twenty-one

I've done it. I've killed Savage!

Rani stared at Ash in disbelief.

Savage was dead.

Any second now... thought Ash.

Any second now and the Kali-aastra would awake, flooding him with supernatural power. He'd given Kali a great sacrifice, a Great Death. The death of his enemy, the man he hated most above all else. Savage's life force would pour into him, giving him the Englishman's abilities. He'd be unstoppable.

Any second now...

The seconds passed.

Nothing was happening.

Why wasn't the Kali-aastra awakening? He'd killed Savage. What more could he do?

He'd killed—

Savage's body glistened.

Ash watched in horror as the wound sealed and the skin smoothed until there was no mark upon it, and Savage began to glow more and more as if beneath the white flesh shone something brighter, something that was reawakening his heartbeat.

"No..." breathed Ash.

Savage opened his eyes and they were a pair of dazzling diamonds lit by a pure white fire within. His teeth transformed into glass and his flesh morphed from meat and bone into crystal, a billion subtle edges and surfaces catching the light and bouncing it between them until Savage was blindingly brilliant.

Savage sighed. He bent and rose. His nails, diamond-tipped, cut long lines in the tiles. The nails accidently tore across his bloody shirt and it drifted off like red ribbons into the wind.

"No..."

Even his hair had transformed, to a crystalline crest that chimed and rang as the minute follicles struck each other.

"What are you?" whispered Ash. The ten skulls, the brands proclaiming Savage's mastery over all magic, were black sooty scorch marks on his flawless, inhuman chest.

Ravana had forged his body from gold to be able to contain the vast, swirling sorcery within him. Magic drew a heavy price from those that used it, ageing and corrupting them, and eventually destroying them. The same was said to be true for humans, even more so. Magic corrupted humans in body and soul, and for that reason it had been believed that mastering all ten sorceries was impossible. But Savage had found a way.

Was this Savage's solution? A body of diamond?

The light dimmed. Crystal gave way to meat and skin. His teeth went from glass back to ivory. Only in the centre of his chest did the glow linger, a beating heart, not of blood and muscle, but something else — a small clump of shining stone.

Savage put his palm against it. "Ah, you have discovered my secret. This is why I am not destroyed by the ten sorceries. I'm protected by the ultimate life force: the Life Giver."

No. Not after all they'd been through. Only a month ago Ash and Parvati had stopped Savage from getting his hands on it. A diamond of legend, created by a god, that had the power to cure any injury, any sickness. Said even to raise the dead. Ash had stopped Savage and hidden it for ever.

But that was in a different timeline. A different universe.

"The Koh-i-noor?" said Ash.

"Indeed. The *Brahma-aastra*," said Savage. "I really, truly cannot die, Ash."

"But Ravana cursed it."

"How to lift the curse was the first thing I asked the demon king when I freed him from the Iron Gates."

Savage pressed his palm against his chest. "I took out my heart and replaced it with the diamond. There was a period of adjustment, but I've never felt better. Literally glowing with good health, you might say."

No wonder the Kali-aastra hadn't awakened. There had been no death. With the Brahma-aastra within him Savage could not die.

❖

Savage beckoned to Rani. "Tell Jackie to go to the orphanage and collect the children. They'll be back to human form now and no doubt confused and a little distressed. Bring them here so we can educate them into their new role."

"As monsters," said Rani.

Savage met the rakshasa princess's green gaze. "Yes, my dear. As perfect little monsters. Just like you."

Ash stepped forward. He had to do something...

Rani blocked him and put her hand up on his throat. She shook her head slowly.

"If you were still the Kali-aastra, then you might have stood a chance, but you are not, not in this timeline. Just when you needed her most, Kali has abandoned you," said Savage. "Now, Rani, please escort our guest somewhere safe and secure. Let him meet the other... inhabitants."

How could Savage be beaten? It was impossible. Ash wracked his brain for ideas, but nothing worked. The guy could probably survive a nuke.

Down they went, into the bones of the mountain. Rani held out a lantern before her as they left the palace above them and entered a labyrinth of crudely chiselled-out passageways, chambers and yet more stairs: dank, narrow, miserable. Icicles sparkled in the passing flames and the amber light was sprinkled upon the frost-coated walls.

This was a place lower than hell, and with every metre Ash went down his heart beat more rapidly. Was there a way out of this? Should he run? He'd been chained again around the wrists, and the manacles were leaden and soaked up hope, leaving him crushed by despair. Maybe he couldn't escape, but he had to try.

"Parvati..."

"That's not my name."

"Where are you taking me?"

Rani pulled at his chains. "Hurry up."

Ash stumbled along behind her in the semi-darkness. *What was that?* He thought he heard something up ahead. Who else was down here? What else?

"Why didn't he send you to get those kids?" Ash asked. He'd heard the tension in her voice when Savage had ordered Jackie to do it. "You were angry."

"What do I care for some orphans?" she replied tersely.

"You tell me."

Rani spun around, her eyes blazing. "They are what they are. Demons."

"They're kids. How old were you when Savage found you?"

"Younger than them. They should be happy for the time they had being children. That is over now." She turned back to face down the corridor. "Come on."

"You don't like it, Parvati."

"That is not my name!"

Ash grabbed her shoulder and Rani hissed. Her tongue danced between her fangs and Ash gulped. He'd gone too far. But this was the only chance he had. There was something good, compassionate, deep inside the rakshasa. He knew Parvati, and whatever timeline or world or age she might exist in, she and he had always been friends. No matter what.

❖

"Listen to me. Savage is going to destroy those kids' lives – corrupt them, twist their minds and feelings and souls... and you can stop him. You're a demon and you've told me that demons don't have feelings or compassion or love, but that's not true. Savage feeds the monster in you, but there's so much more. I've seen it."

She snorted. "So you say, but this other rakshasa, this Parvati of yours, she must be a weak and feeble thing. I am a queen of demons. Who is this other Parvati? Some vagabond? What does she have that I do not?"

"You know what she has."

"Humanity? Compassion? Love?" Rani's eyes were murderously narrow. "Those are things I do not want, I do not need."

"They're yours for the taking. Just help me. We have to stop Savage."

She shook her head. "It's impossible. Savage cannot be stopped." She raised her lantern and revealed an iron door ahead of them. "He has planned for this a long time."

A moaning echoed from beyond the door. The sound – low, mournful, trembling with anger – chilled the blood.

Ash stared. "What's in there?"

Rani unlocked the door and pushed him inside. He fell hard, gashing his knees on the bare rock.

Rani put the lantern inside the cell. "Some light, for what it's worth."

Ash couldn't see far in. The cell was some natural cave. The walls undulated and shimmered with ice. Deep within the endless darkness, beyond the feeble lantern light, he heard feet shuffle. Voices — many — came out of that black void. "What's in here?"

Rani paused at the half-closed door. "Savage has been experimenting to perfect his drug for ten years. Here's where he keeps the failures."

She shut the door and bolted it.

Ash gazed out into the darkness. "Hello...? Who's there?" He backed up against the wall. "Come out into the light."

And they did.

Chapter Twenty-two

The first slithered. It dragged itself over the damp rock, through the dripping pool, with spindly white arms that ended not with hands but bony hooks. Its eyes were huge bulbous things: white, sightless. The mouth was a puckered hole with black gums and a few yellow teeth. Weeping sores covered the sallow, sickly skin that sagged over twisted muscle.

Ash, back against the door, stood ready. The chains of the manacles were heavy, dense iron. He swung them from side to side, prepared to fight.

More creatures emerged into the lamplight, each more malformed and grotesque than the last. One had a mangy pelt and a single wing, neither beast nor bird and no longer human, his skull deformed into a beak and pressed sideways so he kept on turning his head at angles, weird glazed eyes blinking and unfocused. A reptilian tongue darted above the curved jawbone. Another lumbered closer in an ape-like gait, a pair of puny bow-legs supporting a massive torso and arms thicker than Ash's waist. Its head faced almost backwards and patches of a mane sprouted over the cheeks and scalp. A single eye sat in the centre of its brow.

They moaned. They hissed and snarled and spat. Some had no eyes at all and sniffed, their necks stretched long to taste Ash's scent in among the foulness. Bones lay broken and excrement stank in the alcoves.

Claws scratched the stone. Teeth, fangs, snapped with hunger.

How many were there? Shapes moved beyond the light, further and further into the darkness. The caverns could go on for ever.

A man – Ash thought it was a man – scuttled forward. He had six arms and no legs, so he moved like an ant. A swollen head with tusks jutted from the shoulders, and he snorted as he ran up to Ash, beady red eyes set at odd angles in his face. He stopped a few metres from Ash, watching, salivating.

Ash glanced at the bones nearby. These creatures weren't fed by Savage. They fed off each other.

The six-armed man charged. He rushed in low and rammed Ash in the guts, crushing him against the iron door.

Ash gasped as a tusk dug into his thigh and he slammed his fists into the creature's head. He drove a knee into its

❖

jaw and its teeth cracked. He did it again and they all fell out. The six-armed man spat them out and ran back, readying for a second attack. Ash struggled to stand, his stomach heaved and a thin tear bled down his leg.

The air oppressed him as the creatures clustered around. They stood upon each other and hands grasped out, bony fingers or talons jabbing at him, trying to snatch a piece of flesh. They cackled and groaned and jabbered with famished excitement.

A long, serpentine tail wound itself around Ash's ankle. He pulled and beat at it, but it held on. Six-arms charged again, catching Ash in the ribs. He went down and Six-arms pounced on top of him. Cold, strong hands grabbed Ash's other leg and began to pull. Nails ripped at his clothes and sank into his limbs.

Ash wedged the chain into Six-arms' mouth. He heaved it back, bending the neck away from him, but the creature was immensely strong and was able to add its weight behind it. Spittle, green and putrid, dripped over Ash's face. Those red eyes widened, glowing with bloodlust.

A tongue licked Ash's foot. He thrashed out as he felt teeth on his toes.

Sweating, panting, he pushed. The chain dug into the monster's mouth, deep into the sides and his tongue thrashed over the iron as Ash forced him further back. The bloodlust gave way to pain, to fear.

Ash pulled his legs free and tucked them under Six-arms' body. Then, with a kick and shove, he threw him back into

❖

the heaving mass of horrors. He scrambled to his feet, crouching low, glaring back at the dozens of eager, hungry eyes.

They came closer. Six-arms vanished into the crowd, screaming, defeated, and they devoured him. A cluster of creatures surrounded him and tore him, literally, limb from limb, flesh spattering the rocks and other monsters.

Ash shivered, trying not to puke. He picked up a splintered bone. It was little better than nothing. "I hope you bloody well get food poisoning," he snarled. It was all he had left — his defiance. No way could he take them all.

It was a grunt, from somewhere further back. A grunt that was some sort of laugh. Someone clapped their hands and grunted again. "Food poisoning? I like that." The grunt rumbled out again. It was a deep, rocking sound that shook the air, raising echoes that boomed from the darkness. "Food poisoning!"

The mob of monsters fell silent, but for the odd crunch or slurp.

"Make way!" A stick whacked flesh and Ash watched the crowd part. Some were reluctant, still casting hungry looks at Ash and licking their lips, but make way they did.

"Make way..."

A man came forward. The bones within the wrinkled and scarred oak-brown skin had been warped so that his back curved sharply and his head, matted with dreadlocks and tilted on a scrawny neck, seemed ready to snap at the merest sudden move. His eyes were gone, the face grooved with deep scars running from his forehead, through the empty eye sockets and down to the bearded jaw. He walked towards Ash clutching a bamboo stick.

Ash looked at the scarred eye sockets, and knew those eyes would have been blue.

"Food poisoning?" The blind, mutilated man came to a stop facing Ash. "Funny, boy. Funny."

Ash reached out and touched him. "Rishi?"

Chapter Twenty-three

"So, you're the Eternal Warrior? Interesting," said Rishi. He passed a bowl towards Ash. He must have sensed Ash's reluctance. "Mushrooms. The only things that grow down here. Perfectly edible. Perfectly vegetarian."

He couldn't believe it was Rishi. Not the one from his timeline, of course. He'd died rescuing Ash, but having Rishi back, any version of him, meant they were still in with a chance.

Ash rubbed his wrists. They'd managed to smash off the manacles, but he was bruised and aching. He picked up the bowl and sniffed it. He ate one. Not bad. He ate another. "Yes. In my timeline we defeated Ravana."

"Now, that I would have liked to see." Rishi picked up a second bowl. "So I exist in this other timeline also?"

"You saved my life. Mine and my sister's. It was you who told me about the Kali-aastra and what I was."

"Glad I did something right."

Ash looked at the old *sadhu* and, for the first time in ages, felt hope. "What happened?"

Rishi sighed and put the bowl down. One of the others sniffed at it and licked the few specks of left-over mushroom. "Savage returned to India ten years ago. First thing he did was buy that old maharajah's palace downriver from Varanasi. Renamed it the Savage Fortress."

"Same in my time. But he didn't get it ten years ago. He only bought it a year or two back."

Rishi grimaced. "He started digging and found the Kali-aastra. He knew exactly where to look. Then he headed off to Rajasthan. I followed. Alone."

"What about Parvati?" asked Ash.

"She was just five, Ash. Her rakshasa soul hadn't awoken. She was living as a human child with a family who loved her. A few siblings. I'd been keeping an eye on her, watching out for the first signs that she was changing. But I knew I still had a few years. Best let her enjoy them, don't you think? The nightmares, the old memories would come soon enough, show her what she truly was — whose daughter she was. It was kinder to let her have some happy years first."

"What happened in Rajasthan?"

Rishi nodded. "I tried to stop Savage, but what could I do by myself? He caught me and let that vulture Jat eat my eyes. I never saw Ravana, but I heard him. I heard the world scream at his rebirth. I wish I'd died that night."

Ash touched the sadhu's arm. "Then what?"

Rishi grunted. "Savage held me prisoner at the Savage

Fortress for a few months while he studied with Ravana. Then, when he'd learned all he could..." Rishi drew his thumb across his throat. "He used the Kali-aastra to kill Ravana once and for all. There was a lot of confusion that night. I managed to escape, got as far as Varanasi before they caught me. So I was brought here."

"But what about your magic? Couldn't you just blast yourself out? I've seen you hurl lightning bolts."

"Powers my god Shiva bestowed upon me. But they are powers of the sky; I cannot access them so far beneath the earth." Rishi frowned. "Then, as Savage began his experiments, they started to arrive. Poor villagers, lost travellers. He tried out his alchemy on them, and those that didn't die were left here. I did my best to look after them but, well, you've seen. A few hang on to their humanity, but only a very few. By the time Savage has finished with them they are barely human, in more ways than one. What you see here are the... least damaged."

"You have to be joking." Ash looked about him. He'd never seen a more gruesome group of monsters. Even when he'd witnessed the demon nations and seen every rakshasa gathered, awaiting Ravana's rebirth, the horror hadn't been this great. But those were true demons. These pitiful things were neither one nor the other. No wonder nature rejected them.

"The worst disappeared deeper into the mountain. Sometimes they creep here, steal a few of my people. You can hear them in the darkness, and the screams of the ones they take. The mountain shakes and we lose a few under the collapsing chambers and rockfalls. I cannot imagine what sorts of creatures dwell in the very pits that make even a mountain tremble in fear."

"How far in have you gone?"

"Not far. Every now and then we search to try to find those kidnapped, but it seems even the shadows are hungry, and members of the rescue party are killed. But sometimes, Ash, sometimes..." he smiled, "... I think I feel the wind on my face. It is cold and fresh and smells sweet, like the breath of a god. Oh, at that moment I feel almost free." Rishi touched his own cheek. "I dream about sunlight. What it felt like. To be warm again."

Ash sank back against the wall. His stomach rumbled and protested. It wanted more than a few wrinkled mushrooms. He was too tired, too bruised and too hungry. He looked at the old man. Rishi, the legend. He'd struck a cow the first time Ash had met him. Out on the hot, dusty streets of Varanasi. His eyes had shone bright blue. Now they were gone. Only one man shone now and that was Savage. He'd eaten all their hopes, gorged himself on the lives of everyone who'd tried to stop him, and made himself whole, young, immortal and all-powerful.

"How did Savage awaken the Kali-aastra?" The weapon of the death goddess demanded a great sacrifice before it could be used.

"Himself," said Rishi.

"What?"

"Think about it, Ash. There are two of you, so there were two of him. The version you knew, who cast the Time Spell, and the version that existed in this timeline."

❖

"That is seriously messed up. Why didn't the other demons have their revenge on Savage when he killed Ravana? Why did they let him get away with it?"

"He had the demon king's heir."

"Rani," said Ash. It all made sense.

"Yes, Rani. She is the queen, the *rani*, of all the demon nations. A puppet of Savage's to be sure, but still, in name, she rules as her father once did. Savage will tire of the arrangement. He was never one to stand behind the throne when he could sit upon it."

Ash frowned. "What do you mean?"

"He plans to kill her. It is Savage's nature to betray. Surely you know that?"

Yes, of course he did. Savage had conned Parvati out of her father's scrolls back in the nineteenth century. He'd killed Ash before the Iron Gates. He'd tricked him in order to get into Lanka. For all his grandeur, power and ambition, Savage was just a thief. Plain and simple. "I've got to warn her," said Ash.

"Why would she believe you?"

"If it just makes her mistrust Savage, even a little, puts her on her guard, that's good enough."

"Why do you want to? She's as evil as he is. They deserve one another."

"No, Rishi. I know Rani. She might call herself queen of the demons, but she's been my friend for hundreds of reincarnations. She's my friend in this one too, but she just doesn't know it yet."

"It must be a most powerful friendship."

Ash stopped. How many times had she saved his life and he hers? Countless times, over more centuries than history knew. "It is." He walked to the iron door. "When is she down next?"

"Who knows? This is the first time she's been here in months." Rishi hobbled over. "But what's the rush?"

"Savage has perfected his drug. He's going to launch it in a few days. What you have here is going to happen all over the world."

Rishi went pale. "He is insane."

"I won't argue with that."

Ash looked down into the deeper caverns, into the blackness. He licked his lips. What had Rishi said? Wind on his face.

"What is it, boy? What do you think?"

What was down there? There was only one way to find out. He made up his mind and grasped Rishi's arm. "I think it's time we got the hell out of here."

Chapter Twenty-four

"Don't look," said Parvati, but much too late.

They hung from hooks, swaying, cocooned in plastic. Ashoka's flashlight caught on pallid faces and empty eyes.

But what was worse was the way they... sloshed. Fluids had run from the bodies and collected at the bottom of the bags. A few had sprung leaks so the blood and fat and gore dripped steadily into pink puddles on the hard, ceramic floor. Thin rivulets ran to chrome drains and Ashoka felt sick thinking about what they must have swum through to get here. The odour of disinfectant burnt his nostrils, but it still failed to mask the putrid, humid stench of decomposition. A chunk of bile stirred high in his throat. "Those chimneys..."

"They're burning the bodies."

Ashoka stumbled back into the lift. He stared at the floor, trying to clear his mind. "You knew?"

❖

"I suspected. I've come across this sort of operation before."

"Oh, Jesus – Lucks!" Was she here? Or his mum? His dad? *No. No, not after all this.*

He couldn't raise his gaze. He was too terrified of what he might see, *whom* he might see. But how could he not look? He needed to know. What was better? To live in ignorant hope or to risk seeing Lucky hanging upside down in one of those bags?

"You go back. I'll look for them," said Parvati. But even her voice faltered.

"No, I have to come. I have to see."

Parvati took his hand and led Ashoka into the lab.

They weren't human any more. Not just in death, but in what had been done to them. Their flashlights shone upon scaled skin and fur and there were feathers and odd, misjoined limbs, sometimes human, sometimes not, that had grown out of bellies or chests. One old man had teeth within his eyelids.

But no one Ashoka recognised.

They walked silently among the corpses. Goosebumps prickled over his bare arms as the chilled air blasted out, and yet Ashoka sweated, lost in this inverted forest of the dead.

The lights came on. Parvati pulled him behind a storage cabinet. Blue neon tubes flickered and hummed and then bank upon bank awoke, filling the white chamber with cold irradiance. The doors at the far end slammed open, a trolley clanked over the threshold, and Ashoka heard voices talking in what he thought was Cantonese. He peeked a glance as they walked by.

The trolley was three decks high, stainless steel, and the

❖

two men with it unhooked and lay a body on each shelf. They might as well have been picking the Christmas turkey for all the interest they took. They heaved and got the trolley rolling back out. The last man flicked the lights back off.

A few seconds later Ashoka and Parvati followed through the same big double doors and found themselves in a corridor of red-painted brickwork and concrete. Drainpipes ran along the ceiling and Ashoka spotted the dark stains where joints had leaked. The two men and the trolley vanished around a corner.

They crept along the corridor, eyes peeled, Parvati ahead with her knife out. Ashoka felt he was leaving a trail of sweat; every muscle was tight and his nerves were shredded. The doors off the corridor were stainless steel and heavy, down a tall step to prevent contaminants running out into the corridor. The entire underground complex stank of antiseptic. Ashoka caught the distant roar of a furnace and gulped. The pitch rose and he knew what was being burnt within.

They were getting nowhere. Sooner or later those two guys they'd taken out would be missed, or would wake up, or be found wrapped under the desk, and then all hell would break loose. What they needed was a set of floor plans.

Ashoka peered through a glass panel in one of the doors... and met the gaze of a man looking back. The man frowned through a pair of thick spectacles, then his mouth dropped open. A clipboard clattered on the floor.

"Parvati!" Ashoka shouted.

She moved, hurling the door open. She jumped over a

steel table as the man dashed towards the far wall and the red alarm button upon it. He stumbled over a stool and it clanged like a hammer on tin as it bounced on the tiles. Parvati sprang in front of him and wove her hands around his arms, twisting them over his shoulder and driving him to his knees so he screamed.

Ashoka checked the corridor, then locked the door and hung a coat over the glass panel before joining them.

He stared at the line of cold steel tables. They weren't flat, but sloped into a central gulley that ran to a small drain at the foot. Not just tables – dissection slabs. Over each hung a small camera and microphone, and a gas mask dangled from a valve. The slabs had four sets of straps, one at head level, then shoulders, waist and ankles. But you didn't need to strap down corpses.

They're for live experiments.

Neatly arranged beside each was a tray of medical instruments, including electric saws and drills. The slabs were thankfully empty, but even walking past them Ashoka felt sick. Jars filled nearby shelves. He didn't dare look at what was in them.

"You're breaking my arm!" cried the man. He panted with fear and panic, and stared from Parvati to Ashoka and back. "This is restricted access."

Parvati held him with one hand and peered at his security tag. "I can see why, Dr Wells."

Ashoka went to the man's desk. The laptop was open and there was a paused video clip on the screen. It showed Dr Wells, dressed in a head-to-foot blood-spattered bio-suit,

❖

standing over a man strapped to the slab. Or what was left of one.

Dr Wells paled. "And that is not for public viewing."

This is real. This is not some computer game or movie or fake footage. That is a person on that slab.

"Who was he?" Ashoka asked, his voice tight.

"Who was who?"

"The man lying there."

Dr Wells frowned. "I don't know. He just had a test number. It says so on the log."

Rage pounded in Ashoka's temples. "What did you do to him?"

"Please," whispered the doctor. "I just work here. I don't make the decisions. I just—"

"Follow orders?" hissed Parvati. She bent his arm back a little more. Dr Wells whimpered.

"What did you do to him?" said Ashoka. "Or should I press 'play'?"

Sweat covered Dr Wells's face and it was an unpleasant ruby hue, almost as pumped as his bloodshot eyes. "We were testing Lord Savage's new cure. A retro-anti-virus. Number one."

"RAVN-1," said Parvati. "Savage's sick joke."

"What's it do?" asked Ashoka.

"Cures. Everything." But he was hiding something.

"That's not possible." Ashoka glanced at the screen and the twisted mess of a human. "Those bodies, they had scales. Wings. That doesn't look like any sort of cure to me."

Dr Wells cleared his throat. "We've been experimenting

190

on melding the DNA structure from different species. Adding their strengths and abilities to those of a human. There have been some... negative results."

"What are you turning them into, if not humans?" asked Parvati.

Dr Wells didn't reply until she twisted his arm some more. "It turns people into demons. Rakshasas."

Parvati leaned over the man, her face centimetres from his. "You can't."

"We've found a way. Given early enough, the drug infects the child with a rakshasa soul."

Ashoka grabbed the man's throat. "You've tested this on kids? I should kill you right now."

Parvati touched his hand and Ashoka reluctantly forced his fingers apart. "But the person on the video, he's an adult," he said. *And all those bodies hanging in the storage chamber.*

"The effects on adults are... varied. They've not had the initial dose, so it's a tremendous shock to the system. Some transform, partially. Most have a psychotic breakdown as the rakshasa soul tries to enter them."

"You mean it drives them mad?"

"Yes. In layman's terms, they turn into bloodthirsty crazed monsters. Usually with cannibalistic tendencies."

"So what's the cure?" Ashoka asked.

"Cure?"

"How do you save the ones infected?"

"There isn't one. Savage never wanted one developed."

How utterly insane. "How long to make one?"

Dr Wells blinked in surprise. "Years, if it's even possible.

You don't understand – this is the melding of magic and science. Everything we do is groundbreaking. We have no map of where this will lead, let alone any real idea of how to get there."

Ashoka gazed at the screen again. Then he searched the desk until he found a data stick. "I want everything copied on to this. Everything."

"I can't—"

Ashoka snarled. "You do as I say or the next person on that slab will be you."

Dr Wells needed no further encouragement.

"Test subjects," Ashoka said. "You said you have test subjects."

"A few left." Dr Wells pointed to a door at the far end of the room. "We were going to euthanise them now the tests are over."

Ashoka started towards the door. "Over?"

"Yes, we've finished developing RAVN-I now."

Ashoka glared at the man. "My sister... my parents were brought here."

Dr Wells glanced over. "I only work the evening shift. I... I don't know who's in there."

Ashoka was by the door. "Give me the code."

"1839. They're all the same."

The corridor was narrow, with doors down either side. Each was barcoded and had a small shutter and key pad. He went to the first cell.

1839.

Bolts hidden between two solid steel plates slid out of

❖

their sockets within the door frame, and Ashoka took hold and heaved.

"Hello?"

Empty. There was a basin and a toilet and a mattress on the floor. The place was bare and cold and reeked of misery.

Ashoka took another step further down the corridor into the darkness.

Chapter Twenty-five

*A*shoka's eyes were growing accustomed to the gloom. The dim lights were hazy and red and sickly. The heavy antiseptic didn't hide the other smells that lingered there: the sweat, the stale air and the damp dread. An air-conditioning vent droned and rattled over his head like a wave of insects. He cleared his throat, trying to loosen the tightness he felt there. He forced himself further in, even though every instinct yelled at him to run and run far, so afraid was he of what he might find.

"Is anyone there?" he asked.

Voices murmured. Someone scratched at the door from within, and cackled. A fist banged frantically against the metal, and sobs shook inside.

1839. 1839. 1839. 1839. 1839. Ashoka punched the numbers into each door, pulling at the handle before rushing to the next. "Come out. Come out. Please."

❖

One by one, blinking and afraid, they emerged. They wore medical smocks and paper clothes and were dishevelled and frail-looking. Men and women and children, mostly local Chinese, taken by Savage and his lackeys for his experiments. And these were the lucky few.

Lucky.

"Lucks?" Ashoka whispered her name, afraid if he said it too loud his hopes might shatter. "Lucks?"

One man came up to the doorway, stared with slack-jawed amazement, sobbed and pulled at his own hair as he dared to step out into freedom.

"Lucks?" Ashoka raised his voice. "It's me."

A woman clutching her son brushed past Ashoka, stopping only to look at him with a mixture of fear and relief. Her son pressed his face against her and looked nowhere.

Ashoka's heart beat so loudly he trembled. This beat was the thump of some dance. He was breathing hard, trying to stay focused, trying to stop the horror from overwhelming him. Or perhaps the dance, this mad frenzy within him, was making him gasp. Ashoka wiped the sweat off his face. "Lucks?"

Please let them be OK. I don't care about anything else.

What would he give for them to be OK? Everything. Here in the gloom, with the corpses in plastic bags and the ash rising from the chimneys, Ashoka promised all he had to any god that might be listening.

Mum. Dad. Lucks. How could he live without them? It was too horrible to contemplate.

Contemplate it now.

❖

No. He couldn't think like that, but as he opened door after door and didn't see them the dreadful thought wouldn't go away. Some cells held captives, afraid and ill and blinking in the light, but others were empty. He'd come too late for them.

Was he too late now?

As Ashoka crept forward, so did the nightmare that they were gone.

All that he'd taken for granted now came back to haunt him. Those times he'd barged past his mum in his rush to be somewhere else. Those times he'd ignored his dad while he concentrated on some new computer game. Those times he'd shut the door on Lucks because he didn't want to play with her. Those times he'd wanted to be alone.

You're alone now. How does it feel?

Cell after cell clanged open.

All empty.

Ashoka's heart shook. It couldn't end like this. He hadn't even said goodbye. He hadn't said how much he loved them, how much they meant to him; how much he needed them.

A last cell. A last hope.

1839.

He swung the door open.

"Lucks?"

"Ashoka!" A girl ran at him, hugging him with all her might. She buried her head into his chest and Ashoka cried as he held her. "I thought I'd lost you."

"Son?" A man stumbled out from the back of the cell, hand in hand with a woman with ragged hair and a torn suit jacket. "Ashoka?" she said.

It was them. It was them!

He felt reborn. He'd been given a second chance to do his life right, to do it better. He felt light enough to float away. He hadn't realised how much fear had weighed him down.

His parents ran to him and all four of them huddled together in the depths of Savage's slaughterhouse. Ashoka smothered himself in his mother's hair and hugged his father tight. He'd doubted. He'd been afraid. He'd thought he'd lost them forever and here they were. He'd never let them out of his sight ever again. The nightmare was over.

"I thought I'd lost you," said Ashoka. "I'm sorry." He should have been with them. He should have stopped all this. He wiped his sister's tears. "I missed you, Lucks."

Stupid thing to say, but what words could ever express how much she meant to him?

"It's over now, we're going home," he said, holding Lucky's hand, looking at each of them.

How could a few days make such a difference? It wasn't that they were malnourished or ill, but they must have lost hope, and that was the poison that had flooded their veins. Despair. What had they seen? What had they heard? Did they know what took place on the other side of the door when Dr Wells and his staff took one prisoner after another?

"Let's get out of here." He led them back into the laboratory.

Ten others stood around the room, some huddling by Parvati.

Parvati's face glowed with happiness when she saw Ashoka with his family. "Well done, Ashoka."

❖

Ashoka hugged his sister closer. "Now let's get the hell out of here. Have you got all you need?"

She waved the data stick at him. "Got it all. It's worse than we thought."

"With Savage it usually is. What's up?"

Parvati took him to the screen and the map illuminated on it. "See these dots? More of Savage's poison factories. He's been testing on whole villages. Six are in China."

"He's double-crossed the Dragon Court..."

"No surprises there." Parvati smiled and it was sly and very serpentine. "Ti Fun's not going to be happy." She tapped the walkie-talkie. "I'll call him."

One of the prisoners scowled. "What about him?"

They all turned to see Dr Wells trying to slip away into the corridor. Ashoka ran and grabbed him, pushing him against the wall, the other prisoners gathering round menacingly.

Dr Wells looked desperately at Ashoka. "Please, I've done what you asked."

One man held a scalpel up menacingly. He spat and said something with a snarl and Dr Wells whimpered and pressed himself further against the wall as if hoping to disappear through it. "Please..."

Thump thump thump. There was a beating in Ashoka's ears and in his chest. It beat harder and harder. Ashoka stumbled, steadying himself as shadows danced in the corner of his vision. His dad braced him. "Son?"

Exhaustion. That was all. He'd been running on adrenaline

❖

and now he'd found his family it was all catching up with him. "I'm... fine," he said with an effort.

Parvati looked concerned too. "You don't look—"

And that was when Dr Wells slammed his fist on the alarm.

Chapter Twenty-six

Klaxons screamed and emergency lights came on, casting them all in a hellish crimson gloom.

Parvati spun and the doctor had barely lowered his hand when she struck. He held up his hands to try to block her, but she grabbed him and her fangs slid out.

"Last mistake you'll ever make," she said. "Time to die, scumbag."

"Wait," said Ashoka. "We need him."

Parvati didn't let go. "We have all the data."

"Which could be filled with scientific gobbledegook. We'll need him to be able to make sense of it. He comes with us."

"Fine. Tie his hands." Parvati shoved him into the arms of one of the other prisoners. "We need to get out of here. Now," she said, her fangs retracting into her mouth.

Any second now a band of heavily armed and exceedingly angry security guards were going to burst in and fill them with a lot of bullets.

"The lifts," said Ashoka, but his dad shook his head.

"No, son. The lifts will stop working in emergencies. It'll have to be the stairs."

Ashoka looked at the ragtag fugitives, who were all staring at him. How come he'd suddenly been made boss? It's not like he had a clue what he was doing...

"Grab those lab coats – they'll help us blend in. Parvati and I will go first; you wait a level below until we give the all-clear. You and you..." he picked two of the strongest-looking, "... help the stragglers."

Parvati took his arm. "We shouldn't wait for everyone. The deal was to save your family."

"It's all of us or none."

Parvati laughed. "You heroes are all the same." She flipped out her dagger and prepared herself. "Time to embrace your destiny, Ashoka."

"Any tips?" Ashoka wiped the sweat from his hands and took his bow off his back.

"Avoid the bullets."

"Er... thanks." Ashoka wiped the sweat from his hands again. He tightened his grip on the bow and notched an arrow. He only had four, so he had to make each one count.

They ran to the staircase door, Parvati just behind him. The lights blinked on and off and the alarm was deafening in the narrow concrete confines of the corridor. Another

❖

laboratory worker rushed out of the room opposite, but Parvati hissed at him and he rushed straight back in, locking the door.

People were bursting out into the corridor, clutching laptops or folders. Other patients, experiments, stumbled around in a panic, bewildered by the noise and lights. Ashoka barged through them towards the staircase doors.

Don't think.

Don't think of the guards and guns and bullets and grenades and gun smoke and fire and—

He slammed the doors open, bowstring pulled to his cheek and eyes peering down the line of the arrow shaft. He was expecting a hail of bullets.

Instead all he got were the alarms ringing above him and more red flashing lights. The stairwell echoed with footsteps as panicking staff rushed past. "All clear," he shouted to Parvati, who ushered the others up the stairs.

More and more people emerged from all levels, rushing to the staircase. Ashoka tensed as he spotted a pair of heavily armed guards, but they ignored him and ran up the stairs two at a time.

Ashoka joined his family, taking hold of Lucky's hand. "Stick together," he shouted, his mum and dad following close behind.

Suddenly the staircase shook. The steel frame groaned and bolts popped out of the wall as the stairwell shifted. Massive, jagged cracks split the concrete wall and Ashoka gasped as a man tumbled screaming from the floor above.

"What's going on?" Ashoka clung to the railings as the

❖

whole column of steel quivered. The walls rippled and cracked.

"An earthquake?" said Ashoka's dad, his teeth rattling as he clung on to his wife.

Ashoka caught up with Parvati. "We can't be trapped underground during an earthquake!"

"I don't think this is an earthquake..."

"What is it then?"

But before she could answer another tremor tore the stairs below them clean off the wall. A man tottered on the step, balanced with one foot on the upper level. He had files stacked up to his chin and wobbled, unable to decide whether or not to let go of the paperwork. He hesitated too long and was thrown into the air as the upper deck peeled away. He grabbed for the edge, but missed by a few centimetres and tumbled away, screaming.

Electrical cables tore off the walls and sparks jumped and crackled in the blinking darkness. Earthquake or not, they had to get out of here right now.

"One more floor!" Ashoka shouted. He pushed Lucky ahead. "Go!"

They ran as the staircase rocked back and forth. Chunks of concrete fell away. A cable touched the steel railings and sparks erupted in all directions, showers of lightning spraying around them.

He waited until his family had passed him, then ran.

As another tremor shook the building, they stumbled through a brand-new rent in the wall and found themselves outside at last. Rain lashed down and high winds buffeted

❖

them, drawing their breath away as the building creaked and the two tall chimneys swayed. Clouds rolled overhead and there were flashes of lightning. Ashoka grabbed hold of Lucks as she was blown backwards; his parents were huddling together. "Where to?" he shouted over the howling gale.

Parvati gestured towards the beach. She waited behind, helping the other prisoners out of the gap in the wall, everyone forced to link arms or hold hands against the mighty winds that roared through the chemical works.

The wind howled through the quivering cables and rain pelted down, nearly horizontal now, and hitting as hard as marbles. The drops exploded against the steel cylinders that creaked and buckled as the ground trembled and split asunder. Long chasms opened up, and down fell buildings, tanks, vehicles and people.

The endless steel fence flapped like paper and the supports tore free as waves, dozens of metres high, smashed upon the shore.

"What the hell is going on?" Ashoka yelled, trying to be heard.

Parvati shouted something, pointing to the sea, but the wind swept her words away.

Suddenly gunfire exploded all around them. Ashoka covered Lucky as people dived to the ground, screaming.

Guards drew up in a ragged line in front of them, blocking their escape. Dogs snarled and barked, saliva dripping from their heavy jaws.

"Down on your knees!" shouted one of the guards. "Now!"

"Get behind me," snapped Ashoka to his family and the others. He raised his bow.

"Put that down, boy!" The guard levelled his sub-machine gun at him.

He'd take out one, maybe two. Enough to make a gap for them to run through. The bowstring tensed as he pulled back. Wind buzzed through the cables.

"Put it down!"

More guards joined, forming a line of steel across the beach.

They'd almost made it — but almost wasn't enough.

"Ashoka, I've been trying to tell you..." said Parvati, touching his arm gently. "Look." She pointed to the sea, to the swirling clouds and the crackling lightning. "Look at what's making the storms..."

Ashoka looked out to sea. The waves, black and green, smashed against the shore. They struck the buildings nearest the water and dragged rubble away. Pipes broke and great jets of gas and flames burst into the night sky. The two chimneys swayed, one bent now and fire blossoming along the cracks. Then, slowly at first, it fell, crushing a line of parked tanks.

The ship *Pandora* yawed, and crates tumbled off its sides. Waves knocked it against the quayside, smashing up the walkways, and they in turn rent gashes into its low hull. The three other ships were flung against each other and the decks were a mess of rolling barrels and tumbling crates that had broken free of their straps and buckles. Men were tossed overboard or crushed by debris. But there was something else

❖

at work. As one wave rose over the decks Ashoka glimpsed something driving it.

"It's not the waves..." muttered Ashoka. He gazed at the sea along the seafront. The waves were rolling higher and higher, but not because of the winds. There were shapes under the water and they were coming closer.

Cloaked in seaweed and frothing seawater, an immense claw reached out of the pounding waves. Each nail was almost five metres long and thick as a tree trunk. Scales glistened marble, black, green, purple, shimmering and iridescent and ancient.

Dragons crawled from the sea.

Chapter Twenty-seven

*A*sh had rested and eaten. He had his manacles and a crude spear as weapons and the lantern to help him on his way. "Let's go, Rishi."

Rishi stayed where he was.

"Rishi?"

Rishi raised his head and faced the direction of Ash's voice. "What's your plan? We escape, *if* we escape, then what?"

"Go after Savage. Stop him." Wasn't that obvious?

Rishi nodded. "Yes, but how will we stop him?"

"I'll think of something," said Ash.

Rishi sat down. "But when? When it might be too late? No. Let's think about it now. While we can."

Reluctantly Ash lowered himself down on the rock beside the sadhu. "This would be so easy if I was still the Kali-aastra."

❖

Rishi drew his fingers through his tangled beard. "Ah, yes. The Kali-aastra. Killing seems to be the answer to most things, doesn't it?"

Ash frowned. "It is what I am. Kali made me this." He scratched his thumb. "I need a Great Death to awaken the powers of the Kali-aastra. Then we'll be able to deal with Savage."

"A Great Death? That's what powers you, is it? You'll never defeat Savage if this is what you believe."

"What do you mean?"

"When did you awaken the Kali-aastra the first time? When you died. When you gave your life to save your sister's. When Rama faced Ravana, who offered his life to awaken the Kali-aastra?"

"Lakshmana. Rama's brother," said Ash. Lakshmana had taken off his armour, urging Rama to strike, but Rama hadn't been able to do it. He couldn't kill his own brother. "What's your point, Rishi?"

"Love. It is love. Not death. Death is easy, Ash. Let me tell you a story. One of Kali."

"Is this going to take long?"

"Shut up and listen," said Rishi. "You might learn something." He crossed his legs and got comfortable. "So, imagine a battle. Rakshasas cover the earth, their bodies dead and broken, and who stands, alone and victorious?"

"Er... Kali?"

"That was a rhetorical question but, yes. Kali. She has slain them all. Such is her joy, such is her exultation, that she begins to dance. She dances with such fury that the very foundations of the universe begin to crumble."

"And that's a bad thing, right?"

Rishi sighed. "The more you interrupt, the longer this will take. But yes, a very bad thing. The gods are afraid. They entreat her to stop, but she does not hear them. Then her consort, Shiva, has a plan. He places a baby at her feet. It cries and that noise penetrates Kali's madness. She stops her dance and looks for the source of this sound. She sees the baby and comforts it. The universe is saved by a child. A thing so small, so helpless, so without use, but enough to stop the goddess of death."

Kali. Loads of rakshasas. A crying baby. "And the point is...?"

Rishi frowned. "If you don't understand it yet, you will eventually."

"That's not fair. I don't do the brainy stuff. That's usually Parvati's department."

"In this Parvati cannot help you. She is confused between love and hate. I blame her father, obviously." Rishi took up his staff. "What powers the Kali-aastra is not the death, but the life you take. It is not the hate you feel, because hate is plentiful in this world, but the love you have, something so much rarer. Whose life is great to you? Yours, of course. But then your sister's, your parents'. Parvati's too. These are people who mean everything to you."

"Are you saying I'd have to take their lives to reawaken the Kali-aastra? Well, that's not going to happen. Ever."

Rishi shook his head. "Answer me this. Who defines what a great life is? By love? By achievement? By status? Is a king's life greater than that of a slave? A wise man's greater than an infant's?"

❖

"You're saying it's the people I care about. My friends and family. Their lives mean something to me."

"Are they the only ones, Ash?" Rishi gestured to the others in the cavern. "Why not a stranger's? Are not all lives great? Each person is unique to the world. Their lives flicker only briefly in eternity, but will mean something to someone. They will be a person's father or mother, someone's child. Someone will have loved them, will have raised them, and cherished them. Once you understand that, then you will understand the full power of Kali."

"So what do you want me to do? Give Savage flowers when I next see him?"

Rishi smiled. "It is a paradox, I admit that."

"You sound like an old hippy."

"That's because I am. It doesn't mean I'm not right." Rishi stood up. "These are things I should have taught you much earlier. Unfortunately I died before I had the chance. It's nice to get a second opportunity."

Ash stood up. "Now, without sounding like a cliché, we need to get going. We've only twenty-four hours to save the world. Maybe forty-eight. I've kind of lost track. And there's the time-zone difference I'm not completely clear about."

Rishi stood up. "No time to waste, eh?"

Ash looked into the cave. "There are three tunnels. Which one?"

"The left one." He paused and turned to face the other prisoners.

They'd gathered silently, near and listening, forming a circle around the sadhu. He'd tried to get them to come, but they were afraid. They knew how the world would treat them, looking the way they did, being what they were.

"I'm sorry I failed you," said Rishi. "You came down here, victims of Savage, and needed me. You needed me to help you, support you, tell you that whatever he did, it could be made better, that what he changed didn't really matter. The soul is immortal, so is goodness, so is evil. These are things we should hang on to, but it's hard when you feel so broken. Savage beat me. He made me believe hate and rage were stronger than compassion and pity. It's easy to believe that when you are suffering and hurt and weak. Strength comes not from hands or muscles or having big arms and wide shoulders, but from the heart, and that is what Savage destroyed in me. My heart should have been big enough to take you in. It wasn't. I'm sorry."

Someone growled. Another mewed and someone else sobbed. They came forward and touched him. Rishi held out his arms and brushed along the limbs and hands and faces of his people. He lingered, wreathed in them, but slowly they retreated to their alcoves and caves until only Ash and the old man remained in the flickering light of a rusty lantern. Rishi drew a deep breath and straightened. He held up his head and fixed his bamboo stick under an armpit. "Follow me," he said.

Ash grinned. "Yes, sir."

Chapter Twenty-eight

"I'm sure we've been here before," said Ash. "That lump of rock looks very familiar."

"I know exactly where we're going," said Rishi. "I'm just... getting my bearings." He tapped the wall next to him. "Most strange. There should be an opening right here. Perhaps Savage has used his magic to change the route. To confound any escape."

"Or maybe we're just lost?" Ash added a few clumps of moss to the lantern. The wick hissed and smoked, but then the flame brightened. They'd tried to conserve the oil by walking in darkness, Ash being led by Rishi. But after tripping ten times and bashing his head twenty, Ash decided using some oil for light was better than permanent brain damage. Brittle patches of a white moss grew on the rocks and by the small cold pools that lay in the chambers and passages, and it burnt well enough to replace the now consumed lamp oil.

"How many paces since that last junction?" asked Rishi.

"Three hundred and twelve." That was Ash's other job – counting how far they'd gone. Rishi said he'd memorised the route by paces and turns and, so far, he'd been right, more or less.

"Let's try this—"

A roar trembled down the winding passageway. It was far and faint but deep, and lasted several minutes. The cold air quivered and its icy touch raised the hairs on Ash's nape. Other sounds, cries, shouts, screams, joined as a chorus of the damned. "What was that? A Balrog?"

"Come, quickly," said Rishi, and they scurried down the corridor and within a dozen paces saw a side passageway. They turned down it. The roar rose up again, but its echoes died away more quickly. Despite the cold, Ash was sweating, and his fingers ached as they gripped the lantern in one hand and the spear in the other. The labyrinth below the mountain played tricks. He was constantly hearing things, or seeing distant lights, or catching some strange smell. Echoes bounced back and forth irregularly, as if reluctant to enter the darkness, then struggling to escape it.

Sometimes they descended, other times they climbed. They'd go left and left and left for ages, following the curve of one wall, with Ash struggling to keep count as their steps went into the thousands, then abruptly they'd change direction and have to start all over again. Could they backtrack if they had to? He wasn't sure. He just had to trust Rishi's memory.

Now, after wandering for hours upon hours, doubts were creeping in. Did Rishi *really* know what he was doing? And was he limping? "Let's rest," Ash said.

"No, I can go on," said Rishi, tapping a wall.

"I can't." Ash put the lantern down and took out the last of the mushrooms. "Here. Eat something."

"I'm not hungry." The old man was acting like a stubborn mule.

"Fine. All the more mouldy, stinking mushrooms for me. Yummy."

"There's nothing wrong with those mushrooms."

Ash put a clump in Rishi's palm. "Try them for yourself. I'd rather eat the moss."

Rishi chewed methodically and struggled to swallow them; the mushrooms were as stiff as leather, but he forced a smile and smacked his lips. "Delicious. Now eat some yourself."

"I'll save mine for later."

Rishi's face creased in anguished realisation. "You let me eat them all, didn't you? Stupid boy."

"I can afford to lose a few grams. You can't."

"We need you strong, Ash."

"A few wrinkly fungi won't make any difference." Ash turned the spear over in his hands and jabbed at an imaginary target. "Strange how I can still do all the punching and kicking stuff."

"They are human skills, ingrained in your muscles, in your blood. It is the preternatural powers, the massive strength, the inhuman speed and the death touch, that you've lost, the things that were extensions of Kali's power and

214

wholly dependent on you still possessing her aastra. Even without it I doubt there's a mortal alive who can defeat you in combat."

"Shame the bad guys aren't mortal."

"Yes. A shame indeed."

Rishi didn't need to say it, but the meaning was clear – if Ash faced any one of Savage's rakshasas he'd be torn to pieces.

They set off again. As they delved deeper into the mountain, they found remains, piles of bones, partial skeletons and skulls. Some had been cracked open like eggs and others ripped by claws and teeth. The bones looked well chewed, not a strip of flesh left on them, and sucked clean of marrow.

And it was getting hotter, the air stuffier and moist. And the smell. At first it was just a faint odour on the faintly stirring breeze that occasionally rippled down through the passageways, but it didn't carry any freshness with it, none of the stark, cold mountain air Ash was expecting. Instead it stank of putrescence, of decaying meat and bilious gases, of bodies heaving and sweating. Some passages smelled worse than others, and they hurried past those quietly.

Then, as Ash was dragging himself down another seemingly identical passageway, Rishi grabbed his arm. "This is it," he said excitedly. "Can you smell it?"

No, he couldn't. Nothing but his own sweat.

Rishi raised his head high and slowly turned, sniffing. He smiled. "Fresh air. I'm sure of it. We're getting close, Ash."

Ash peered down the winding, uneven corridor. Water ran

down the walls, dark and glistening in the faint lamplight, and pooled in the indentations in the ground before running off into other cracks and holes. Ash put his hand against the wall and scooped up a palmful of liquid for a drink. He stopped. It wasn't water.

It was blood.

"The walls are bleeding," he said. "Which is odd." He looked back at the puddles they'd walked through and saw the trail of bloody footprints. "And kind of gross."

Voices cried out. They wailed and howled and the sound of their hunger rolled along the passageways and vibrated through the cracks. The rocks around them split as a shockwave made the entire tunnel quiver. Blood spat and hissed from the walls as great jets spurted over them both. Deep, distant thunder rumbled out of the darkness.

"Well, that's not good," said Ash. "Time to move."

"Too late," said Rishi. "They're here."

Ash spun as a scream blasted his ear. A man, his arms huge and hairy, but his torso ending in long, bony legs and with the hard carapace of an insect, sprang out of a shadow. He'd been lurking within one of the cracks and his body was slick with blood, his eyes white, large and insane. He leaped at Ash's throat, but Ash blocked with his spear and the teeth clamped down on the stick, snapping it in half. Ash kicked the thing off and spun the two sticks around. He rammed them both into the creature's chest. It squealed and tried to claw at him, but within seconds its own blood mingled with the flood now pouring from the walls. Ash left it pinned there and gathered up his manacles.

"Run, Rishi. I'll follow."

"No," said the old man. "We fight."

Ash pushed him ahead. "There's no room for both of us. The passage narrows here. They'll have to come at me one at a time." The ceiling had dropped to less than two metres and at its narrowest point was less than a metre across. "Find the way out; I'll join you."

Rishi wasn't happy, but nodded. "Follow as swiftly as you can."

Ash picked up a thick, long thighbone and faced the oncoming horde. The lantern sat a metre or two behind him and its light didn't venture far. It flickered and shook, as though afraid of the overwhelming darkness that waited all around it.

Ash saw the eyes, too many, shine red in the faint light. Slick bodies, oiled with blood, slid and climbed over the rocks and each other towards him. Fang-filled mouths snarled and snapped, and ivory claws scraped across the red ground. They had tentacles, wings; they had tails and snouts; they were deformed, melded together into a seething single worm-like entity comprising dozens of creatures, human and animal. Faces stared out of the quivering worm of flesh as it slithered towards him. Teeth snapped where eyes should have been, and hands reached out from mouths, clawing and grasping at him in hungry eagerness.

The monstrosity had a name. He'd fought one many thousands of years ago, as Prince Rama. Created by the darkest of Ravana's magic, it was built out of living beings, all merged into a single insane mass of screaming, tormented souls. Hundreds of arms and legs and faces all screaming from a bulbous, ever-mutating single whole. It oozed through the tight passage, splitting and reforming constantly. Ash watched as a dozen torsos pulsed and grew arms, long and short, thin and fat, spindly and massive. Savage really was as powerful as the demon king if he'd been able to create such a monster – a Carnival of Flesh.

Ash couldn't hear Rishi any more; he was alone. Ahead of him were the hisses and snarls of the people of the Carnival. He steadied himself, firming his grip on the thighbone in his left hand and the iron manacles in his right.

He'd hold them off as long as possible. Rishi would make it, and find Parvati and Ashoka, and together they'd stop Savage. That was good enough for Ash.

The lamplight weakened to no brighter than a match.

"Come on then," snarled Ash.

The light went out.

Chapter Twenty-nine

*A*shoka stared as the dragons rose out of the sea. They raised huge waves before them and the winds howled as they swept their heads into the air and roared, controlling the elements with their fury and their power.

Some guards formed a crude, trembling line across the ruins of the fence, some stared at the beasts with slack jaws, others threw down their weapons and ran, or crumbled and cowered, weeping and soiling themselves.

These were dragons.

First one beast, then another, lifted itself on its mighty legs and shook its long pearl-white whiskers free of seaweed and water. Eyes as large as tables, swirling with a myriad of colours, stared down at the puny defence. Bullets from the bravest guards sparked across their scales, but had no more impact than raindrops.

❖

The first dragon, a hundred metres long, rose up to dance within the winds. It had no wings, but writhed into the storm like a snake. Its shadow passed over Ashoka and his party, scales shining like the skies of eternity. Claws scooped up men and tore open buildings and vehicles and then, over the howling typhoon, it drew breath.

A jet of liquid erupted from the dragon's throat and as it touched the first cylinder it burst into white, searing flame, ripping through the steel walls as if they were tissue. The gas within exploded and the air was suddenly black with smoke, to be whipped away by the hurricane winds.

Flames licked the dragon's belly as it slid over the burning wreckage. Huge gouts of fire trailed out of its mouth as it cast an infernal wall back and forth over the factory. Pipes melted, guards were transformed into black dust and the stones under their feet to glass.

The second dragon climbed higher into the storm, lightning caressing its steely body, before it twisted and poured volcanic fire and poisonous gases over the fleeing guards and remaining buildings. Its tail swiped the remaining chimney, which crashed into the sea, shattering two more of the ships into so much wreckage.

"Look!" shouted Lucky. "A boat!"

A powerboat bounced upon the waves. Razor-sleek and bone-white, it cut through the turmoil and swung to a stop a few metres from shore.

Standing on the top deck, his coat flapping about him, was Ti Fun.

"That's our ride," said Parvati.

❖

Ashoka took a firm hold of Dr Wells. "Move," he ordered. "I... I can't swim!"

Ashoka dragged the scientist along.

The smell of burning petrol mixed with the salt and chemicals, which were sweet and foul. Clouds of green smoke and yellow rolled out of laboratories and tanks and ruptured pipes. Men dissolved as acid showered over them, and others burst into brilliant, blinding flames as the dragons swooped and annihilated.

Ashoka ushered the other prisoners in a line towards the boat. He clutched his bow in one hand as he led a couple of kids into the roiling waters. He could barely see for the intense rain. He could barely hear for the winds. But he heard the scream.

A thing, scaled but humanoid, easily three metres tall, waded through a wall of fire. His scales were stubbly green and as thick as armour. A long snout extended from his face and jagged uneven fangs stuck out at all angles. His reptilian eyes locked on Ashoka and he roared as he lifted one of the prisoners over his head. And ripped him in two.

"Look out! Mayar..." shouted Parvati.

Ashoka watched in terror as a guard trying to flee the flames stumbled into Mayar's way, the demon swatting him as if he was no more than a fly, crushing the man's chest with one blow.

The ground shook as Mayar's feet beat down, and Ashoka fumbled his arrow, just grabbing it before he dropped it.

He was twenty metres away.

Parvati shouted to Ashoka to run, but there was no time.

❖

Lucky was just behind him, and if he didn't stop Mayar, he'd eat his sister whole.

Ashoka drew the bowstring, felt the fletching caress his cheek.

Mayar rose up before him, towering over Ashoka. His fetid breath, all offal and slime, choked him. His entire body was covered in impenetrable armoured scales.

Ashoka sighed. His body seemed to sink into itself. He gazed down the shaft to the brilliant steel arrowhead and the rakshasa before him.

I've been here before.

He raised his aim, past the chest, past the throat.

Wait.

Mayar widened his jaws so his tongue hung almost over Ashoka's head.

Wait.

The claws spread wider and wider. There was no escape.

Parvati screamed, but she seemed far away. It was as if another will guided Ashoka.

Wait.

Spittle flew from Mayar's fangs across Ashoka's face. He raised his aim just a notch higher.

Now.

His fingers just slipped the bowstring.

The arrow pierced Mayar's palette. The soft inside of his mouth was unprotected by scales, his only weak spot.

How did I know?

I just did.

The arrow tore through, deep into Mayar's brain.

❖

Mayar dropped to his knees, already dead. His eyes rolled over and blood dribbled from his slack jaw.

Ashoka was suddenly shaking. What had just happened to him? He stared at the dead demon, at the arrow and at the bow in his hand. He felt weak. If he'd been a second too soon, a second too late, he would have been ripped apart. Something, someone, had forced him to hold his nerve until the very right moment.

He stumbled back, away from the dead demon and into the water.

Ashoka's dad scooped a terrified Lucky into his arms as they all waded into the sea. Ti Fun swept his hand and the winds and waters instantly calmed around his boat. Men, the gangsters from earlier, threw out ropes and hauled in the fleeing refugees like fishermen bringing in a catch, fishermen in designer black. Ashoka swallowed a hefty mouthful as the wash from the boat covered him and for a moment he went under into the black darkness of the water, but Toad latched his big sticky palms on him and lifted him out as if he was a minnow. Ashoka collapsed on the deck, coughing. "Thanks."

Toad grunted and gazed contemptuously with his big bulging eyes.

"Out to sea," commanded Ti Fun.

The engines roared and the boat bucked as the prow rose out of the water. Vast spewing jets of water shot from the rear underwater turbines and then, crashing against the storm, the boat accelerated away.

Ashoka, clutching the side, looked back.

All the ships burned. A vast wall of fire surrounded the

Savage factory. The chimneys were gone and instead huge clouds of smoke rolled up into the sky. The rain hissed and steamed upon the blazing world, and still the pipes and labs poured more chemicals and petrol and fuel on to the dragons' flames. Wreckage, both crates and bodies, floated in the inky waves.

Guards and lab technicians clustered along the beach, waving and calling for help. Some waded out and decided to swim for it, despite the huge waves.

Winds screamed and the rain smashed upon Ashoka's bare flesh. His shirt was torn and small cuts bled from all over his chest. He hadn't noticed.

They should sting, but they don't.

Then he turned away from the smoke, fire and death.

The boat bobbed gently in a glass-flat sea. Stars shone upon a velvet black sky and a moon, curved like a maharajah's tulwar, rested low above the water.

Some of the party had already been offloaded to waiting sampans. Others had been dropped off on a quiet, empty beach on the neighbouring island of Cheung Chau. Then the pilot had revved the engine again and taken the rest of them out, beyond the outlying islands, beyond the lights of Hong Kong, until they found themselves in an empty, featureless sea, nothing on the horizon but moon-glinting waves.

Lucky slept, her head on Mum's lap. She, also asleep, rested her head on Dad's shoulder. He had his arm around them both, hugging his wife and child as if he would never,

ever let them go for the rest of his life. They'd been given blankets and food, but they looked exhausted, crushed by their ordeal.

Ashoka had not yet had a chance to talk to them; it had all been so insane, with the storm and the refugees and the dragons. Ti Fun's goons had been surprisingly sympathetic, offering tea and comfort to the terrified locals. Ashoka had helped where he could. But what could he really do?

But there was plenty of time to talk with his family now they were safe.

Ashoka met his father's gaze, and his dad smiled weakly. But his eyes were haunted and wary.

Ashoka went over to him. "You OK, Dad?" he asked.

Dad's smile broke into a low laugh. "Now, that's not something a son should need to ask his dad, is it?" He patted the seat beside him. "Come up here." He pulled him close. "What, too cool to give your old man a hug?"

"What happened, Dad?" asked Ashoka, letting himself be pulled in.

Dad sighed and squeezed Ashoka hard with his free arm. "I thought... I thought I'd never see you again, son. How did you find us?"

"I had help. Parvati."

"That girl? Who is she?"

"Would you believe me if I told you she's Ravana's daughter?"

"Yesterday, no, I wouldn't have. But tonight I watched dragons — real, live, non-CGI'd freaking *dragons* — burn a factory to the ground. So, yes, you tell me she's Ravana's

❖

daughter and I do believe you." Dad ruffled his hair. "I hardly recognise you."

"Nothing's changed, Dad. I just had to toughen up a bit. So I could find you."

"Is it over?"

Ashoka glanced across at Parvati. She and Ti Fun were deep in conversation.

"It is for us," said Ashoka. "We're going home."

His dad closed his eyes. "A police car stopped us. Said the bridge was closed and sent us down a dead end. Men, I think they were men, pulled us out and chucked us in a van. You know what? I kept on thinking it was a mistake. Mistaken identity or something, and they were kidnappers after some rich family and had got us by accident. I thought if I explained it to them, they'd understand and let us go. How stupid is that? I... I live in a world of logic and common sense, Ashoka. I live in a world of reason, of reasonableness. Where things make sense and people are *reasonable*. Things like kidnappings and human experimentation and dragons do not exist in my world. How can you prepare yourself for things like that?"

"I don't know. You can't."

His dad said nothing, he just looked at him oddly. Ashoka straightened his collar. "What?"

"You seem different, son. You didn't freeze, or panic, or stand around wishing it would all go back to normal. You accepted this world. It's almost like you belong in it somehow."

"Last week my only encounter with dragons was when we played the Mountain of Doom at Josh's house. The only heroics I've ever been involved in were through my tenth-level paladin."

"And yet you saved us all."

"That was mainly Parvati. I'm the comedy sidekick."

"You got us all out of that building; you killed that crocodile beast, got everyone on to the boat. You are a hero, son. To me anyway," said Dad.

But Ashoka's attention was already elsewhere.

One of the gangsters who had been guarding Dr Wells had left him and gone over to talk to Ti Fun and Parvati, and even from here Ashoka could see that Parvati was not wearing her happy face. All three descended, and the gangsters cleared a space around the scientist, who looked frightened and very alone.

"What is it?" asked Ashoka, walking over.

"It's not good," said Parvati. "We've found out what Savage is planning. Tell him," said Parvati to Dr Wells.

Dr Wells cleared his throat a couple of times. "Savage has been perfecting his RAVN-I for the last few months. He intends to launch it over the major population centres around the world. The bursts will contaminate vast areas and infect millions of people, mainly children, who, to all intents and purposes, will become demons. The rest will react differently. Most will suffer brief but intense periods of psychotic rage, ranging from violent urges to uncontrollable cannibalistic hunger. The long-term effects haven't been determined, but will range from mild physical deformities to deep-seated and permanent psychological trauma. In short, layman's terms – Savage intends to drag the world into chaos."

Ashoka stared at the scientist. How could he talk about destroying the world so calmly? He was stunned. It was beyond evil.

Ashoka's dad walked over, peering at the screen. "These are the monsoon patterns."

Dr Wells nodded. "RAVN-I will enter the ecosystem via rain and soil. The world's food production will be tainted by the drug for generations."

Ashoka's dad glared at him. "And you sound so proud."

"Do you have any idea how much work and money and effort has gone into this? Even if I say so myself, the project deserves a Nobel Prize."

"Like the one Savage already has for world peace," said Parvati bitterly.

Ashoka looked at the swirling patterns on the screen. They covered all of India and half the Near East. "Savage doesn't need to do this. The world's quite insane enough without him."

"This science could have been used to provide anti-viruses across the whole world," said Dad. "Good grief, you could cure so many people. Think about it. The cure for polio, measles, whooping cough and yellow fever and so much more, just growing in fields and running in taps and falling out of the sky. You could prevent so much misery."

"But misery is where the profits are," said Dr Wells.

Dad grabbed the man and pushed him to the boat's side. No one tried to stop him. Tears ran down his cheeks and his face was pale with rage. "The things you've done, we'll never escape them. God, the screams, and the way they begged.

They even begged for you to kill them in the end. How could you?"

"I was... just..."

"We've already established that line's not going to save you," said Parvati. She put her hand on Mr Mistry's shoulder and he let Dr Wells go.

"Those ships were meant to deliver the drug, weren't they?" asked Parvati.

Dr Wells nodded. "Yes. The delivery manifest is there on the data stick."

"And they're at the bottom of the sea and the chemical factory's destroyed, and we know where the others are, right? So is it over?"

"There were five ships," whimpered Dr Wells. "The *Lazarus* sailed out two weeks ago."

"To where?" asked Parvati, her green eyes glowing.

"I don't know, believe me."

Ti Fun tapped his fingertips on the screen. "I will find out. We have friends in the docks. Someone will know, but it will take time."

"What about the other factories in China?" asked Ashoka.

Ti Fun's gaze was dark. "We'll take care of them. The Savage Foundation will cease to operate in China by dawn."

Ashoka joined his dad on the other side of the deck. He was staring out to sea, quivering with rage and terror. He chewed his lips and fought back the tears. "Don't look at me like this, Ashoka. I'm such a failure."

"Dad, it wasn't your fault."

"Oh, God, Ashoka. I failed. I failed so badly. I couldn't

❖

protect them, Mum and Lucky. I couldn't do the one thing a father, a husband, should do: protect his family. How can I look at them, be happy with them, knowing how useless I was? How impotent. I failed so badly."

What could he say?

There was a huge splash and they both turned around. Parvati and the others were looking over the edge.

"What was that?" Ashoka asked. "Where's Dr Wells?"

He ran to the side. The water lapped and a few bubbles popped on the surface. But not many.

Parvati widened her eyes to imply surprise. "Dr Wells, overcome with remorse, decided that he couldn't live with himself a moment longer."

Ti Fun nodded and gave a melodramatic sigh. "Such a waste. But the guilt was too much." He looked to his men. "It's true, isn't it?"

The gangsters, all lined up, nodded in unison.

"Most tragic," said one.

"We tried to stop him but he overpowered us," said another solemnly. "Much stronger than he looked."

Ashoka looked at them. "So the six of you, and you, Parvati, and you, Mr Dragon, could not stop a feeble old man from diving overboard?"

Parvati smiled.

Ashoka looked into the black depths. Nothing stirred. Dr Wells was, if not sleeping with the fishes, certainly having a serious lie-down. "Fair enough."

Chapter Thirty

*A*sh fought. He didn't need to see – they were all around him. He swung the manacles, the chains clanged and struck flesh and bone. Screams choked the air and the stench suffocated him as much as the press of the bodies. He was torn and bloody from claws and tusks and fangs, but he couldn't fall, there wasn't any room, and Ash's cries joined the chorus of pain. Hands wrapped around his wrists and ankles and threatened to tear him apart but, soaked and slimy with blood and gore, he slipped from their grasp and rammed the now-splintered bone shard deep into the massive worm. A multitude of cries burst out and Ash twisted.

He fought, he bled, he retreated and fought and bled again. He kicked and smashed and stabbed, even as he wearied beyond exhaustion, and yet the Carnival of Flesh came on relentlessly, abandoning bits of its body to thrash and slither over the blood-soaked ground.

The rest of it, the immense single mass of amalgamated flesh, beat and pushed, squeezing itself through the narrow passageway, heaving against the rocks, cracking deeper crevasses into the fractured stone. Broken fragments fell, cutting Ash's shoulders, but what were they compared to the tears and rips that covered him already?

The ground buckled and Ash tripped as a thin chasm opened up along the floor. He winced as his foot caught in the crack, but it barely stopped him. Any second now the entire tunnel was going to come down.

Ash crawled backwards as the Carnival pushed itself through the thin gap, hissing furiously while Ash caught a few seconds' rest. The noxious fumes from the hundreds of twisted bodies covered him like a poisonous cloud. What he'd give for a lungful of fresh air.

The Carnival struggled and heaved, stone split, the cracks shattered in a web pattern across the surface and a deep rut opened in the crumbling floor, as loud and as sharp as a gunshot. A shower of dust and small stones fell.

Ash didn't need Marma Adi to know what was about to happen. He just needed to give it a little help.

A cluster of eyes stared at him and the pulsing mass of flesh and bile and foulness hesitated. Perhaps in one of the heads there was a glimmer of something other than madness. Caution.

The rumbling stopped and the walls settled down.

Ash ran up and swung the manacles into the monstrosity.

❖

It screamed as he hit it again and again. He kicked one of the faces and rammed his fist into a bulbous belly that quivered from the blow. He needed it angry.

"Come on, I'm right here," he said. "Yummy yummy."

The Carnival thrashed and Ash dashed back as a forest of hands and claws reached out for him.

Fresh air. A narrow, crooked slit had opened up during the battle and a breeze blew in. He couldn't see it, but the coldness of the air was delicious relief from the cloying damp heat. Goosebumps rose over his bare arms and Ash threw the manacles and bone aside and ran. Head down and left hand against the wall, he stumbled and tripped, but kept his face towards the wind.

And behind him, around him, the mountain shook. Boulders crashed down and thunder boomed as vast chasms splintered the rock. The yells and screams of the Carnival turned to cries of fear and terror. Feet and hands and slithering meat slapped the ground behind him as bits of the Carnival tore off and gave chase. But even as the stone rained down on to him, Ash didn't pause or look back. His heart pounded and he was gasping, but the air was cold and sharp and clean.

A dazzling line lit the passageway.

I'm almost there.

A hand grabbed his heel and he tripped. A legless creature hauled itself over him, red eyes as wide as its mouth. It wrapped its arms around Ash's waist, trying to hold him down as others came up behind it to feast. They were bony, slick with blood and purple with bruises and built out of

233

different parts so that some ran on mismatched arms and their legs waved out of their shoulders.

"No!" cried Ash.

Not when he was almost there...

But they were upon him, and Ash roared as they trapped his arms and snapped at his body and nails raked his face and—

The tunnel collapsed. It fell away, tilting down towards the widening opening. The light erupted as the mountain face broke, and Ash and Savage's mutants rolled and slid down. Ash heaved one off him and twisted another so that it slammed the wall as they tumbled past.

The tunnel continued to tip and Ash slid faster and there was sunlight ahead. A distant ridge of mountains, pink with dawn, lined up on the far horizon, and Ash yelled as he fell out of the cave mouth. He rolled in the air and his stomach jumped to his mouth as he went into freefall. A second of air time and then he crunched down into snow.

Down and down he tumbled. Snow was shoved into his mouth and ears and blinded him and went down his neck and he couldn't stop. He didn't want to. As the world turned, sky, snow and mountain, he saw the entire mountainside collapse in on itself. Thousands of tons of rock fell and bounced down the slope, any piece of which could totally splat him.

"Ash!"

The slope shallowed and Ash's fall turned into a surfing slide.

Rishi stood upon a large, settled boulder, waving. "I'm here, boy!"

They'd made it!

❖

Ash spat snow out and managed to get up; not easy as it was like lying in a sea of feathers.

He'd come to a stop on a short ledge. To the left and right the slope continued down for a good two hundred metres, maybe more. Behind him was the black wall of the mountain, continuing up to the clouds. A few last boulders rolled past them, but the worst seemed to be over. Of the creatures that had attacked him, there was no sign. *They must have fallen all the way down*, thought Ash. The joy of victory rose within him.

"Come, we must be quick," said Rishi.

"Why? I totally and utterly kicked its butt!"

As if in answer, a deep, long moan rumbled from within the mountain. Dust and pebbles blew from the cracks and holes, a vast exhale.

"No, Ash," said Rishi. "You just made it angry."

Chapter Thirty-one

ingers tore open the mountain. Fingers ten metres long and each built from a dozen people. The thing did not care that limbs broke and bodies were ripped apart as it beat its way free. Blood sprinkled the rock and snow above them as another pair of hands, ten-fingered, eleven, pushed its way out of the mountain prison.

"Go, Ash. Quickly."

Ash stared in horrified awe. How big was it? Five arms now were ripping their way through the jagged cave mouth. The stone crumbled as massive fists pounded the walls from the inside, and the thunder was deafening. Ash took Rishi's arm. "Come on then."

The old man didn't move. He smiled and shook his dreadlocks, savouring the elements around him. "It is good to feel the wind and sun upon my face. To bury my toes within fresh snow. To be free at last. Thank you, Ash."

"Thank me later. Come on."

"Listen to me, Ash, this is important."

Ash took Rishi's hand and tried to pull him along. "If it's more philosophy, it can wait. A long time."

"No. It's about the Kali-aastra."

"What?"

The wind rose, whipping Rishi's dreadlocks all around him. "Savage found it in Rajasthan. He used it to kill Ravana."

"Yeah, I know that. Come on."

"I stole it from him," said Rishi. "There was a lot of confusion when Ravana died. Some of the rakshasas wanted Savage dead, others accepted his rule as long as Rani was there. I was being held in the catacombs below the Savage Fortress, but in the chaos I managed to get out, and get the Kali-aastra. I got as far as the old city before Savage caught me."

"What about the Kali-aastra?" asked Ash. "Did Savage get it back?"

"No. I gave it to someone for safekeeping. Someone who knew all about Kali."

"Who?"

"Who do you think? Ujba." Rishi twisted his hand free. "Now go."

A thousand throats screamed in unison. The Carnival of Flesh, the thing he'd fought, had been the merest fraction of the creature. Up and up it rose, climbing out of the tears in the mountain, spewing from half a dozen different orifices, melding together like wax and assembling itself in an entity of hundreds of arms and legs, all different, all misjoined, all as long as trains and built of so many villagers, victims of Savage's alchemy. Bodies tumbled free like sweat drops and fell screaming to be smashed upon rocks. Vast patches were bruised, purple fields of injured flesh that bled from a hundred wounds as the monster squeezed itself out of the holes and crevasses covering the mountain face, a lava flow of meat and bone.

"Go, Ash," urged Rishi. "Hurry."

Rishi was insane. There was no way he could beat that thing. Ash grabbed hold of his arm.

Sparks burst from the old man and Ash cried out, instantly letting go.

Steam rose from his stinging fingertips.

Lightning crackled across Rishi. Sparks and bolts jumped over the blue-glowing flesh. The air stank of ozone and Rishi pulled his lips back into a fierce snarl. His hair rose and tiny bursts of light shone within the strands. "Free at last..."

Ash wanted to say so much. He wanted to hug the old man. How many times he'd saved him, ever since he'd whacked that cow on the nose in Varanasi in a different world. Rishi was the same. Here and in the past and, no doubt, in the future. Ash fought back the tears. "I don't want to lose you again."

"It's only death." Rishi smiled. "Now run. Look to the living. They will need you."

238

Ash swallowed a large, painful lump and nodded. "Until next time."

Halos of light radiated from the sadhu. Freed from the iron-bound rock, all the magic he'd stored for a decade filled the frail flesh and even his pores sparkled. Every part of him hummed with energy – the power of the gods.

Blind and crippled, Rishi began to chant. Mantras to his god, Shiva. Lines glowed over his skin, the marks of his patron, and the sky shook. The clouds flashed with lightning, disturbed and angry. The Carnival of Flesh raised its many Hydra heads out of the mountain and cried out against the sky.

Ash ran as fast as he dared, wary of the uneven path and the sheer drop on either side. The snow clumped at his feet and he slipped on ice and had to brace himself, but he didn't stop.

But he did look up.

Rishi stood on the ledge, a shimmering outline in a blinding haze of electric-blue light. Looming over him, covering the slope in shadow, came the Carnival, freed from the stone and hundreds of metres high. It swept a fist down upon the sadhu and Ash cried out. But the blow didn't land. The fist exploded, sending bodies and limbs and burning flesh in all directions. The Carnival recoiled, then waved its appendage as it reformed. Ash stared as people seemed to flow into the burning stump, regrowing it out of themselves.

Rishi's staff began to disintegrate, unable to contain any more power. It crumbled to dust and Rishi himself, bright as an exploding star, became a being of light.

❖

Lightning burst down from the black clouds. Huge chunks of the Carnival were instantly incinerated. Even down where Ash stood, the stench of burning flesh filled his nostrils. Bolts struck the mountain and the peaks trembled.

Rishi was just a faint outline within a sphere of searing white light.

Then, silently, the sphere expanded. It grew outwards, slowly to begin with, then faster and faster, till it was ten metres wide, twenty, fifty. A hundred.

Rishi went supernova.

Ash covered his face with his arms as the light became unbearable. It seemed to shine straight through him, lighting his very heart. The heat didn't come from the outside, but from within. Ash gasped and fell in the snow. He curled up and tried to hide from the blistering heat. He felt as if he was about to disintegrate, as if every atom was shaking apart.

Then it winked out.

Light spots danced and burst in his eyes as he opened them.

The clouds had gone. Sun, harsh and clean, shone down over the snow-blanketed plateau and lifted the mountain out of shadow.

The ledge was still there and so were the huge rents in the mountainside. But there was no Rishi, no Carnival of Flesh. There was no aftermath of carnage. No bodies or lingering smells. No marks at all. All had just ceased to exist.

Ash sank into the snow. Whatever had kept him going until now had finally run out. He was hungry, tired, bruised

❖

and bleeding, and a million miles from anywhere. He was not the Kali-aastra. He was just Ash.

Where could he go? As far as he knew, Parvati and Ashoka were still in London. Back home.

Home. He could never go back home, and that hurt more than the bruises and the cuts. He shook. His body, pushed beyond all human endurance, rebelled and didn't want to move. It wanted to give up and just collapse. Ash knelt in the snow.

Where could he go?

Chase after Savage? What was the point? He'd just get his backside kicked all over again.

But the alternative was to curl up and die here. No thanks. Ash gritted his teeth and got up, even though his legs wobbled and burned with fatigue.

Snow and mountains all around. A vast desolation surrounded him. His coat was torn and he'd freeze to death tonight if he didn't find shelter.

A faint smudge stained the otherwise clear blue sky. Ash shaded his eyes and peered into the brilliant glare of sunlight on pristine snow.

He blinked, not sure if the specks were signs of habitation or his own concussion. Could it be a cluster of houses and smoke rising from a chimney? Only one way to find out.

Ash looked back to where Rishi had stood, a hollowness deep in his chest. He wished the sadhu was still here to help him sort it all out, but it was down to him now. No Rishi, no Parvati, no Kali-aastra. Just him.

And Ujba.

Of all the people, in all the timelines, in all the universes, it had to be Ujba.

Ujba was a master of *Kalari-payit*, the ancient martial art. Ash had been sent to train with him and had spent weeks of misery getting beaten black and blue, morning, afternoon and night. That had been bad enough.

But the man was one of the *Thuggee*, the cult of killers who worshipped Kali. And Ujba had tried to recruit Ash. Ash had hoped he'd never, ever see the man ever again.

And now he was the only person who could help him.

Ash straightened his ragged coat and headed down the mountain.

Chapter Thirty-two

$\mathcal{T}$i Fun made sure they were left undisturbed once they got back to the Mandarin. His cars took Ashoka and his family quickly from the docks to a suite set aside for them. Parvati had one of the rooms too. Lucky and Ashoka's mum and dad, while polite, watched the girl warily.

It was well into the afternoon when Ashoka got up. There were people milling around in the main reception room, and he heard Parvati talking with Ti Fun. Ti Fun was not taking Savage's double-cross well. That suited him fine. Let the big boys sort out Savage; that was their job.

He was going home.

Hong Kong shone in the daytime. The endless landscape of glass turned the city into a vast hall of mirrors, each reflecting one another over and over again. In the distance he saw the black Bank of China building, said to have been

❖

designed as a hatchet plunged into the heart of the city. The sea beyond glistened green and he wondered if the dragons were lurking in the harbour, perhaps snoozing as ferries and ships passed overhead.

Clothes were laid out for him. A black suit and stark white shirt. He slipped them on. They fitted perfectly. He even found a pair of black shades on the table. He adjusted his sleeves, checked the silver dragon cufflinks were in place, then came out from his room.

Ti Fun and Parvati looked up. Ti Fun smiled. "I see my tailor got your measurements exactly."

"How are you feeling?" Parvati asked.

"Ready to go home."

Ti Fun stood and snapped his fingers. Two of his goons sprang to their feet. "My private jet will take you all to Birmingham. I have people there who'll keep you safe."

"For how long?" asked Ashoka.

"For as long as it takes," said Parvati. "Until I've dealt with Savage."

"And how will we know you've succeeded?"

Parvati poured out the tea. "You'll certainly know if I've failed."

Ashoka peered at the papers on the table. Dock manifestos from ports all over the Far East. "Any luck finding the *Lazarus*?"

"Not yet," said Ti Fun. "There's plenty of ocean in which to lose one little ship. It could take a few days yet. But I have found all Savage's other factories and chemical labs in China. Something bad has happened to each of them. He'll

❖

not be producing any more of his drug for a long while to come, that's for sure."

Ashoka went to join his dad, who was in another room with some of Ti Fun's men, analysing more of Dr Wells's data. Ashoka watched him hurrying about between half a dozen computers, looking at weather charts, locations of Savage's investments, and shipping news. He doubted his dad had slept at all since they'd arrived here.

"Your father has found a purpose," said Parvati, sipping tea from an antique china cup.

Ashoka stabbed another ball of dim sum with his chopstick. "He wants Savage stopped."

"And what about your sister and your mother? How are they?" asked Parvati.

Lucky had woken screaming. It had taken them ages to calm her down. Mum jumped at every sound or slight movement, her nerves as tight as piano wires. Her eyes, usually bright with humour, were ringed, afraid. She hadn't slept, too terrified of what nightmares might come.

But Ashoka's hands were steady. The visions he'd seen, the corpses swinging in their bags, the men devoured by acid and flame, the stench of death, it... stirred something inside.

A thrill. A burning, shameful thrill.

"That was quite a shot you made," said Parvati. "Mayar was a lord of demons. Only the greatest of heroes would have ever stood a chance against him."

"I was lucky. Really, stupidly lucky." Now that he thought of it, Ashoka could barely stop himself from trembling. Taking out a demon crocodile with an arrow. Waiting until the jaws were practically around his head before letting the arrow go. What had he been thinking?

"I wondered when it would happen," said Parvati.

"Wondered what?"

"You believe in reincarnation, don't you?" asked Parvati.

"I suppose. I've never really thought much about it."

Parvati smiled. "You've been around this world a thousand times, Ashoka. I've been there and seen you. You've had so many lives, been so many people in so many different places. All different, but for one thing. Your destiny has never changed."

"Destiny?" He didn't like the sound of that.

"You are the Eternal Warrior," said Parvati. "War calls to you."

"No, it doesn't. I hate conflict. I can't even stand up to Jack and his cronies at school. You'd have thought I'd be slimmer with all the times they've nicked my lunch money."

"No, what matters are the stakes. I knew Rama. He gave up his throne without hesitation, even though he knew it was a plot, but he obeyed his father's word. He lived in a forest, content, sleeping on leaves when he once had palaces beyond number. He knew the true value of gold, of silks and diamonds – which is nothing. He had Sita, and that was all that mattered. His love for her was all-consuming. But when Ravana kidnapped her his rage and fury knew no bounds. Rama would have set the world on fire to find her. He was at heart a man of peace, but when it truly mattered, he was an unstoppable god of war."

He'd never heard Parvati speak like this. She stirred her

❖

tea, lost in some ancient memory, and sighed. "I have known you for so long. As Rama, the Emperor Ashoka, as a Trojan prince, a Roman slave, a Sikh maharajah and many others. Sometimes we'd meet and you'd be a small child, or I'd be a withered old crone, but I always knew you instantly. I've been beside you. Through all of it."

She looked at him and Ashoka caught his breath. Parvati's gaze was frighteningly intense, flooded with emotion. But she wasn't looking at him, not really, but at his other self, Ash. The boy she'd fought Ravana alongside, the friend with whom she'd gone to Lanka, the warrior for whom she'd travelled through time.

All those sacrifices she'd made, in this life and so many others, for him. Parvati had bled and died for him. And she would again and again.

"Why haven't you told Ash?" said Ashoka.

Parvati blinked. "Told him what?"

"Isn't it obvious? That you love him."

Parvati put her hand to her throat, stunned. "I... I'm a rakshasa. A demon." She got up and the cup rattled as she dropped it on to the saucer. "We are not capable of such things."

Ashoka sank into the sofa. He was just trying to help. Parvati and Ash had feelings for each other that went way beyond mere friendship. The way Parvati talked, it was obvious she'd loved him since the moment she'd first seen him, as Rama. But then Prince Rama was the ultimate good guy, the perfect hero. He probably had that effect on everyone.

Wow, the brand had lost its value if he was meant to

be the same soul as the prince of Ayodhya. Rama had defeated the demon nations. Ashoka could be defeated by a tall flight of stairs.

Parvati looked over her shoulder, towards an object resting against the wall. "Make sure you pack everything."

His bow. It had been cleaned and collapsed back into its 'package' shape. Ashoka went over to it and picked it up.

The tremor ran along his fingertips as they tightened around it. The arrow clip was empty, but he rubbed his fingers together, imagining the fletching between them. "Is that what happened last night?"

Parvati leaned on the sofa, hands under her chin. "You slew one of the greatest demon warriors of all time: Mayar."

"But how?" Ashoka touched the bowstring. There was an energy, a tension, that he hadn't felt before. An urge to use the bow again. He looked around the room, searching for an arrow. And a target. What was happening to him?

Parvati's eyes narrowed. "You performed a perfect shot. I thought you were dead. Mayar almost had your head in his jaws. Then you shot. You waited and waited until the exact moment he was vulnerable. And you killed him. How did you know that was his one weak spot?"

"I just did. It felt like I'd always known."

"As if you'd fought such monsters before?" she asked.

Ashoka paused. "Yes," he said quietly.

Parvati beckoned him to sit. "It was one of your past lives, guiding you. There is no other explanation."

Ashoka sat down, the bow across his knees. Parvati leaned closer so her serpentine eyes filled his vision.

"Is it like this for Ash?" he asked.

"No, actually. Ash can only access the memories of his past lives. What he experiences is ultimately passive. He cannot interact or absorb any of their abilities. I have my own theories about this, but I believe that the Kali-aastra restricts such access. Kali is a jealous goddess and does not want anyone else controlling her weapon. Still, the past lives do come to give clues, hints as best they can, for his problems. But with you, it is different."

"How?"

"You might be able to consciously access the abilities of who you once were. Not just the memories, but the actual skills. I think last night was an example. Some great warrior, an archer, guided your aim, kept you patient until the perfect moment arrived."

Ashoka nodded. He'd felt it that moment on the beach. He just *knew* what he was doing. It wasn't as if someone had told him; he just seemed to have... remembered it. Where crocodile-demons are vulnerable. "You think there's more?"

Parvati shuffled closer. "Yes. You might have access to all the masters of all the arts of war, and many others; all your past lives and everything they knew. And I think I can help you to contact them."

"Really?"

Her eyes grew larger. The pupils dilated until they were two massive pits of darkness. "Will you let me try?"

He looked at her, and felt himself falling, falling into the brilliant green depths of her eyes. "Did this ever work on Ash?"

❖

"No. I tried to hypnotise him once, but it failed. Again I think Kali blocked me. She would never permit a demon's magic to be used on her disciple."

Ashoka's body grew light. He wasn't sure if he was sinking or floating. Maybe both. "OK," he said. "Do it..." And he fell.

Chapter Thirty-three

*A*shoka *smacks his parched lips. He ploughs through the grey sand. Not sand.*

Ash.

The heat bears down upon his shoulders, upon his back, like a physical weight. The sky flickers with fire. The clouds rumble and crackle, black and stung by lightning.

Broken armour, swords and steaming spent bullets scatter the ground. Smoke bellows out of cracks in the earth, acrid and stinging.

He clambers over rubble. There are toppled statues of forgotten gods and empty, ruined temples. Here and there he sees figures, but when he calls they fade to nothing.

Ashoka runs his tongue over his lips, but all he tastes is bitterness.

A wheel strikes stone. A hoof hits rock. A horse whickers and swishes its tail and a shadow looms over him as a chariot rises over the crest of a low hill.

❖

The driver rests the reins on his shoulder. Four white horses, their chests panting and their legs and bellies caked in grey dust, sniff the dirt and forage futilely in this burning world.

The chariot is light and decorated with ribbons, and holds racks of arrows and spears. It creaks as the passenger dismounts. He wipes his face and his armour, bronze and elaborate, though dented and battered by years of hard use, rattles as he lifts his bow from his shoulder. Long, elegant fingers pluck the string and a quiver of trepidation runs through Ashoka.

"Namaste," says the archer.

"Where am I?"

"In a world where we failed." He descends the slope, kicking up grey clouds as he does so.

"Is this the future?"

"The future. The past. The present. It is all the same to us." The archer is Indian, tall with long black hair tied in a simple knot. His features are aquiline, his eyes dark and clear and he moves with feline grace, sure and powerful. The bow is as tall as he is and carved with symbols that never rest, but fight and pulse with radiant energy.

"Us?" asks Ashoka, already knowing the answer.

The archer points behind him. "Us."

Another man sits upon a broken column. His chest is bare, broad and lined with scars. He wears a studded leather loincloth, and a Roman gladius rests on his knees. Brooding blue eyes peer out from under a deep brow. He sips from a water skin, which he holds out. "Thirsty, boy?"

Ashoka gulps it down.

One after another gather here, among the ruins. There comes another Indian warrior, a brutal, savage-looking brigand, the very opposite of the noble archer. He wears a crude breastplate and has a heavy sword, plain and strapped across his waist by a red sash. He runs thick fingers through a black beard, and golden bracelets clank on his wrists. He winks at Ashoka. "Aren't you a little short for an Eternal Warrior?"

"Leave him alone, Ashoka," says the archer.

The brigand snorts.

"What's going on?" Ashoka turns to face each of them. All so different but still familiar. It was as if he was looking into water, the reflection rippling and transforming his face. "Who are you?"

The archer frowned. "Don't you know, boy?" He gestures to the rough-looking brigand. "This is, or will be, an emperor. The Devanampiya."

The brigand laughed. "Devanampiya? Beloved of the gods? I'm just a wolf with a pack. I sleep on leaves and hunt by moonlight." He meets the archer's gaze. "And you we all know."

Ashoka handed the water skin to the Roman. "And you?"

"I'm Spartacus."

Spartacus? Now that was worth a 'WOW'. Maybe even an 'OMG'.

Ashoka, the emperor version, spat. "Just the three of us; I expected more."

The archer shrugs. "Three will have to be enough." He beckons Ashoka. "Join us, Ashoka Mistry."

"What's going on? What am I doing here?"

"Look about you. This is the world Savage seeks to create. His arrogance and hubris know no bounds; he is more powerful than Ravana now, and more foolish. He thinks he is the master of Time, that he can go back and forth, altering destinies and fates. The strands of reality will begin to unravel, child. You must stop him, and we will aid you."

The Devanampiya-to-be scowls. "The boy needs the aid of the gods, not of the likes of us. Even you, archer, for all your courage and skill, cannot stand before Savage unaided."

The archer shakes his head. "This is the age of men. I went to war to make it thus. It is in men I place my trust, not in the gods. They do not give their aid freely, and more often than not the price is too high." The archer's face twists in momentary pain but then breaks into a soft, warm smile as he puts a hand on Ashoka's shoulder. "I put my trust in you."

"Me? You've got the wrong Mistry. You want Ash, not me. He's the hero."

"Ash is the Kali-aastra," says the archer. "And Kali owns him body and soul. She will not permit us to aid him. He is lost to us."

"Lost? How?" Ashoka doesn't like the way this is going.

"Ash walks the path of death. We can do nothing for him."

They gather around him. "We are you, and you are us. Three and one. Thus we will give you what is ours. Knowledge, skill, talents at war — we will pass them on to you. Such things are thunderbolts through the heart and will burst and end in an instant, so be prepared. Use them well, Ashoka Mistry, use them wisely, for wisdom is the one thing that we cannot give you. Yet it is more powerful than the sharpest swords and more precious than rain in the desert."

"No," says Ashoka. "I am not a hero. I have found my family. I want to go home."

The archer looks at him sympathetically. "You cannot hide from your destiny, Ashoka. I know. It comes and finds you no matter what. How long do you think you and your family will be safe if Savage wins? A day? A week? He will hunt you down and they will suffer beside you."

Ashoka knew he was right, even though he wished he wasn't. "I'm not saying he shouldn't be stopped, but you should get someone else to do it. Someone who has a chance of succeeding. You send me and I'll fail. I guarantee it. I can't beat Savage."

"With us perhaps you can," says Spartacus.

"Look, I never signed up for any of this. I'm sorry, but my job is done."

❖

"You are the Eternal Warrior. Your job will never be done," says the archer.

"That's not fair." Ashoka sits down. The weight of it, the idea, is enormous. The Eternal Warrior. Never to escape war. Never to know peace. Is this it? Is he at war now for eternity? "I should have a choice."

Spartacus grins. "If we had a choice then we'd have all said no. What man would want this duty? None. All of us want peace, boy. But peace is a fragile thing. It doesn't take much to break it. Ambition. Jealousy. Greed. These things destroy peace, and they lie within the hearts of all men."

"So what's the point?" says Ashoka. "Why fight against them?"

The archer puts his hand on Ashoka's shoulder. "Because we must have hope. You are our hope."

Ashoka wants to go home and close the door and have everything go back to how it was. But he knows that's impossible. He looks around at the faces of the three men. His heart beats violently and he stands up. "What do I have to do?"

The men smile at him.

"I could tell you," said Spartacus, his face lighting up with amusement, "but you'd forget the moment you awoke."

Chapter Thirty-four

*P*arvati snapped her fingers. "Ashoka?"

Ashoka blinked, the images of that gloomy place already fading. His throat tingled with the water he'd drunk, the feel of leather on his lips.

"Ashoka?" asked Parvati. "Are you all right?"

"I met them, Parvati."

She looked confused. "You were only under a few seconds."

"I talked to them. For ages. It seemed like ages."

"Time and memory are curious things. Who did you see?"

"Spartacus. The first emperor and... Rama. I met Rama."

"Then I envy you, Ashoka. How was he?"

"He seemed... sad. I think he realises his duty never ended, not even with death. Weary too."

"He was aware of his legacy even back then, back when he fought my father. Few men know what a burden it is to be a legend in the making. More than a legend, an ideal for mankind."

She loves him, even now, thought Ashoka. Is that why she has stuck with the Eternal Warrior for so long? An eternity of unrequited love? All that sadness locked inside.

Ti Fun came back in and one of his men dropped a set of suitcases by the door. "The flight's this evening."

In twelve hours they'd be home. But Ashoka couldn't get the faces out of his head. "Who else have I been? What other talents could I draw upon? I mean, what if I'm the reincarnation of Bruce Lee. I'd be able to fight like him, right?"

Parvati shook her head. "Impossible."

"Why not?" asked Ashoka.

"Bruce Lee? He's not dead," said Ti Fun. "He and his son work for us."

Ashoka's jaw fell open.

"Can we get back to the matter at hand, please? You were saying, Ashoka? The past lives?" interrupted Parvati.

"They said they'll help me. I'm coming with you."

"No, you're bloody not," said a voice from behind. It was Ashoka's dad. "You're coming home with us."

"Dad..."

Ashoka's father stared at them, livid. "You're filling his head with madness. I heard. Eternal Warrior, Rama, destiny... He's just a boy. Leave him alone."

Ashoka didn't want to disagree with his dad, but this was bigger than his dad could understand. "You weren't meant to hear all that."

❖

"So what were you going to do? Sneak away without us knowing? Send us a text? How could you do that to us? After everything we've just been through..."

But Ashoka could barely hear him. The faces of the men, his vision, were so clear in his mind. He'd been fighting for thousands of years. His heartbeat quickened with dim memories of battlefields and palaces and enemies and allies. Parvati appeared again and again. He'd known Ti Fun before. Was there a place, an age, he hadn't been? Ashoka looked at the floor, and the marble mosaics decorated with dancing dragons. He rubbed his toes on the smooth, cold surface.

Just like Pompeii.

The vast masterpiece of Alexander fighting Darius. He'd trodden over the fallen warriors, their faces contorted with despair and rage. Whose side had he been on? In the end there were but two. The living and the dead.

Ashoka looked up at his father. "This is something I have to do."

"No, it's not, Ashoka," his dad pleaded. "You belong with your family."

Ashoka met his father's gaze. He was both younger and older than this man. Voices whispered, out there on the edge of his dreams — men, women and children; gods and demons. "*Dharma*. It is dharma. My right way of living. Rama tells me, Dad. I have to listen to him. You told me how you felt when you couldn't protect Lucky and Mum. You shouldn't suffer; it was not for you to do. It was for me. I failed. I didn't come quickly enough."

"Ashoka, none of this makes sense. You're just fourteen."

"I can make a difference, Dad, I know I can. I don't know whether I'll succeed or fail, but it's my duty to be there."

There'd been as many defeats in his lives as there had been victories. In Thermopylae, on the road with Spartacus. At Wounded Knee, in the mud of the trenches, in the deserts of Arabia.

"You know I love you, Dad, you and Mum and Lucky, and I don't want to leave you. But if I don't go, I'll fail you more than you can imagine. Savage has to be beaten, once and for all. You take me home and he'll win."

"You think you can stop him?"

"I have to try, Dad. There's so much evil and misery in the world, you said so yourself. It's down to the brave to stop it, to make a stand for those who can't. Otherwise we live in a world of demons, where the only law is to feed on those weaker than yourself."

"You can't change the world, Ashoka. It is what it is."

"It is what we make it, Dad." He took his dad's hand. "You have to be brave, brave enough to let me go."

Dad blinked back tears. "What shall I tell your mother? What about Lucky?"

Ashoka hugged him, feeling his dad's heart trembling, his own tears wet on his cheek. "I'll tell them."

And so he did. He went into the bedroom where Lucky and his mum were packing their suitcases. His mum looked shattered, but smiled as she saw him, and Lucky ran over and gave him a big hug. "We're going home!" she said. "We're going home!" She repeated it, as if she almost couldn't believe it.

❖

Mum pushed her clothes down and zipped up the suitcase. Ti Fun had got them a new set of luggage and enough new clothes to reboot their wardrobes for the next decade. Lucky had a toy tiger in her backpack. Mum glanced over. "You packed already, Ashoka?"

"No."

"You'd better hurry up. Though I suppose the plane will leave whenever we want. Still, I can't wait to go. To be home again." She smiled. "Do hurry up."

Ashoka took a deep breath. "Mum, Lucks, I need to tell you something."

Ashoka stood on the tarmac of the runway, watching the jet lift off into the night sky. He waved and waved as the plane disappeared into the darkness, only its tail and wingtip lights still shining. He waved until they too were gone.

Mum had sat quietly, but Lucky had cried. She was angry and scared. She'd thought she'd lost him once and couldn't understand why he was staying. He belonged with them. He was only fourteen.

Fourteen and ageless.

Now, standing there, the fumes swirling around him, sharp and sweet, Ashoka's heart ached. They had left. They were his family and they bickered and argued and his parents had strict rules about homework versus gaming time and Lucks was a pain in the butt and much smarter than him and they were the best things in his life. But the reason he wanted to go straight after them was the very same reason he had to stay. He'd held Lucky's hand and told her that, and eventually she stopped crying and blaming him and nodded.

He wiped his face clean of tears and met Parvati's gaze, soft and warm. Despite her protestations, she was human. She put her hand in his and their fingers entwined.

Chapter Thirty-five

"*Reggie Sahib! Reggie Sahib!*" *A fist bangs on his door.*
Reggie shakes himself awake. The bed creaks as he gets up, pulling the mosquito net aside.

"*Reggie Sahib! Come, come!*"

It is still night. The room is deep dark and it takes Reggie a few moments to find the matches. The candle lights, but struggles to brighten. The shadows are reluctant to leave him. As ever.

Where are my glasses?

Reggie feels over the table beside his bed and finds them. He unfolds them gently — the wire frame is old and the tiny hinges delicate — then hooks them in place. Still it takes a few moments for the room to come into focus.

Outside there are cries and angry shouts. Why are the villagers up?

A woman begins to wail.

What's going on?

Reggie does not look for his boots but takes his shawl and goes to the door.

Little Sabu stands on the veranda. He points to the mob assembled at the centre of the village. "Reggie Sahib, come quickly!"

"Get me my stick. Over there."

The boy grabs Reggie's walking stick and throws it at him before dashing off to the crowd.

Reggie takes one step down, then another. Quickly? He scoffs. Men of sixty are never quick about anything.

More of the villagers stumble, tired and bleary-eyed, from their huts. Reggie shuffles closer. Men brandish sickles and clubs and Hussein waves his father's old sabre in the air. He spits and snarls as they drag something through the mud.

A tiger? Have they caught a tiger?

The village is surrounded by jungle and they have lost cows and goats to such beasts before.

Then he sees Bibi Uma. She screams and pulls her hair as she holds her husband in her lap. His face is white and his eyes wide, blank. Green and sickly yellow bile fills his mouth.

Reggie kneels beside her. He does not need to check the pulse to know he is dead. But this is no tiger kill. His body is unblemished. All Reggie sees are two blackened puncture wounds on his forearm.

A snake bite.

"Who did this? What happened?" Reggie asks. Not even cobra venom has this effect.

Hussein drags their captive along. "She killed him." He kicks the figure. "A rakshasa!"

In a circle of torches a young woman lies covered in mud and leaves. Blood drips from her face and she is covered in bruises. Thick rope ties

263

❖

her arms and legs and she has been dragged by the noose around her neck. The villagers threaten her with their crude weapons and spit upon her and beat her with their fists.

"Back away!" yells Reggie. "Leave her be!" He brandishes his stick with both hands. "How dare you!"

He knows these people! He's lived with them for years... and this? How can they do this? He stares at them as if he's never seen them before. Friends now yell and glare at him, their eyes red with fury. This is madness. He shakes his stick, knowing that any one of them could easily wrench it from him. But he is the village doctor and no one dares defy him. "Get back."

Hussein glowers and is slow to lower his sword. "She killed Kumar. I saw it."

"He was killed by a snake," says Reggie.

Hussein points the blade at the woman. "See for yourself."

What does he mean? Reggie shakes his head and puts his hand on the woman's back. "What is your name?"

She does not face him. Instead she stares at the dirt and Reggie barely hears her response. "Parvati. My name is Parvati."

"What happened?"

She shrugs. "I live in the jungle. Men came. They attacked me."

"The jungle? Why do you live in the jungle? It is a dangerous place, Parvati."

She laughs. "Dangerous? To others, perhaps. Not to me."

"I don't understand."

She turns and her green eyes are filled with malevolent, cruel light. Her irises are huge and within them the pupils are narrow vertical cuts. Scales cover her face and her tongue is forked and flickers between a pair of thin, long fangs. Even in this light Reggie sees the venom slick upon them.

264

He can barely breathe. Reggie's heart pounds within his thin chest.
"What are you?"

Parvati sighs. "You know what I am."

Ash travelled south for five days. First he smuggled himself
on to the back of a truck taking wool south. He'd lain in
the deep, smothering comfort of the piles of smelly fleeces
during the day, thankful of its warmth as the truck crossed
the mountains. And then the dream had come.

Reggie, working in remote villages and shanty towns,
tending and caring for those too poor for proper medical
help, valuing each life as greatly as the next. He'd served
maharajah and beggar with equal devotion. Even a rakshasa,
like Parvati.

What is he trying to tell me? Ash wondered as the truck
pressed on.

The journey took him around endless hairpin bends,
steadily descending to lower altitudes. Breathing came more
easily as the air thickened, and at night Ash sneaked out to
snatch food from bins at roadside shacks.

He bailed out a few miles from the border with Nepal
and crossed via a river, wading knee-deep through the freezing
flow.

He rejoined the road, the one main road that ran all the
way to Kathmandu, and helped a bus load up suitcases and
backpackers in exchange for a meal of thali and tea and a
lift to the capital. They reached there at nightfall and Ash
went to sleep on the bus-station roof with the orphans and
beggars. No one approached him. Despite washing in the

river, he still had blood under his fingernails and a look in his eye.

On the fifth day he was up at dawn. The mountains he'd crossed were far away and pink in the morning sunlight. He'd given his coat to an old man begging at the roadside and hitched a lift south-west with an English family, into India, and to Varanasi.

Where it had all begun. This was where he'd found the Kali-aastra and met Savage and entered a world of demons that he'd never known existed.

He was dusty, he hadn't changed his clothes since Bukrong monastery, and they were now rags hanging off him. He'd listened to the radio all day, half expecting to hear about some disaster as Savage launched his Ravan-aastras, but the only news of interest was the destruction of one of Savage's chemical works in Hong Kong and incidents at his plants elsewhere in China. Savage was on the radio, explaining it was the work of terrorists and that he'd not be deterred from his goal to save the world. He'd sounded tense, quite unlike the cool and confident Lord Savage they were all used to. He was seriously annoyed, and Ash wondered who'd got so under his skin. Could it be Ashoka and Parvati? He thought about them, and wondered where they were, and if they were safe.

He should go and find Ujba. That was why he was here. But he had to admit, there was another reason.

Ash stood at the gates of Varanasi University, watching the students wander in. The campus was huge and sprawling with parks and many facilities, all small independent kingdoms, as well as the accommodation for the staff. There

❖

were apartment blocks for the junior teachers and a large mansion for the rector, with a walled garden with palm trees and a veranda with cotton parasols and servants. There was a second walled compound for the rest of the senior staff, and Ash found a palm tree leaning up against the outer wall and climbed up on to the top. He picked a likely spot, then dropped down three metres into a thick clump of tall grass on the perimeter.

Water spouts spun, spraying the lush green gardens, which were filled with flowers and fruit trees and monkeys and hummingbirds darting from one orchid to another. Ash picked an orange off a branch and bit deep. The juice dribbled down his fingers and he licked them clean.

The university was doing well, thanks to Savage's contributions.

The houses were new and modern. Two storeys, each with a garage and a long glazed facade, and paths lined with rose bushes. Ash walked along, keeping close to the foliage, and found the house he was looking for.

The sign on the door read, in English and Hindi, 'Head of the Department of History, Professor Vikram Mistry, BSc, MSc, PhD, Fellow of the Institute of Archaeology'.

Wow, he'd been promoted. He'd always wanted to be department head.

In his timeline, Uncle Vik and Aunt Anita were dead, victims of Savage's lust for power. Another reason Ash wanted to see them. What would he say? They knew Ashoka, not him. It didn't matter. He had to see them. He went to the door and knocked.

❖

No answer. Strange. Uncle Vik was a man of habit, and right now Aunt Anita should be getting dinner ready. But there were no smells of curry and frying vegetables. No hiss of ghee. They were out. Maybe he'd wait for them inside – he looked like a beggar and didn't want some security guard chasing him off campus. He checked under the second flowerpot and found the spare key.

The evening light, red and sombre, shone through the windows and lay long rosy carpets across the floor.

The air-conditioning hummed, keeping the rooms pleasantly cool. Minute portraits from the Mughal reign decorated the hallway and Ash moved into a large study. A desk sat at the far end and there was an empty armchair in the shadow of a partially open curtain. The ceiling was high and heaving bookshelves lined the walls. There were maps, dozens of them, pinned up, each an excavation of some ancient city or tomb. Uncle Vik's neat, small handwritten notes covered the maps, and stamped in the corner in red ink was the Savage coat of arms. Artefacts rested on a row of pedestals against the windows. Small pots, coins and statues. Ash picked up an iron figurine of a dancing girl with bangled wrists, her hand resting on a jaunty slim hip.

He rubbed his thumb. It was an old habit, it didn't mean anything, but... it itched. He scratched it again.

The hairs on the back of his neck stiffened as if a cool breeze from the Himalayas had followed him here.

"I know you're here," he said. His voice came out oddly, faltering, as he addressed the darkness. "Here to kill me. Fine. I can't stop you. But let's talk first."

❖

She was right in front of him, sitting in an armchair. It was as if she had willed herself to become visible. Ash was sure he'd looked there just now and it had been empty.

Rani had her two tulwars lying unsheathed on her lap. Her fingers were curled around the hilts. They were silver and swept into fangs, the points deadly and the edges sharp enough to shave electrons off atoms. She watched him through half-hooded eyes, her lips trapped in that permanent sneer, thanks to her scars. Slowly she relaxed her grip on the swords. "Speak."

Ash took a deep breath. "How did you find me?"

"You're sadly predictable."

"You know me well then." In so many lifetimes.

"Don't flatter yourself, Mistry. What is this? A last-ditch attempt to appeal to my humanity? I'll save us both the effort. There's nothing human to appeal to."

"Then why not kill me, if there's no point?"

"You might beg. I like that. It amuses me what sort of thing mortals come up with."

"Like what?"

"Oh, how they've children, a family. That they'll stop doing whatever it is that's brought me to their door, that they'll leave and never be seen again, or give me money, or it's a case of mistaken identity. They didn't do whatever it is that's upset me. They usually get down on their knees. There's plenty of sobbing and praying. Lots of requests for divine intervention. A few defiant curses." She smiled. "Never made a difference but, I don't know, I suppose I'm curious to find out if anything ever will."

❖

"Not even once?"

"Not even once. I really am as evil as you imagine." She glanced at the doorway. "Why don't you just run? I'll even give you a head start."

"Thanks, but I'm pretty tired. I think I'll stay here." Ash met her gaze. "What do you want, Rani?" He watched her face harden, saw the flicker of pain in her one good eye. "I know, you want to get out of the shadows."

Rani said nothing, but she tightened her grip on her swords. One misstep and she'd behead him, but he had to tell her. "I've known you a long time, Rani. I knew you as Rama, as Ashoka, and a dozen other of my past lives. Deep down you've never changed from what you are."

"And what's that?"

"Alone," said Ash. "Outcast to both worlds, demon and human."

"Who says I need anyone?" But she bristled.

"You've stuck by me for hundreds of lives, Rani. You've saved my life in most of them. You rescued me when Savage caught me—"

"That wasn't me. That was the 'other' girl. *Your* Parvati."

"It doesn't matter. You are the same. People fear you. I'm sorry, but that's the way the world is. Humans have their prejudices. But Savage feeds your hate, Rani. He doesn't want there to be good in you so all he allows you to see and do is evil. He tells you that you're nothing but a monster, but I know you better than that. I've seen you be a hero. Not once, not a dozen times, but a hundred. You fought at Troy to defend a civilisation that wasn't yours. You made peace with Rama and saved the rakshasa nations from extinction. You risked your life for me at Ravana's rebirth. You've taken the bullet for others who never valued you. I can understand why you feel that way, that the world will never understand you. It's easy to hate us. We mortals haven't done a good job of looking after ourselves, or of the world itself. Maybe it would be better if the rakshasas were back in charge. I don't know. But not like this, not the way Savage wants it. He thinks he'll bring order to everything, but he'll only bring annihilation."

"He's seen the future, Mistry. He knows."

"It's a future of his making, Rani. All those apocalypses ahead of us, it's Savage that brings them."

"How can you be sure?"

"Because that's all he is capable of." Ash shook his head. "I'm not afraid of you. I never have been. You're the best person I've ever known, Parvati. In all my lives."

Rani looked away. "Is that what you wanted to tell her? Why haven't you?"

"Never seemed like the right moment. Funny how the prospect of imminent death puts things in perspective."

Rani stood up and with a sudden flick of her wrists sheathed her swords in scabbards across her back. "Leave. Leave before I change my mind."

"You're letting me go? I thought you were going to kill me."

She smirked. "What's the point? You're the Eternal Warrior. You'd only come back." She laughed. "We'd meet in some future and I'd never hear the end of it, would I?"

Only now did Ash realise how much he'd been sweating

through their talk. "Come with me. I can't stop Savage by myself."

"I don't think I can either. He's more powerful than my father."

Ash had to agree. "He knows all the ten sorceries. He's got the Brahma-aastra buried in his chest."

Rani raised her eyebrow. "What about the Kali-aastra?"

Ash stopped. Was that what she wanted? Was this some fresh ploy of Savage's? Had he sent Rani here to trick him into revealing it?

Rani laughed. She laughed the way Parvati laughed. The way she did when she was unguarded, happy. It was a sound rarely heard, but it did something to Ash's heart, made it bigger. How he'd missed it. She tutted. "Honestly, Ash, I can practically hear the gears of your brain working. Our familiarity works both ways. You're wondering if this is an elaborate double-cross, aren't you?" She shrugged. "Honestly, what is the world coming to if you can't trust a half-demon assassin raised by an evil sorcerer and daughter of the greatest terror the world has ever known?"

Ash had the decency to blush.

"Well?" she asked.

He looked at her. He knew this girl. He trusted her. "Come with me."

Chapter Thirty-six

They made their way into the old city, leaving behind the elegant environment of the university and entering a labyrinth of ancient temples, uneven houses leaning over narrow alleyways, shops that were little more than alcoves in doorways. Skinny cows, left to roam free, wandered along, nibbling at rubbish piles. Street food sizzled in huge iron pans as the vendors came out for the evening trade. The city had many temples and they passed by chanting pilgrims and doorways ringing with bells and saffron-robed monks and shaven-headed mourners coming from the burning *ghats*. Varanasi was India's holiest city and it was good karma to be cremated here, upon the banks of the sacred Ganges.

"Where are we going?" asked Rani.

"There's an old maharajah's palace along the river made

of red brick. I stayed there when I was last here. Back in my timeline, that is."

"And you think that's where you'll find the Kali-aastra? How?"

"An old friend told me," he said.

He knew the way. Despite the different timeline, this was the old city. It never changed. They came out along the river and Ash saw it. "The Lalgur."

The crumbling old building stood up against the river. The walls were of red sandstone, immensely thick, and the corners were decorated with worn carvings. Posters and advertisements had been plastered over the ground floor, and the river itself was overlooked by many balconies, some of them broken and perilous. Nevertheless, children sat on the edges, quite unconcerned by the long drop. A few turned to stare down as Ash and Rani approached a door. Ash lifted the old elephant-headed knocker and banged. He looked up at the kids. "I'm here to see Ujba. Tell him Rishi sent me."

They muttered among themselves, then ran off.

"You'd better wait here," said Ash. "This guy's not a fan of demons."

"I'm shocked." Rani flicked her forked tongue out. "Don't be long."

The door creaked open and a small boy looked out. "What do you want, English?"

Ash grinned at him. "Take me to Ujba, John."

The door opened wider. "Do I know you?" asked the boy.

Ash entered and took a deep breath. He took in the musty smell of the damp walls and the dhal and rice cooking in the simple kitchens at the back. His ears filled with the chatter of the kids and their whispers and their light bare feet scurrying across the stone.

John gestured along the darkened corridor. "Wait here. Ujba's busy."

"He's training down in the basement," replied Ash.

John frowned. "Who are you?"

Ash met his confused gaze. What could he tell this other version of his friend? Nothing that would make things clearer. He merely touched his shoulder. "I know the way."

Kalari-payit, the world's oldest martial art. It was here last year that Ash had been taught it, by Ujba. He came to the narrow steps leading to the basement. From below came cries and shouts and the clash of weapons. Heat swept up and with it the heavy smell of sweating bodies.

They stopped as soon as Ash appeared in the hall. Dozens of boys wearing loincloths, their bodies shining, paused in their fights and exercises to stare at this intruder. The floor was hard-packed earth, a rectangular pit with a walkway on all four sides where the weapons hung and the students rested beside clay jugs of water.

In the centre of this stillness stood a muscular man, his thick legs planted firmly, his bare chest broad and heavy with blocks of muscle. He had a moustache and a yellow scarf hung across his shoulders. He wiped his face then peered at Ash with small, black, evil eyes.

Just because they both served Kali didn't mean they were friends. Ujba was a Thug, one of the sect of killers that believed murder was a prayer to the black goddess. But no one else alive understood the mysteries of Kali better than him.

"Who are you, boy?" said Ujba.

"A friend of Rishi's. I've come for the arrow he gave you."

"I do not know of this Rishi. Nor any arrow."

"The Kali-aastra."

Ujba's jaw clenched and his thick fingers tightened into fists. "Go away, boy. If you know what's good for you."

Out of the corner of his eye Ash watched one boy step forward. Lean, lithe and covered with sleek muscle, he dropped down into the pit halfway between Ujba and Ash. The boy glanced over his shoulder, seeking permission from his *guru*, his teacher.

"*Namaste*, Hakim," said Ash. How many times had they fought down here? How many days had he stumbled off after a beating? The hard lessons he'd learned from Ujba's best student. He scratched his thumb.

"Give me Kali's arrow," said Ash. "I need it."

Ujba crossed his big arms. "No."

"Don't force me," said Ash. "It'll be better if you give it to me than if I take it."

Ujba turned his head a jot. "I'd like to see you try."

Before the lesson they would have had to complete a complex salutation ritual. It had been more than a mere bow or slam of fists; it had been an intricate pattern of kicks, sweeps and punches. All directed at the corner of the room, at the shrine to Kali.

Honour Kali. That's what Ujba said at the beginning of each lesson.

❖

There she was, a black statue of the goddess. She was skeletal, her body stained with blood and garlands of marigolds around her neck and covering her boyish chest. She stood, ready for battle, glaring, her mouth wide open, her fangs revealed and her long tongue eager for blood. Her eight arms were outspread and she carried a weapon in each. A sword, a spear, a noose and the severed head of a demon. A bow, a discus and an arrow.

An arrow with a bone-white shaft, black eagle-feather fletching and gold arrowhead.

The Kali-aastra seemed to pulse with power, shining brightly with a glow from within itself, despite its gloomy setting.

Ujba sacrificed to it daily. The blood of an animal washed it and it gained power. Small amounts, but Kali was a greedy goddess and all death fed her.

Ash dropped into the pit, opposite Hakim.

"How badly do you want it, English?" asked Ujba.

"Pretty badly."

Someone tossed two weapons into the pit. The katars clattered against each other before they came to rest between the two boys. Hakim, his eyes never leaving Ash's, bent down slowly and picked one up. He kicked the other towards Ash.

Hakim was a bully. He terrorised the other kids and beat them up mercilessly for the smallest mistakes. Ash knew he made John's life a hell. No one stood up to him, no one could beat him.

But Ash could. Easily. Even now, without the powers of the Kali-aastra, Ash knew every move Hakim could possibly make. Hakim had been taught by Ujba, the priest of Kali.

Ash had been taught by Kali herself.

❖

Hakim needed a lesson in humility. He deserved it. Ash had the power to break him into a million pieces.

Ash stepped forward and Hakim rose on to the balls of his feet, limbs loose and katar held low, ready for a strike. Ash walked past him.

Their eyes met, Hakim's hot and arrogant and boiling for a fight. Ash just shook his head. "I won't fight you, Hakim." He stepped past, his back exposed, and went up to Ujba. "Give me the Kali-aastra."

Ujba towered above him. He blocked the way to the statue and his shadow loomed in the weak candlelight that flickered down here. Ujba looked at Ash. He was evil, he was a killer and he was Ash's guru. A guru deserved respect.

Ash bent down and touched Ujba's feet.

Without looking up, his head bowed, he pressed his palms together. And waited.

Ujba could kill him easily.

Ujba grunted. "Take it."

The arrow shone. Droplets of blood glistened along the bone-white shaft and on the golden point. Kali held it lightly, poised to place it in her bow. Then Ash reached out and lifted it from her fingers.

Ash shivered as energy seeped through him. His heart pumped faster, spiking with the thrill of Kali's power.

The aastra was awake. It stirred Ash's senses to new levels and he tightened his grip.

Of course. Savage had awakened it when he'd first found it. He'd used it to free Ravana, then later to kill him. All that power remained within the golden arrowhead.

❖

It was the one weapon capable of destroying Savage. And it was in Ash's hand.

Ash drew his thumb across its edge. The point was perfect. No broken slivers missing. Unlike the Kali-aastra back in his timeline, whose missing piece was embedded in his thumb.

He had hoped that when he grasped the arrowhead his own aastra might have responded, maybe even awakened. But Ash felt nothing. It remained dormant.

Did it matter?

Not now. Not now I have this.

They parted silently to let him leave. There was a small nod from Ujba, nothing else. But as he passed by Hakim Ash retrieved the remaining katar and tucked it into his belt. "I've a feeling I might need this."

Rani wasn't outside. There were shouts and commotion in the alleyway. Something was wrong. People were milling around doors, and radios were being turned up and groups gathered at open windows, watching the TV sets within.

Rani was among the audience outside an electrical shop. Ash couldn't see what was going on, but he sensed the anxiety, saw the grim, set faces. "Rani," he said, reaching out to touch her. "What's going on?"

She stared at the screen, but it was a blur of flames and shadowy figures being filmed via a crude camcorder. "Something's happened."

"Where?"

"Kampani."

Chapter Thirty-seven

It took four days for Ti Fun to track down the *Lazarus* and its destination, the Indian coastal city of Kampani. Ashoka's response had been, "Never heard of it."

And now, after a flight and a two-hour bus ride he was here, and gave Parvati his first impression: "What. A. Dump."

It could have been India's new capital, but instead was the world's biggest slum. The British government had been based in Calcutta until 1911, then decided to move. The choice had been here or New Delhi. New Delhi had been picked, and while that had risen with elegant buildings and wide boulevards and museums, Kampani had faded out of history. A port city with the mountains of the Western Ghats behind it and the Arabian Sea before it. But ships didn't come here with cargo and business. They went to Mumbai for that. Ships came to Kampani to die.

The beaches were a huge, endless graveyard of steel. Ocean liners were stripped down, panel by panel, by workers who covered the carcass like a million ants, their acetylene torches illuminating the rusty oil-covered frames with pinpricks of white, blue and orange. Bare-footed children and women rummaged around the black sands collecting nails, bolts, small springs and anything else of even the smallest value to be sold to the nearby workshops and factories. As the hull was taken away, the ships lay there, the ribs of their superstructure exposed, dead giants being devoured inch by inch. The city stank of fumes and the evening sunset was painted with brilliant colours thanks to the pollution.

A seemingly endless wall of cliffs overlooked the beaches. The homes were everything from rickety huts to brick dwellings with a couple of levels built into the cave mouths, and electrical generators powered a whole sub-city that lived within the caverns and tunnels, people too poor even to live in the shanty towns of corrugated iron and beach-washed wood. Parvati had hired a place here for them to stay in, basically a shed. They'd needed somewhere that overlooked the beach and this wasn't the sort of town that attracted five-star hotels.

"Home, sweet home," said Ashoka. "Or should I say, 'Hovel, sweet hovel'?"

"Your stay at the Mandarin has spoiled you." Parvati unlocked the padlock and pulled out the chain wrapped around the door handle. "It's discreet and near the docks. This is what we want." She paused. "Just check under the mattress for scorpions."

Ashoka spread out his arms and almost touched the walls.

❖

A single bare light bulb hung off a length of copper wiring, and two small beds, hardly wide enough to lie flat on, were stacked up against the wall, which was made of washed-up bits of wood and metal sheeting. The roof was a wooden frame covered with black plastic. There was an upturned wooden box to use as a table, on which was a small cracked vase with a few dried flowers in it.

"This would be so much easier if Ti Fun had come. Or at least lent us some dragons," said Ashoka. Instead it was just the two of them, again.

"Ti Fun's powers are tied to China, as are the others. If he came here, he wouldn't be able to raise so much as a breeze."

Ashoka flicked the switch and the wires hummed and fizzed as the bulb slowly brightened.

"You have a look about while I set up and pay the rent," said Parvati. "Just don't get lost."

Oil, salt, frying ghee and the stench of open drains filled the air, but a cool breeze drifted off the sea. They'd chosen well — a hut on the hills that overlooked the beach and docks. Beneath, and above, climbing up the cliffs, rolled an endless shanty town. Buildings packed together, supporting each other, built right on top of each other, with whatever materials the inhabitants had been able to salvage. Old warped wooden planks, plastic sheeting, corrugated iron panels and brick, concrete and even paper, packed into bags. Cables hung and looped from the pylons that ran down to feed the ship-stripping workforce. Seagulls called and picked at the refuse as rats and dogs fought in the alleyways.

A boy leaned on a windowsill, watching Ashoka. Behind him

a cluster of kids sat around a tin bowl eating mashed-up lentils and rice with their fingers. A radio hissed in the background.

Evening descended, and as the sun dipped below the horizon a blanket of darkness stretched over the city. Huge walls of floodlights burst into life down on the beach. A thousand hammers clanged. Saws screeched and a piece of hull the size of a football field groaned as it was lifted by two cranes, their gears howling with the effort. Generators hummed, chugging out thick black smoke as they powered the various sections of beach, each serving its ship. It was the music of destruction.

How many people lived here? A couple of million, clinging to the cliffs and the beaches? More? The shanty town went on and on, along the edge of the sea and all the way back to the mountains.

Thick smoke rolled up the slope, stinking and stinging, drifting through the gaps between the walls and flapping tarpaulin.

Savage had chosen well. The population density meant even a small burst of RAVN-1 would infect huge numbers.

The hull panel boomed as it dropped on to the sand, shaking the earth even all the way up here. The dust hadn't even settled before men were attacking it with their torches, slicing the skin of the panel into smaller, more manageable sections. A new chorus of beats and clangs rose up into the darkening sky.

"You humans thrive on this." Parvati sat down and they watched the scene below. "On destruction."

"No. It's death giving life. Look at all these people. All

❖

living, growing because of what's happening down there. I didn't realise it was possible to live on a diet of steel and smoke, but maybe it is."

"You're a glass-half-full sort of person, aren't you?"

"Could do with a clean-up. Can't imagine all this pollution's good for anyone, but there's money to be made, I suppose."

Parvati nodded. "It wasn't that different in London, if you go back a few centuries."

Ashoka listened to the beat. "India's changing. Who knows what it'll be like in a few years' time?"

"Provided we stop Savage."

Back to business then. "What's the plan, boss?"

Parvati opened up a map. "The *Lazarus* isn't a big ship, so it could dock pretty much anywhere. Then he's got to offload the stuff and get it distributed around the city. Then he's set. He'll want to set them off as soon as possible."

"Meanwhile we watch and wait?" said Ashoka.

"We'll take turns," said Parvati. "I'll go first; you get some sleep."

Chapter Thirty-eight

Ashoka yawned and pulled his blanket up to his chin as he sat leaning up against a rock, high on a ledge overlooking the beach. He swilled the soup around in his tin, as if the motion might warm it up, then drank it all. Parvati had done her shift so now it was his turn. Another hour and he would hand over to her again. He picked up the binoculars and searched the sea, as he'd been doing for the last three hours.

A sea mist swamped the low, sloping cliff, turning the dawn sky grey. Strings of fairy lights, torches and lamps illuminated the narrow paths through the shambolic city of huts and hovels. Bells chimed from the many small temples and incense merged with the acrid smell of burning rubbish and the smoke coming out of the shipping junkyards. Seagulls and rats and human rubbish pickers crawled over the mountains of debris.

Being on watch was utterly boring. He played games to keep awake, guessing which seagull would win as a pair squabbled over some rotten piece of fruit. Or he'd make up names and stories for the workers still peeling the hulks apart throughout the night. Their shifts were longer than his and he recognised more than one who'd been working the evening before. Ten, twelve hours nonstop.

Fishing boats bobbed out on the horizon, each followed by a cloud of gulls, chancers looking to grab a fish as the men hauled up their fields of netting.

A black cloud puffed from the funnel of a distant ship. It rode the waves awkwardly, as if too heavy for its size. Low in the water it pitched unevenly over the sea, the prow sinking one moment before rising up again, spraying water over its decks. It blasted its horn as a fishing boat strayed into its path.

Ashoka sat up straight and steadied the lens. He tried to match the rolling motion of the vessel so he could read its name.

His heart jumped as he read *Lazarus*.

The *Lazarus* was a rust bucket. The hull hadn't been painted in years and long streaks of oil ran like tiger stripes down its orange, corroded panels. Black smoke belched from the single funnel.

There was something on the decks, all covered in tarpaulin, but even from his vantage point Ashoka could see the crewmen were stepping gingerly around their cargo. Lifeboats swayed on lanyards, a pair overhanging both the port and starboard sides. The bridge, from where the captain watched the route and steered the ship, stood up stubby and smoke-stained at the rear of the ship, its windows catching the glimmering light of the rising sun.

Ashoka ran down the cliff path and banged on the shed door. Parvati opened up and must have understood the eagerness in his face. They dashed up the slope and he handed the binoculars over.

"It's a tramp steamer, looks late-Victorian," said Parvati. "The seas around here used to be full of them. They'd turn up at a dock looking for trade then and there; take you and your cargo anywhere around the world. It's not big, a crew of a dozen, no more than that."

"We can handle a dozen, can we?"

Parvati smirked. "I can."

Ashoka scanned the decks. "You think Savage is on it?"

"There's only one way to find out. Let's go."

They watched until the *Lazarus* dropped anchor, a couple of miles offshore. Then they returned to the shed, and while Parvati assembled her weapons Ashoka unzipped the bags. He lifted out a black-jade jar, the size and shape of a large Coke bottle. He could just about hold it with one hand. The glossy black surface distorted his reflection, widening and deforming his face. The top was plugged with wax and a paper seal covered in red Chinese writing. There were three more identical jars in his backpack and Parvati had the same.

Presents from Ti Fun.

Dragonfire.

"When we said we were going to destroy the ship, I thought he was going to give us explosives."

❖

Parvati put her own binoculars away in her backpack. "You know how to use that stuff?" She gestured at the jar he carried. "It will melt anything. Tear off the seal and smash it open on the deck and that ship will be settled at the bottom of the sea within five minutes. You watch — it will be on fire as it goes down. Dragonfire's amazing; water doesn't quench it — it burns in a vacuum. We're lucky Ti Fun was feeling so generous."

"And we've got eight jars of the stuff." Ashoka wasn't remotely happy lugging it on his back.

"Best to be thorough. That ship will be filled with RAVN-1. I want to make sure we destroy it all."

Gear collected, they headed down to the beach. The sun hadn't cleared the mountains and the sky hung grey and sombre with the mist rolling off the sea. The city still slept, but breakfast fires shone in a few windows and the early-morning hush was occasionally broken by a cockerel greeting the new day and dogs barking.

The fisherman was waiting. Parvati handed over the fistful of rupees and the three of them pushed the boat down the beach and into the placid early-morning waters of the Arabian Sea. Ashoka clambered on board as the fisherman settled into long, slow strokes of his oar.

"This is so cool," he said. If only he'd had a commando or two in his past lives, he'd be sorted. Coils of knotted rope lay at his feet, a grappling hook with its steel flukes covered in cloth to muffle the noise, and alongside Parvati's urumi was his bow and a quiver with a dozen brand-new steel-tipped arrows. The shafts were made of some lightweight

❖

compound and could fly for miles and still punch through sheet steel.

But Parvati's gaze was on the distant ship. "We'll be there in ten minutes. I want you to stick close behind me, understood?"

"But, Parvati—"

"Close behind or wait in the boat, understood?"

Ashoka folded his arms. "Fine. Understood."

The ship loomed over them, far bigger than it had appeared from the shore. The deck was about ten metres above the small rowboat and the outward curve of the bows trapped them in darkness, hidden from the casual gaze of any crew members.

The shore was two miles back. The sea mist rested upon the water, letting their boat close in unobserved.

The *Lazarus* was quiet but for the waves lapping against it. A deep, low rumble echoed from within the idling engines, and the links of the anchor chain occasionally clunked together as the ship rose and sank with the swell of the sea.

"Stand back," said Parvati. She stood up on the rowing bench, took the rope and grappling hook and began to swing it in a slow circle, gently lengthening the rope enough so it just scraped the surface of the water. Then she did a sharp, swift single spin and hurled the hook upwards, the knotted rope trailing behind it.

The hook sailed over their heads and on to the deck where it thunked hard on the metal. It sounded like a dinner gong.

Parvati winced and Ashoka grimaced. That must have woken the whole crew.

❖

The rowboat bobbed, the fisherman ready to paddle away at the first sound of an alarm.

But nothing. It was an old ship and it creaked and moaned and made a hundred different noises over the day and the crew couldn't inspect every single strange sound. After waiting a minute, Parvati slowly pulled the rope until it caught. She gave a sharp tug and locked the other end around her waist. "Up you go."

"Me? Shouldn't you go first?"

Parvati steadied the rope, holding it taut so it was as straight as a pole. "Unless I weigh down this end you'll end up swinging from side to side as you climb. Now up you go. When you get to the top, keep your head down and stay quiet. I'll be right behind you."

Ashoka inspected the rope. It was thick damp hemp and every metre there was a knot. It looked doable.

"Remember to use your legs and feet to support your weight. Don't pull with your arms, it'll tire you out."

"Feet. Right." Ashoka took hold, hugging the rope as the boat bobbed up and down. He kicked off his shoes. This would be easier barefoot. He checked his arrows were fixed to the bow clip, then slung it over his shoulder. The steel bowstring dug into his shoulders, but he felt safer having it already prepped.

And up he went.

He clung on, scrabbling with his feet to try to get some purchase on the wet and slimy rope, hunched against it like some frog. It was harder than it looked, and despite Parvati's efforts the rope swung in all directions, dragged this way by the ship, that way by the movement of the rowboat, and another way because of his shifting weight. Halfway up and his arms and shoulders ached.

He hated climbing. It was the worst part of gym. True, he hated cross-country more, but at least he knew how to run, albeit slowly. He might be last, but he would finish. But climbing was a nonstarter. He looked down. Maybe he should just wait in the boat. But Parvati glared back at him. "Don't stop," she hissed.

Halfway there. I'm halfway there.

Ashoka shuffled his feet up to the next knot, then pushed with his legs and slid another metre higher. The deck railings were visible above him. Not far to go.

He heard voices and froze. A couple of men, just chatting. But what if they saw the grappling hook? It was probably right by their feet. He curled up and hung on. A cigarette stub, still alight, flew over the edge and sailed past him and into the dark sea. The voices receded.

Parvati gave the rope a twitch and Ashoka climbed the last few metres and a moment later was pressing against the hull. He reached out with one hand and grabbed hold of the railing, then a second later slithered off the rope and on to the deck of the *Lazarus*.

Wow, his gym teacher would have been impressed. But now his limbs really did ache. His arms felt as if they were water, he could barely make a fist, and he was bathed in sweat. The steel deck was warm with residual heat and his bare soles felt the engines tremble below. Spotlights shone on the roof of the bridge, but Ashoka was well hidden behind a stack of wooden boxes.

Crates and barrels and other small cargo and equipment had been lined up against the railings, held in place with ropes and webbing. Vast sheets of waterproof tarpaulin covered the deck itself, obscuring what lay underneath.

A chain clattered behind him and he turned.

Three sailors stood watching him. Dressed in oily, stained patchwork clothing, they stared at him, their stubble-dark faces grim and highly unfriendly. One had a baton, another a net of webbing, the third a long chain, each link two centimetres thick.

He needed to think of something quick, something to put them at ease and give Parvati time to get up here and save his butt. Ashoka smiled. "Er... hello?"

"What are you doing here, boy?" said the guy with the big wooden baton.

Come on, Ashoka. A witty quip would be perfect right about now.
"Er...?"

"You thinking to stow away, boy?" said the one with the net.

"Savage doesn't like stowaways," said the man with the chain. "We find any, we feed them to the sharks."

I am sooo dead.

The man slammed the baton down on Ashoka. The blow clanged and he shuddered. He clutched his head, expecting it to shatter like an egg, but it was all in one piece, no brains leaking from his ears.

The baton had struck the railings instead of his skull. Lucky break. He wasn't going to get another one.

No time to draw his bow, he shoved out, knocking the man away. The baton clattered on the steel deck.

❖

The man shook the numbness from his fingers as Ashoka picked up the wooden stick. Then the man grinned and drew a big, big knife from the back of his belt. "Gonna carve you up for the fishes, boy."

Scratch that. I'm totally mega-dead.

Ashoka curled his fingers tighter around the stick. It was about half a metre long, thick and skull-crunchingly heavy. It felt right in his palm. Ashoka slowly rose to his feet.

Salute them, boy. And say the words.

Words came to him. Words that had been dust for over a thousand years. Ashoka didn't know Latin, but the phrase had been drummed into him. In the training camp. In the arena. On the sands that had soaked up his blood, all those lifetimes past.

Ashoka raised the baton and said the words: "*Nos morituri te salutamus.*"

The guy with the machete frowned. "What?"

We who are about to die salute you.

Chapter Thirty-nine

*H*e *adjusts his grip on the gladius. His shield is lost and there are three against him.*

I've fought worse odds.

The baying of the crowd fades until all he hears is his own breath, low, slow and deep. He watches and waits, saving his energy. Let them come to him.

Three against him. The first a retiarius, *a net fighter, swings his net over his head, preparing for the throw. His trident is missing; no doubt he hopes to snare him and have his two companions finish him off. Spartacus edges to the side, keeping the man to his right and between him and the second gladiator, a* thraex. *He wields the curved* sica *sword with confidence, an experienced warrior. Spartacus will need to watch out for him.*

The third opponent is a laquearius, *but instead of a rope he carries* a steel chain. He will hope to entangle Spartacus's own weapon and pull it from his grasp.

Let him try. I've not survived so long relying just on my sword.

The eyes betray intent. And with a glimpse Spartacus knows. Fear, inexperience, lack of training. These things can decide the victor as much as skill at arms.

The retiarius throws his net too soon.

Spartacus ducks and surges forward, the net sails over him. The retiarius backs away, now weaponless, eyes darting to his companions for aid. He opens his mouth to scream...

Spartacus shoves the man back with his shoulder and down he goes, flipping over the railings. There is a cry and a splash.

Gladius and sica clash, the blades a finger's width from his throat. The thraex is bigger and heavier than him, and uses his weight to press down. He glares, spittle drooling from between his clenched teeth. Spartacus, pushed to the railings, feels them bite into his back. His feet slide to the edge.

A bolt of steel rattles overhead and Spartacus twists. The heavy chain smashes the thraex across the shoulders and he grunts, his grip weakening for a fraction of a second.

That is a lifetime in this game of death.

Gladius slips free and strikes the thraex's head, once, twice and a third time across the jaw and the man loses his teeth and his consciousness.

The chain flicks and traps Spartacus's sword arm.

Mistake.

Spartacus throws his gladius in the air, catches it with his left hand and rams the tip into the laquearius's belly. The man yelps and curls up, *knees knocking the ground. Spartacus turns in a swift, powerful circle and the blow to his chin lifts the man back up to his feet and back down, flat on his back.*

The arena erupts in celebration. Spartacus points his gladius at the editor of the games, in acknowledgement, in defiance, as the mob chants his name to the heavens.

Chapter Forty

"Ashoka?" Parvati nudged his back. "What have you done?"

Ashoka stared at the two unconscious men. His baton dripped blood and a tooth was embedded in the wood. The machete lay at his foot. He kicked it over the edge. Parvati just stood there, dumbstruck. She blinked, as if her eyes must be deceiving her. "I... That was amazing."

The roar of the crowd still echoed in his head. Chanting his name.

Spartacus.

Parvati nudged one of the unconscious crew with her toe. "Past life, yes?"

Ashoka nodded. He sank down on a crate. His head swirled with images and memories, the blur of faces in the arena, the smell of the sweat and the dust and sand in the

❖

air. The relish he felt as he struck, the drunkenness of victory. He felt euphoric. He felt sick. "What's happening?"

"Aftershock. Get used to it."

"I'm not sure I want to." Ashoka dropped the baton and clutched his head, trying to breathe more slowly, trying to calm down. Now he was terrified. "Those men were going to kill me!"

Parvati patted his back. "Shall we toss them overboard?"

"They'll drown. They'll die."

"And that is bad because...?"

"Parvati, no. We'll tie them up and dump them in that lifeboat. No one will see them there." Ashoka stood up. "What happened to the other one?"

Parvati peered over the edge. "Swimming back to shore, I think."

There. He was up and not shaking. Wow. That had been weird, but already the memories of the gladiator were fading away. He picked up his baton, but it felt different, uncomfortable, less familiar. Not a weapon but a piece of clumsy wood. He didn't know how to fight with this. Not any more.

It took a couple of minutes, but eventually they had hauled the two men into the lifeboats, tied and gagged.

Parvati sounded a low whistle as she looked under a corner of one of the tarpaulin sheets covering the cargo. "Savage doesn't do things by halves, does he."

It was a missile. Sleek, narrow, black and shiny and just under two metres tall. The guidance fins were bright red and the surface decorated with strange symbols. Engraved on the warhead, which was made of glass and filled with green liquid, was some Hindi lettering.

"The Ravan-aastra. Tasteless and blasphemous," said Parvati. "There must be hundreds."

Ashoka peered under another sheet. She was right. The deck was covered with the missiles, all standing rank upon rank, metal and glass soldiers ready to bring death and horror to India. He tapped the cylinder and looked at the exhausts. "These are short-range rockets. Not enough fuel to get them across the country from here. Savage would need to fire them pretty close to the target city to be effective, but there are enough here to take out twenty cities at least."

"Hire a convoy of lorries and spread them out over the country. Thank God we found them now. Once distributed, we'd never have tracked them all down."

Ashoka took out one of the jars. "Let's get busy. I'll go down the right—"

"Starboard."

"Whatever. You go down the left—"

"Port."

"*Whatever.* Save one each for the bridge, OK?"

"That wasn't the plan, Ashoka. We stick together. Remember?"

Ashoka grinned. "Things have changed. I kick butt now."

"Fine. Let's hope the next past life you summon isn't Charlie Chaplin." Parvati gave a mock salute and went on her way.

Ashoka entered the ranks of the Ravan-aastras. He worked his way along the deadly cylinders towards the centre of the

299

deck. He tore off the paper seal and settled the first jar gently on the floor. Out came his pocket knife and off came the wax plug. He'd leave them like this, then throw the last one from the bridge. That would burst into flame and set off the ones on deck in a chain reaction. He hoped that would give the crew enough time to abandon ship. He put two more deep among the missiles and emerged at the prow of the ship. A large covered mechanism stood at the very front of the deck, supported by a thick steel column and connected to power cables running along the rusty steel floor.

Ashoka pulled the sheeting off.

Four Ravan-aastras sat loaded in a missile launcher, each missile garlanded with marigolds. The launcher had been bolted in place and was so new Ashoka could smell the paint. It was military hardware, designed to be fired from warships at targets onshore. It confirmed his guess that the missiles were all short-range: Kampani was just a couple of miles away.

There was no obvious 'fire' button so Ashoka guessed that it would have to be launched remotely, probably by the captain on the bridge. He needed to disable it, but there was no way he could lift one of those missiles off by himself. He looked around and found a toolbox. He quickly grabbed a couple of screwdrivers and rammed them into the gears so the launcher couldn't move or change its aim, then he set to work uncoupling the power cables from the driver motor. He whacked the receiver box with a large spanner until it fell to pieces on the deck. He kicked the pieces off into the sea and slung the sheeting back over.

❖

Those missiles weren't going anywhere.

The backpack was a lot lighter now he'd got rid of three of his four jars so he jogged back and found Parvati waiting at the foot of the steps leading up to the bridge. She put her finger to her lips and then signalled 'four', pointing up.

Four crew up there. Ashoka nodded and let her lead the way.

This James Bond stuff was easier than he'd thought. Maybe he should apply for a work placement at MI6 during his holidays.

The bridge overlooked the deck and was raised about six metres above it. The windows were thick, tilted downwards, and gave the crew an almost 180-degree view. A small array of radio and satellite equipment hung off brackets on the front and the roof. The steel structure had seen better decades, but was still sturdy, despite the pockmarks of rust, and the door was heavy with a watertight seal.

Parvati sneaked a peek through the porthole window in the door, then crunched down and whispered, "I'll go in. Keep this door closed in case one of them tries to make a break for it. I'll give you the all-clear when I'm done."

"Don't kill anyone," said Ashoka.

She pouted. "You're no fun." Then she changed into a cobra and slithered into a run-off pipe just under the door threshold. Ashoka grabbed hold of the door handle with both hands.

There'd be a drain, a gulley, in the bridge to allow any water to drain out. Ashoka could imagine Parvati sliding along the steel pipe, through the bends and slopes and up the drain into the room. He reckoned she'd be out about—

A man yelled.

About now, in fact.

A loud, terrifying hiss followed and the door jolted as someone tried to open it. Ashoka braced himself against it, gazing at the petrified face yelling at him from the other side of the glass. The man, cap askew and face white, banged on the door. "Open the door! Please! Please!" His breath steamed up the porthole window. Then he screamed again as he was dragged away.

Something smashed. Something heavy, a body maybe, thumped against the door. The window overlooking the deck cracked as one of the crew was hurled against it. Hisses, screams, cries and thumps, and the sound of things cracking, breaking and bruising broke out, and someone rattled the door handle desperately, sobbing on the other side. There was a pitiful whimper. "Please, oh God, please..."

Then a single, long, high-pitched scream. Then all was silent.

The weight on the door handle dropped away.

"All clear," said Parvati from the other side.

Ashoka turned the handle, dreading to see the carnage. It sounded as if she'd torn them limb from limb. The walls were probably drenched in blood and internal organs. The bile was rising up his throat in anticipation. He opened the door.

The bridge was cramped with screens and controls and there was a rack of very new and shiny gas masks hanging

❖

on a wall. In case of any leaks of RAVN-1, Ashoka supposed.

Parvati sat on the captain's chair, her foot resting on a body. Four others, one on the control panel, lay unmoving. A tea tray lay on the floor among broken crockery. The wall was dented and the main window fractured like a spider's web. She wore the captain's hat. "Warp factor ten, Mr Sulu." She grinned. "Always wanted to say that."

"I thought I told you not to kill anyone." Still, the walls were surprisingly blood and gore free.

"Just unconscious. I promise."

"All that screaming! It sounded like they were facing their darkest nightmares."

Scales spread over Parvati's face and her fangs stretched down to her chin as her eyes glowed with green malevolence. "I gave them my fright face. You'd be surprised how effective it can be, given the right environment. Low lights, alone in the sea. It creates the right ambience. Never underestimate the power of theatrics." She handed over her backpack. "Let's get these four into the lifeboats."

It wasn't easy getting four unconscious men down a narrow, steep and slippery staircase. Ashoka dropped one and winced as he rolled down to splat on the deck with a moan.

Parvati stifled a laugh. "I'll drag them into the lifeboat. You set this off on the bridge," she said, passing him her last jar.

Ashoka went to the top of the stairs, tore the seal off a jar and threw it over the deck. It smashed among the missiles and a white bloom of fire sprang up instantly, flooding the

303

❖

deck with light. It burned like a magnesium flare, blindingly intense, each spark generating another, before settling into a brilliant blaze of golden flame. Another jar caught and burst over the ship with devastating whiteness. Droplets flew into the water and sank, glowing fairies going for a midnight swim.

A fire alarm burst into life, clanging across the bridge, the decks and no doubt into the cabins of the rest of the crew.

Ashoka opened the door to the bridge and entered. The lights on the console blinked and the alarm was deafening in here. It didn't matter; he wasn't staying long. He ripped off the seal from his final jar, cut the wax plug out and then poured the contents over the ship's controls.

The door slammed shut. Ashoka ran to it. It wouldn't open. What was going on? He kicked the steel door, heaved his entire weight against it. It didn't budge a millimetre.

Sparks exploded as the dragonfire ate into the metal and the wiring. Ashoka coughed as black smoke rolled up into the ceiling in a dense layer just above his head.

The PA system hissed and crackled. "I'd be careful breathing any of that. The plastic on the wiring is quite toxic when burnt."

Ashoka stared at the speaker. "Savage?"

"Ah, young Ashoka. What a shame we meet under such sorry circumstances."

Ashoka wrestled with the door. "Let me out!"

"Dear boy, that won't do at all."

Ashoka ran to the window and started hitting the glass.

❖

Parvati was just climbing up into one of the lifeboats. She met his gaze as she put out a foot towards the deck—

The crane arm swung the lifeboat out, away from the ship and over the water. Ashoka and Parvati stared as the rope unwound. She stretched out, but too late, and the lifeboat fell away into the sea.

The flames covered the floor and Ashoka covered his mouth, choking as the smoke stung his eyes and filled his lungs. He grabbed one of the gas masks and put in on, pulling the straps tight.

"Poor magician I'd be if I couldn't manipulate matter," said Savage. "Did you really think I'd leave this last ship unprotected? After you'd sunk all my other plague ships? Still, dragonfire, very good."

Glass shattered in the heat. Ashoka stood up. He had to jump. But a wall of flame stood between him and the broken windows. Molten steel dripped off the ceiling and ran over the floor. The structure groaned as holes opened up under his bare feet. He could barely stand, the ground was so hot.

"I've waited too long for this. This is the first day of a new world, Ashoka. My world. Observe."

The missile launcher up in the front of the prow groaned. The gears clunked, grinding against the screwdrivers he'd wedged between them. The missiles rose, aiming themselves towards the shore.

Among the flames, separate from the hundreds of missiles exploding on the deck, floated another four Ravan-aastras, slowly turning to face the city a mile away. Flames ignited within their exhausts.

"*Bon voyage,*" said Savage.

The four missiles in the launcher burst off, momentarily flooding the deck with white exhaust. Ashoka watched as they rose into the sky, wobbling as their guidance systems adjusted, then, like four shooting stars, descending towards Kampani. Out of the flaming deck rose more missiles, and one after another they ignited. The roar was so loud the ship shook, Ashoka fell back against the red-hot door and cried as his skin burnt.

"What do they look like?" asked Savage. "I imagine they are quite beautiful."

The water, the sweat on him, started to steam. He had to get out. The ship lurched and a jet of water and steam erupted from the centre of the deck as the dragonfire melted straight through the hull and boiled the water beneath. The wall of seawater washed over the bridge, the flames flickering, just for a second.

And Ashoka dived. The heat engulfed him and for a fraction of an eye-blink he thought he was going to burn. Flames licked his skin, scalding droplets stung him and the smoke blinded him... and then he was out, in the air. He opened his eyes to see the sea rushing towards him and he gulped a single breath before diving in.

Down he went, flailing wildly, trying to work out which way was up. All around him burning chunks of metal sank into the water, each glowing like a fallen angel; bright, ethereal, spots of light among the utter darkness of the depths. The sea groaned and shook as the *Lazarus* broke apart and began to sink. Ashoka kicked and pounded the water, desperate to reach the surface as the ship threatened to drag him down in its wake.

He gasped as fresh air filled his chest. Waves covered him, but only for a second.

"Ashoka! Here! Here!"

Parvati waved at him from her lifeboat. He made his way over to her, through the burning wreckage, and pulled himself aboard.

On the horizon they watched as the sky filled with fireworks of green light. One after another they burst and a glowing green cloud swelled over the city, a miasma of horror. It spread wider and wider as more missiles exploded, adding their lethal contents to it until the whole coast was covered.

Then, slowly, dreadfully slowly, the mist descended over the city.

Chapter Forty-one

Ashoka and Parvati reached the shore and watched helplessly as Kampani turned upon itself. The air was thick with poisonous vapours and all Ashoka could hear were screams and howls as the children mutated into monsters.

Ashoka stood immobile on the shore, his breath fogging the gas mask he dared not remove. How could he deal with something so horrible? Bodies tumbled off the ships, the adults who'd succumbed to RAVN-I. They crashed and splatted, hideous red sacks of bone and blood. Some had been transformed and bore strange deformities, extra limbs that had burst from their torsos, or faces with twisted skulls, or horns, wings, scales. It was all a blur, and Ashoka was thankful that the mist hid what else was going on. A pack of once-children feasted on a body, their eyes glazed with bloodlust and savage hunger. They turned their eager, smeared faces towards Ashoka, but Parvati hissed and they backed away, recognising a demon far more terrible than they.

Fires broke out. People ran to the sea, waving at boats, screaming to be rescued. Howling packs of rakshasas chased the slow, tearing them apart with nails and teeth as their cries rent the city.

"It's hell," said Ashoka, too dumbstruck to move.

"We've got to do something."

"What?"

She grabbed his arm and marched up the beach towards the city. "Think! We need to rescue those we can and get them somewhere safe, somewhere we can defend."

How could he think? Rivulets of blood streamed down from the shanty town and already the dead were piling up in doorways. Wings, dark and huge, swooped overhead, as hellish shrieking raptors swirled and dived upon their prey. Ashoka stared as a creature, a two-legged hyena, fur bristling and blood-splattered, emerged from a hut, fangs dripping. It threw back its head and howled with joy. Then its yellow eyes fell upon them. The grin became a snarl, then it faltered as it saw Parvati. It bowed before her. "Rani, I didn't realise—"

Steel flashed between Parvati and the hyena and its head slid off its neck as it slumped to its knees. Parvati twisted the urumi again and, like a living thing, it wrapped itself around her waist.

Ashoka broke free and stumbled towards the hut.

"What are you doing?" Parvati asked.

"I... I need to check. There might be someone in the hut."

❖

"There isn't."

"I should look. Maybe if I look…"

"There isn't, Ashoka." She held out her hand. "There isn't."

Silent tears ran down Ashoka's face as he turned around and around. What world had he fallen into? Rakshasas, those that had followed Savage since he'd inherited Ravana's crown, rioted throughout the city, all restraint gone. The age of darkness had arrived and after waiting, hating, for more than four millennia they hungered for revenge on mankind, the race that had all but annihilated them. There would be no pity, no quarter, nothing but rage and frenzy.

Parvati peered ahead. "We'll go into the cliffs. There are plenty of caves."

Ashoka wiped his face. "Right. The caves. The caves. We could hide in the caves. Then what?"

Parvati's face said it all. She was as frightened as he was; the mask of self-confidence slipped and all he saw was despair. It was gone in an eye-blink, and her mouth was a hard, thin line. "Let's just get through this."

Chapter Forty-two

*A*sh stepped carefully out of a crooked path between a row of ruined shacks. Rani was at his shoulder, her swords drawn. The air tasted bitter.

What have you done, Savage?

It had taken them three days to get to Kampani, three days since the explosion that had changed the world for ever, and the city was still smothered in smoke. Countless fires dotted the sea of huts and hovels, and screams and howls drifted on the wind.

Ash searched the alleyways, hand grasping the katar he'd taken from Hakim. A strange, deathly calm cloaked the city. After seventy-two hours of rioting and massacres, even the most bloodthirsty rakshasas had had their fill, and the demon hordes now drifted aimlessly, wallowing in a perverse stupor. Daylight was clouded with smoke that hid the sun and left

Kampani under a grim shadow, robbed most of the older rakshasas of their full strength and speed, and many of the newly created demons, the children who'd succumbed to RAVN-I, had returned, frightened, lost and bewildered, to their human form. But their tainted hearts held on to the firm knowledge that as the shadows stretched and darkness fell they'd change again; that the monster within them would claw its way back to the surface and another night of slaughter would begin.

What can I do? thought Ash.

There was no antidote, no cure. No going back. Corpses littered the beaches, bloated, discoloured and mutilated beyond all recognition. Even now rakshasas prowled the shore, looking for titbits, fighting with the seagulls. Whole flocks of crow and raven demons dined on the plump eyeballs and soft organs of the dead.

With each step Ash's hate grew. If any man deserved death, it was Savage. Somehow he'd find a way to make Savage suffer for all this.

Rani walked beside him, searching the ruins of houses and tumbledown shacks. She had said nothing since they'd entered the city. This had been her dream not long ago, a city of rakshasas to rule over.

They approached a house, sturdier than most of the buildings here. Instead of driftwood and corrugated iron, this was made of bricks and whitewashed. It had a gate, though that had been torn off its hinges, and in the small patio beyond, clothing still hung from a nylon washing line.

And then Ash heard it.

❖

A sniffling. A caught breath.

He stepped into the single room that was kitchen, dining room and bedroom. Two bodies lay sprawled over blood-soaked mattresses. A man and a woman, or what was left of them. Ash drew a bedsheet over them both.

He turned towards the cupboard as the door creaked.

"Come out. I won't hurt you," he said. The shadow of Rani loomed in the doorway, her green eyes luminescent in the half-light. Ash put down his katar and held out both hands. "Come out."

The door widened a few centimetres and a dirty face with huge brown eyes peered through the gap. A little girl.

"What's your name?" Ash asked.

"Lakshmi," the child whispered. The door opened some more, but she didn't step out.

"My sister's called Lakshmi," said Ash. "Come out, Lakshmi."

"I'm scared."

"So am I," Ash replied. "But maybe if we both hold hands we won't be. Want to try?"

The girl paused. Then slowly she nodded. She held out her hand.

There were no fingers, just long curved talons, as dark as jet. Scales covered the skin, vanishing under red-stained sleeves.

Her hair was matted with dried blood, and while she'd wiped her face, her collar was sprinkled with reddish-brown spots.

Rani hissed and clutched his shoulder. "She's turned. Leave her."

Ash shook her off and took Lakshmi's hand. The needle-pointed tips of her talons scratched his palm. He smiled at her. "I don't know about you, but I'm feeling better already."

"Ash..." warned Rani.

Ash didn't look round but carried on smiling at the girl. "Forget it, Rani, she's coming with us."

She wasn't more than five, just skin and bone, so Ash scooped her up while slipping the dagger back in his belt.

Rani glared at him. "Why are you doing this? She's an abomination. Neither demon nor human. All she has ahead of her is madness."

"She's both. Like you." Ash met Rani's fierce gaze. "You found a way; so can she."

But as he stepped back out into the ruins he wondered why he'd done it. The child smelled of death and sickness, the odour of RAVN-1 clung to her. But if he didn't at least try to help, even just one person, then he might as well give up here and now.

Why else had they come here? To wait for Savage?

And where was Savage? He'd have thought the aristocrat would want to be here to claim his victory.

The poisonous mist had dispersed but the city was under quarantine. The army surrounded it and the government had declared the area off limits while they tried to understand what had happened. But the net was porous. Refugees still slipped out through the cordon at night or between gaps where the troops had been spread too thinly. Ash and Rani had sneaked past a roadblock while the soldiers had been on their dinner break. Getting back out with a little girl wouldn't be a

❖

problem. "Let's get out of here." They left the house and turned back towards the cliffs. Ash handed Lakshmi a water bottle from his shoulder sack. "You hungry? I've an apple—"

The rock clipped his head. Another flew through the air and struck his shoulder. Ash stumbled and Lakshmi screamed as they heard footsteps hurrying from behind.

Ash dropped the girl to her feet and covered her as more stones flew at him. Rani's swords slipped from their sheaths and men yelled. Blood dribbled into his eyes, he felt fuzzy, but still he glimpsed the crude spear stabbing towards his belly. He knocked it aside and rammed his fist into the man's face. A dozen, maybe more, burst out of the alleyways around them. Everywhere he turned, knives and clubs and spears jabbed at him. He and Rani stood shoulder to shoulder, weapons drawn, with Lakshmi behind them. The crowd tightened around them, each unsure about being the first to attack, each waiting for someone else to make the first, probably suicidal, charge.

Rani swept her swords across the decreasing gap between them and the mob. "Get back, scum."

They were locals, humans, armed with whatever they could find. Each man looked weary, more than a little frightened, but firm. Ash could charge straight through them, but some would die. He wasn't going to do that. Rani on the other hand...

"Just let us go," he said.

"You go, but not the rakshasas. They die," snarled one man with a crude axe.

Rani laughed. "Come and try."

❖

More clustered around the back till in all there were about twenty in a tight little dead end. Another rock flew over from the back, but Ash swatted it casually away. None of these people were fighters. They were caught in that tension between fleeing and charging; one small thing could send them either way.

"I need you to calm way down," Ash urged.

There was a commotion at the back. Feet shuffled and people parted. "Get out of the way!" said a girl.

She pushed through the ring and looked at Ash with her bright green eyes. And smiled. "'Calm way down?' Is that the best you could come up with, Ash?"

"Parvati!"

His face broke into a smile. It really was Parvati. How was that possible? He'd left her in London. "What are you doing here?"

"Saving the day, as usual."

Ash hugged her, squeezing her in his arms and lifting her off her feet. "Parvati!"

He couldn't help grinning, and Parvati looked pretty pleased too, her lips turned upwards a few degrees, which for her was a big smile. Eventually Ash put her down, but he couldn't stop looking at her. Parvati was here and suddenly it all felt all right.

"My lady, he attacked us," complained one of the mob. "He broke Himesh's nose. He's—"

"—one of the good guys," interrupted Parvati. She looked at Ash's two companions, winking at the little girl, then faced Rani. The smile vanished. "You, on the other hand, I'm not so sure about."

❖

The two demon princesses faced each other. Rani's face was torn by scars, her left eye white and blind, her hair cropped short. She was the cracked mirror reflection of Parvati's cold beauty, and there was no mistaking their epically lethal similarity. If the atmosphere between them got any colder, it would start snowing.

Ash cleared his throat. "She's here to help, Parvati."

"You trust her?" Parvati asked.

"Like I trust you. With my life."

Even Rani looked surprised at the statement. She didn't know how to respond to Ash's declaration of faith. But she spun her tulwars and slid them back into their sheaths. Not that it made her any less dangerous.

"Well, we're not down here to top up our tans," said Parvati. "Let's get back to base."

"You've got a base here?"

Parvati pointed up at the cliffs. "More like a refugee camp. We go out during the day to find food and supplies, fill the bottles with clean water, then get back before dark. That's when they come."

"How bad is it?"

Parvati grimaced and she looked tired by it all. "Pretty awful, Ash. We lose a few more people every night. The caves have an endless network of tunnels and fissures — no one knows all of them and we're not enough fighters to defend all the ways in. And I swear new ones open up, walls shift and cracks appear where there weren't any the day before. My people just... disappear."

"You think it's Savage using his magic? Changing the tunnels?"

❖

"If it is, then why doesn't he just finish us off? No, I think its other rakshasas who've learned a few sorcerer's tricks, nothing major but enough to manipulate elements at a local level."

"Ashoka still around?"

"He'll be pleased to see you."

They hiked up the slopes past abandoned barricades made of rocks, wooden planks and metal sheeting. Some had been welded together and studded with spikes, dried blood encrusted on them. The fighting had been at close quarters and vicious.

Three rows of walls protected the cave mouth, each higher than the last, and men patrolled with crude weapons and home-made armour. A trench had been dug in front of the first wall, and its bottom lined with long spikes. A couple of guards were dragging impaled bodies off them.

Parvati waved at the watchtower, a platform built into a natural ledge, and the steel gates rattled open. She glanced down at the pile of corpses, not much interested. "From last night. The city's split in two. The worst affected, those consumed by demonic possession, are outside these walls, feeding on each other and any unfortunate souls who've not found refuge with us. Can you believe it, but some decided to stay at home? No point arguing with fools, so we left them to their fate. Torn apart, devoured, just to protect what? A few pots and pans. I'll never understand humans."

She marched under the walls and Ash saw the second line of defences, murder holes and the glow of fires on the battlements above. Parvati followed his gaze. "We pour hot sand on anyone who comes too close. It's brilliant. Gets into all cracks and between armour. Better than boiling oil – not that we have any."

More soldiers joined them as they passed the second gate. Parvati and her men offloaded their armour and the bigger weapons, but each man kept something to hand. Water and food was passed around and they dropped away to join their own people until it was just Parvati, Ash, Rani and the little girl Lakshmi, who refused to let go of Ash's hand even when a woman tempted her with a bowl of hot, sweet rice.

Parvati splashed water on her face. "Where was I? Oh, yes, the city. So, we have the infected outside. Joining them in greater numbers every day are the true rakshasas, those that follow Savage."

Rani nodded and accepted a bowl of food. "Yes, each major city had a battalion of rakshasas allocated to it. Once the city had been infected with RAVN-I, the rakshasas serving Savage would act as *agents provocateurs* and commanders. They'd rally the new demons to their service and organise them into a proper army, destroying any local resistance before it could present a threat. I was meant to lead the army in Rio."

Why was he surprised? Savage's background was service with the East India Company. Military conquest was his *modus operandi*. "So all those other target cities – London, New York, Beijing – have hundreds of demons all just waiting for the green light from Savage?"

"He's had ten years to plan this," said Rani.

"Kampani's become a hot zone for the rakshasas spread

❖

over India. They're all making their way here, swelling the opposition."

"What about Savage?" asked Ash.

Parvati shook her head. "No. Not yet."

"He'll come," said Rani. She looked at Ash. "For you, he'll come."

Parvati stopped at the third wall — the highest and best guarded. The gate was topped with barbed wire and the men on the battlements had guns. There was even a harpoon fixed on a ridge, no doubt taken from some whaling ship that had been dismantled down on the beach. "But now you're here, Ash, we've got nothing to worry about, have we? Fighting a thousand demons, ten thousand. All in a day's work for you, isn't it?"

"Er, I wouldn't put it quite like that." Especially now he no longer had the use of the Kali-aastra. "I'm just an extra pair of hands."

"You look exhausted," said Parvati. "We've a few hours before dark. It might be a good idea to get some rest."

They entered the tunnels. Light came from oil lamps and bare bulbs strung out along wires nailed to the walls. There were cramped alcoves where families nestled together with their few belongings. Men watched him with grim, hard expressions, the women with weary despair and the children with bewilderment.

How long would they last? Ash felt chilled at the thought. What sort of a life had they had? And was this how it would end?

They huddled together. Wanting to be close. Rishi was

right. All lives are great. Everyone was important to someone.

He scratched his thumb and pushed further into the caves.

The sound of metal hammering on metal echoed through the dingy labyrinth and the air stank of ozone as welders assembled better defences and new armour for the fighters. Ash ducked his head as part of the tunnel constricted, and kept his eye on Parvati. If he got lost here, he'd never find his way back out. They passed through vast cathedral-dwarfing caverns where hundreds camped among the stalagmites and streams of water dribbled along well-worn ruts in the limestone. In the torchlight these places glistened like cities built by fairies, all sparkling with amber, with emerald, with sapphire colours.

People came to Parvati with questions, and for blessings. She had both human and demon in her camp, slumbering side by side and sharing their food. Fear, desperation and a hope that with numbers they'd be safe had helped them put their differences aside.

Spider rakshasas spun hammocks for people to sleep in, and wolf rakshasas growled over a game of cards with a group of soot-stained welders. A few spotted Rani, stared from one demon princess to another, and a large, old cat rakshasa, his eyes milky and his fur patchy, bowed and touched her feet in humble greeting.

Hammers struck and sparks flew in one of the deeper chambers as blacksmiths and welders constructed arms. Roughly made swords from thick iron ships' panels, spears from metal poles, edges and points keen, lay piled by the

❖

entrance. In a cave opposite, a man distributed flour and rice from sacks no doubt scavenged from the town.

"You organised all this?" Ash asked. There was a mini-city here at work.

"The caves have always been inhabited," replied Parvati. "There are even old temples down here, carved right into the rock. But yes, until a few days ago it was just a refuge for those too poor to even live in the slums."

"And you've rakshasas here too?" asked Rani.

Parvati laughed. "I think they mistook me for you. Not all follow Savage. They want an alternative and were only waiting for me — you — to make the break from him. Enough remember what happened in the last war between demon and human."

Ash looked around at the rakshasas. "Are they all true demons?"

"No, some are victims of Savage's chemical attack. These with us are the ones who've managed to hang on to their humanity, their sanity. There is blood on their hands, that is inevitable with the first change, but they still cling on to their mortal identity. Though for how long I don't know."

"Ash?"

A figure sat beside a small oil lamp. He turned an arrow in his hand, fingers smoothing down the fletching made from plastic bottles. The arrowhead was a jagged shard of glass. A bow lay across his lap, made of steel and strung with wire.

Rama.

That was Ash's first reaction. The figure wore a breastplate, and a sword rested against the wall, the single curved edge silvery bright. Disassembled arrowheads, some glass, some metal, some stone, had been spread out over a tattered sari and the archer had all the materials for arrow-making arranged at his feet: shafts, fletching, glue, thread, arrowheads and spare bowstring.

Ash's heart trembled. If Rama was here, then they had hope. The world had hope. The first and greatest of all Eternal Warriors.

"Ash?" the archer repeated. He stood up and gripped Ash's arm. "Blimey, am I pleased to see you."

"Ash... Ashoka?" Ash stuttered.

"Of course. You look like you've seen a ghost."

Ashoka? How could this be Ashoka? Ash shook his head. "You've changed."

"Changed? Understatement of the year, brother. Understatement of the century."

Thick muscles quivered along his bare legs and arms, which were criss-crossed with fresh scars. The breastplate had been beaten from an oil drum and there was still a logo, a chariot, upon the chest. The front and back pieces were held in place by ribbons tied through loops over the shoulders and a deep blue sash was wrapped around his waist. His trousers were studded with irregular steel and iron discs that rustled as he moved. Ashoka blushed. "I must look like a clown."

Ash blinked, still shaking his head in bewilderment. "You look like a bloody god of war."

Ashoka blushed even brighter. "Look at this face. Enough to frighten kids." He shifted so the uneven light caught on a deep crevasse that ran from his forehead to just below his eye. The stitching was simple but effective, but the scar was going to be large and permanent. "From my first fight with a rakshasa. A big panther. It almost clawed my eye out."

Parvati handed Ashoka a waterskin. "You should see him, Ash. A week ago he could hardly peel an orange without cutting himself, and now even the rakshasas beyond the gates speak his name with fear. They think Rama has returned."

"I can believe it," said Ash quietly. He looked at the arrow in Ashoka's hand. "You made this?"

"Yes. Simple when you know how."

"And you know how?" The fletching was perfectly even, the shaft true and the arrowhead delicately chipped to a needle-fine point. This was the work of an expert, a master. "How?"

Ashoka looked embarrassed, so Parvati spoke. "He's the Eternal Warrior."

But so am I, he wanted to say. They were the same person but as different as night and day.

"You're the Kali-aastra," said Parvati, touching him softly on the hand.

He was a thing of darkness — that's what she meant. The weapon of Kali, a killer. Things had happened to him that had never happened to Ashoka, forced him into a world of darkness. Ash was the shadow to Ashoka's sun. The guy in front of him was a slightly less plump version of the nerd whose life he'd saved in that alleyway less than a fortnight ago. Back then he'd emptied his guts at the sight of a little blood, but this Ashoka... his demeanour, his gaze, his confidence were that of a warrior, a noble.

❖

"Say something, Ash," said Ashoka.

"Er, have you met Rani?"

Rani looked at Ashoka with the same bewilderment verging on awe. She felt as Ash did, that they had Rama walking among them. She huffed and adjusted her scabbards to hide her stunned expression and nodded in greeting. Then she glanced at Ash. "Give it to him."

Yes. Ashoka was this universe's Eternal Warrior. Destiny couldn't have been clearer if it had sent eagles to fly around Ashoka's head. Ash took out a cloth bundle.

Ashoka unwrapped it and the golden glow of the object within illuminated his face. "This what I think it is?"

Ash nodded. "It's yours. You'll only have one shot."

"Look at us," said Ashoka. "Two Eternal Warriors and a pair of demon princesses." He smiled. "How badass are we?"

Chapter Forty-three

R eggie lifts his sputtering candle and shines its wavering light to the chair in the corner of his room. "Sit over there. Let me have a look at you."

"Why?" says Parvati.

"You're hurt."

"That is no concern of yours."

Reggie gathers his bag and puts it on the table. "It is. Now sit."

"They intend to kill me." Parvati hesitates at the door. "It is hypocrisy to patch up my injuries now only to hang me in the morning."

Reggie snaps the bag open. Instantly the smells of his herbs and chemicals break over him. "Why must you be so difficult?" He pulls out a roll of bandages. "And who said anything about hanging you?"

Reluctantly Parvati sits on the wicker chair.

Reggie pours water into a tin dish and then with his pipette squeezes five drops of iodine into it. He rolls a cloth into the water until it is soaked and then turns to look at her.

Her fangs and the scales that covered her face have gone. She would be human but for her eyes, which remain those of a serpent. There is a swelling above her left eye and cuts upon her arms where she defended herself. She walked to Reggie's bungalow, so her injuries are most likely superficial, but he will keep her here tonight to be sure.

"What were you doing in the jungle?" asks Reggie. He gently wipes her face clean of blood.

"I wanted to stay away from people. It's safer that way."

"What happened?"

Parvati shrugs. "Men came. Their mistake. They attacked me. Their bigger mistake."

"So you killed one?"

"I had to."

Reggie sucks his teeth. "That I do not believe."

"You know nothing of the ways of the world, old man."

Reggie rinses out the bloody cloth and starts on the wounds along her arms. "I've seen more death than you can possibly imagine."

Parvati smiles. "I doubt that."

Reggie meets her gaze. "You killed that poor man. Why? Because killing is easy. What does it take? A pull of a trigger? A thrust of a sword? It takes nothing."

Parvati winces. Reggie doesn't know if it's because of the sting of the iodine or his words.

"He would have killed me if I hadn't killed him first."

"He was afraid. He didn't understand. And you didn't give him the chance."

There is a long cut down her shoulder. Reggie adjusts his glasses to have a closer look. "This I will need to stitch."

"Be my guest." Parvati turns in her chair. "What does it matter who he was? He was just a peasant. India's filled with them."

❖

"He was a man. He breathed the same air as you. Trod the same earth." Reggie heats the needle in the flame of the candle. "He worked hard and fed his family and slept under the stars hoping for a better life. A life you have denied him."

"So his life was worth more than mine? I am a demon after all. I am evil."

"Who am I to judge who is good or evil?" Reggie bites his lips as he threads the needle. His eyesight grows poorer every year. "I cannot see into your heart."

Parvati shifts so she can glance over her shoulder. "You are different from the rest."

"The rest?"

"Yes. I've known you from before, and will no doubt know you in the future. You've been great warriors, great kings. This version of you is new."

"I've fought. I found it a waste of time and effort."

Parvati laughs and it sounds bright in the gloomy room. Reggie smiles. "You should laugh more often."

"I've missed you," says Parvati simply.

"Child, you have never met me."

Parvati shrugs. "You never remember. That's the curse of being the Eternal Warrior."

"Eternal Warrior? You have me mistaken for someone else."

"No. You are he. In this life a healer. That's good. I wonder why." Parvati flexes her arm slightly. "You are good at what you do."

"I've had enough practice."

"In many wars?"

Reggie nods. "Too many. And they have all been pointless and tragic and I learned only one thing: no man's life is greater than another's."

✳

❖

Ash woke. Lakshmi lay asleep beside him, a rag doll curled up under her chin. An oil lamp sent waving shadows over the cavern wall.

Reggie is wrong, he thought. You could judge whether a person was good or evil. You didn't need to look into their hearts, just measure their deeds.

Sure, it would be nice to live in a world where everyone could love one another, but that world didn't exist. He doubted there was a world like that in any timeline, in any universe.

Sometimes killing was all there was.

What would Reggie do here? Open the gates and let the rakshasas in? Give them tea and cake and hope everyone would just get along?

Ash got up silently, so as not to wake Lakshmi. He passed by other sleepers. He stepped carefully over the incumbent bodies and the snoring men, their arms draped protectively over their families. Most had their weapons lying alongside, ready to be snatched up at a moment's notice. They'd fallen into the pattern of their enemy, resting during the day, fighting at night.

Ash followed the breeze to a cave mouth high up on the cliff. Someone sat on the ledge overlooking the city.

"I've been looking for you," he said.

"I've been waiting," said Parvati.

A sun, a huge blood-red drop, settled its lower edge upon the horizon. Its reflection stirred upon the waters of the Arabian Sea and its beams were cut by the skeletal ship frames beached and abandoned on the shore. Campfires

❖

sparkled upon the beach and from a thousand patches of Kampani as the shadows lengthened. Drums beat in the distance and conch horns bellowed, still faint and distant.

"The city's waking," said Parvati. "They'll come when the last rays fade from the sky."

Ash sat down beside her so his heels dangled a hundred metres above the rocks.

"We'll be ready," said Ash.

"We'll be as ready as we can, but we aren't enough. Two patrols haven't come back and the guards on the southern tunnel are gone."

"What happened to them?"

"Killed or run off, who knows? The result's the same." She continued to look out over to the setting sun. "Why did you come, Ash?"

"Where else would I go?"

"We're going to die here. Tonight. You do know that, don't you?"

"I've fought against worse odds. Thermopylae, for instance."

"You died there too." She made a face. "Actually, I think I might have been responsible. I was fighting for the Persians. It was a confusing time for me."

"What about Troy? We were on the same side in Troy."

"Yes, the losing side."

Ash frowned. "I see a theme developing here."

"You're the Eternal Warrior. You're not the sort to die peacefully in your bed."

"You would have thought that with all this experience I'd be better at surviving."

❖

"Sometimes survival isn't the point." She looked at him and she had tears in her eyes. "I've really liked being here with you."

Ash put his palm to her cheek and wiped the tear away. "We'll meet again. Reincarnation has its benefits."

"But you and I won't be the same. I knew you as Rama. As Ashoka, as a gladiator, and many others. This one, you..." she poked his chest, "... is my favourite. You know what I mean."

"More than Rama?"

"Rama? Everyone loved Rama. How could you not? He was perfect. But you know how most felt in his presence? Unworthy. How could you measure up to what he was?"

"So you're saying I'm not perfect?" Ash clutched his chest. "Now you've really hurt my feelings."

"Oh, just shut up, Ash." Parvati bit her lip, gazed at him with her eyes narrowed and filled with doubt. "There is so much I want to say to you, but it would take a lifetime to say it. I wish I had a lifetime to be with you. All these centuries and yet it all comes down to this, a few moments beneath a dying sun."

Ash's heart beat hard and his breath held in his throat. He'd said things to Rani, things he should have said to Parvati. His lips were so dry. He didn't want her to say any more, but he wanted, hoped, desperately, she'd say the things he couldn't find the right words for, speak for both of them.

C'mon, Ash. Just tell her.

A horn blasted out below. The sun had dropped beneath the sea and the last of its red light faded from caressing the clouds, letting them turn black.

331

❖

Cries rose from the dark city, and drums and howls and screams. Torches danced and whirled in feverish exaltation.

Ash got up as he heard footsteps approach.

Ashoka stood at the cave mouth, bow in hand. He pointed towards Kampani. "We're needed below." Then he turned and left.

Ash brushed the dust from his trousers. His head was spinning with what Parvati had just said. How could he answer? If anyone felt unworthy, it was him. He should go after Ashoka.

"Wait, Ash." Parvati stood beside him. She took his hand and pressed it against her cheek, her eyes closed.

If there was a moment he wanted to last for ever, this was it. Ash felt the warmth of her skin against his and watched the strands of her hair gently drift in the breeze.

Parvati kissed the back of his hand, then let it go. What else was there to say? Nothing.

More and more burning torches joined the vast star field gathering across the city. Thousands of spots of light approached the cliffs. Dark wings swooped overhead, heralded by brutish, coarse shrieks and cries. Banners made of flayed skins flapped on frames of bone.

The demon nations marched to war.

Chapter Forty-four

"Parvati and I will hold the main gates," said Rani. "You and Ashoka are to protect the people within the caverns. The rakshasas will creep in from every opening and crevasse. Then they'll make smash and grabs from the tunnels. Spiders and scorpions will form the vanguard."

"Why?" asked Ash.

"They can get into the smallest places and are poisonous. They'll cause a lot of mayhem very quickly. But they'll try to take control of the bigger tunnels to allow the other, larger predators in. Once that happens..."

"All bets are off," said Parvati. "Save who you can. There are some fishing boats hidden in a cove about ten miles north along the coast. Try to get as far from here as possible.

Ash was confused. "Why haven't we loaded people up on them already?"

Parvati sighed. "There aren't enough, Ash. And who would stay and be left behind? Look around you. There are so many families here and we've only boats enough for a hundred, maybe not even that."

Rani nodded. "We fight until there is no hope."

"There's always hope," said Ashoka.

Parvati looked at the men gathered in the cavern. They wore armour, carried their weapons and torches, gripping them so hard their knuckles were bone white. Every face, every eye, held fear, dread and determination. They were fighting for their loved ones, their friends, their families. Ash knew every one of them would fight to the bitter end.

"Follow me," said Parvati. She looked back at Ash. "Goodbye, Ash."

Ash forced a smile, trying to look as casual as he could. "See you later."

Arms and armour rattled and clanged as the troops, roughly half the warriors present, tramped out behind the two demon princesses. The rest looked to Ash and Ashoka.

Ash wasn't wearing any armour. He'd been trained in Kalari-payit and that meant being fast and flexible. He had two weapons, his katar and a sword, both newly sharpened.

Ashoka drew out the golden arrow.

Ash took a deep breath. "You ready?"

Ashoka didn't respond. He just turned the arrow around and around between his fingers.

"Savage is coming, Ashoka. I know he is. This is the end, and he'll want to witness it. He'll want to see us die and will want to gloat."

❖

"And I'll take him with this." He raised the golden arrow.

"No matter what, that's to be saved for Savage. The Kali-aastra is the only thing that can take him out. Understand?"

Ashoka nodded. "Understood."

"It all comes down to you tonight, I'm afraid," said Ash. "We both know that."

"You're the Kali-aastra too," said Ashoka.

"Not any more. It's not awakened. The last time I awakened it I had to sacrifice myself. I'm not sure that trick will work twice."

Ashoka nodded, and turned to his men. "We'll take the upper levels."

Ash watched him leave. So confident, so inspiring. No wonder they thought Rama walked among them. With a man like that fighting beside you, you might believe you could beat anyone: man, demon, even god.

More horns echoed from the distance. The men with him looked around the cavern, trying to work out which direction the sound was coming from. It didn't matter. It was coming, and that was all they needed to know.

Ash drew his sword and turned to his people. "I feel I should have some speech prepared or something. I don't, sorry. I've fought since the day man first picked up a rock. I've fought for every cause there's been. Freedom. Tyranny. For glory. For gold. For a patch of earth. It's all rubbish." He tested the blade. Someone had taken a lot of care making it very, very sharp. "Just think of your wife's touch, your child's smile, your mother's kiss. These are the only things worth fighting for, worth dying for. You'll see sights that'll

❖

turn your guts, make you shake, make you want to flee. Fear is natural, but you must stand fast. Think of them, and you'll find the courage to challenge the gods." He settled the sword in his hand. "Come with me."

He tried to summon faces to his mind. He had fleeting thoughts of his parents, of Lucky, the family he loved. But one face came clearest of all, the one person he'd fought for throughout the ages.

Parvati.

Chapter Forty-five

Total war. No respite. No quarter. No pity, compassion, humanity. Ash fought until his sword broke, his katar was blunted, and then he picked up rocks. Everything was a blur. He fought until his body was a mass of pain, muscles exhausted, skin cut and bleeding.

That was the only way to fight demons.

He watched men torn from limb to limb, their heads severed from their necks, organs ripped out by claw and fang. The rakshasas were deformed monstrosities, walking nightmares of chaos, half glimpsed in the firelight of the tunnels and caves. Spiderish *things* scuttled across the ceilings, tangling their victims in webs and reeling them away into the dark. Wolves stalked the chambers, fresh blood on their snouts. Vast waves of rats scurried through the passages, squeezing and overwhelming the fleeing refugees, consuming them with thousands of bites.

There was a cluster of men with him now. They paused, catching their breath, trying to work out which way to run, whose screams to follow. Ash trod on a discarded blade, a single flat slice of steel with one edge sharpened and cloth wrapped around the end for a handle. Sweat turned to steam on his burning, feverish skin. The caves became a furnace, filled with hot, stale air. He'd gathered refugees, wedged them between his men for their protection.

"Time to break for those boats," he said to no one in particular. He patted the nearest man on the back; his name was Nabeel, he thought. "Make for the lower levels and come out via one of the caves down there. Then stay close to the cliffs and you should be able to make your way to the boats. Understood?" He waited. The man didn't move. "Well, go on then."

"You're not coming?"

"What? And miss all this fun?" said Ash. "Good luck." He slapped the man on the back and set off in the other direction.

Where were the others?

Ash wove through the dark tunnels. Sounds of fighting trembled from down paths, through rents in the rock, out of secret chambers. He moved steadily upwards, towards the main gates. The tunnels widened and the bodies piled up.

No sign of Savage. He'd been so sure he'd be here, coordinating the battle, watching it unfold. But perhaps he was so sure of victory he couldn't be bothered to witness it.

Ash was going to die without any chance of revenge. That angered him.

Claws struck rock and a pair of yellow eyes shone ahead of him. The creature hissed and in the dimness Ash saw black scales flex as it tensed its legs. Then it charged, a giant lizard, low to the ground, thrashing its tail from side to side, long red tongue darting between its jaws.

Ash flicked up a discarded spear. He jumped sideways, kicked off the wall and thrust the tip square between the creature's shoulders at the base of the neck. Spinal column severed, the lizard collapsed. Ash stood on its head and heaved the spear all the way through. The beast gurgled and coughed up dark red blood. Ash twisted the spear back out.

He ran until he met a crowd of refugees. They were fleeing, pouring out of side tunnels into the wide thoroughfare that led to the main gates, carrying what few belongings they had or just running empty-handed but with blind panic in their eyes. They knocked over those who were too slow, and Ash had to push and shove to help a man back up before he was trampled. There were lupine howls from behind and the people ran like sheep.

We're being herded.

But he couldn't stop them. Ash shouted for them to turn back, but no one could hear him over their own screaming.

Then, carried by this tide of fear, Ash stumbled out into the main cavern and to the third gate.

Two Carnivals of Flesh tore at the walls, huge, cumbersome behemoths crouched so as to reach into the low-roofed area of the rear of the central cavern. Harpoons bristled over their bodies and another boomed from its launcher, punching through a metre of melded flesh, sacks of blood bursting out, the broken bodies twitching and falling off the Carnivals as they reassembled themselves around the fresh wound.

Parvati and Rani fought side by side upon the battlements, knee-deep in the dead. The urumi sang its song of slaughter and Rani's fangs, her two lethal tulwar swords, reaped heads and limbs with each swing.

Ash watched Ashoka jump from ledge to ledge, his bow launching arrow upon arrow. He kicked off a spider rakshasa and knocked back a pair of rodent demons with a thrust of his bow. Men fought beside him, fighting beyond their exhaustion and fear with broken weapons or their bare hands. Ashoka was the eye of the storm.

But he can't beat them all, thought Ash. *There are just too many of them.*

The refugees flooded out into the melee, pushing from the rear, unaware of the vast demon army in front of them, just desperate to escape those behind.

The gates themselves had been ripped down. Ash struck left and right, but it made no difference; when one demon fell, another two, another four, took its place.

Ashoka spotted Ash, and the danger. He signalled and shouted for the people to stop, but it was hopeless; his voice was drowned out by the cacophony of battle.

Metre by metre they were pushed forward. Soldiers abandoned their posts to protect the swelling mass of frightened civilians, their own people.

What could he do? It had turned into a rout. Ash grabbed

❖

a woman who was trying to hang on to a dozen crying children. "Stick with me!" he shouted. She stared, then dumbly nodded.

The first and second walls were utterly demolished. The trench was so thickly filled with dead demons you could just walk across it now. Ashoka scrambled down the cliff face and beat his way to Ash's side. His face was a mask of blood, yet he smiled. "Still alive, I see."

"Pleased to see you too," said Ash. "The Kali-aastra?"

Ashoka drew it from his quiver. "Safe. But..."

"No Savage yet."

Then the refugees stopped. The soldiers paused and Ash pushed his way forward.

In front of the cave mouth stood, waited, the demon army, swollen so large that there was hardly a patch of sand visible from the cliff all the way to the sea. Countless torches illuminated the hungry, bloodthirsty faces of jackals, of bears and crocodiles and things neither one animal nor another, but built out of evil fury and hate. Swords and crude knives and claws and talons and teeth caught the amber light of the flames, and the moon shone down on horns and scales and fangs.

Behind them the howls lessened; their job was done. The cave complex had been overwhelmed. Ash caught a glimpse of movement above him and saw the roof was teeming with black hairy spiders. The wings of bat rakshasas beat the air as they swooped in and out of hundreds of alcoves and cracks too high and inaccessible for humans.

Parvati and Rani joined him. Rani's armour hung by its

straps and Parvati's scales were soaked with gore. Ashoka stood ready, another arrow notched.

"What are they waiting for?" asked someone.

Ash looked around. The ruined gates were filled with their people. Even the elderly men had weapons ready. Children hefted rocks in their small fists. How many of them remained? A few thousand? But every one of them was going to go down fighting. They'd gone far beyond fear and now all that remained was steel resolve. "The rakshasas are afraid of us."

Parvati shook blood out of her hair. "They want to finish this, but they know however they do it, it will cost them. No one wants to be the first to die."

Rani spoke. "There's been enough death." She stepped forward, into the no-man's-land between the two armies.

What's she doing? They'll kill her.

Ash stepped forward, but Parvati stopped him. "Let her try."

There were about twenty metres between them, a space where dwelt only the dead, demon and human alike. And into this silence went Rani, swords aloft, head proud and defiant.

A spear thrown, an arrow fired or rock hurled true, a sudden charge, and it would be over. But no one moved.

The only sound was the waves beating against the empty ship hulls down on the shore.

"You know me," said Rani. She didn't shout but her voice carried to every ear. "You knew my father. Many of you fought beside us in our last war against humankind. You know what followed.

"War is coming; this is but the first battle. The seeds we sow tonight on these sands, seeds of hate, of cruelty and pain, will only lead to the most bitter of harvests." She cast her gaze over the demon army. "Is that what you want?

"Rakshasa or human — I don't choose one side over the other. I choose both. Rakshasas, we are creatures of eternity. We remember and know so much, have acquired wisdom over centuries. And how do we use our wisdom? In games of tyranny. Humans, we live for the moment. Our passion drives us to achieve so much in our brief lives, to reach such heights, but how we squander that fire and chase the most temporal of things: wealth, fame, illusions that last as long as a candle flame.

"You have a choice today, and only today." Rani turned her swords in her hands. "Take up your weapons and slaughter each other. One will conquer the other by dawn's light, but the victor will know no peace. No restful sleep will come to him, nor to his family. There will be no comfort and he will watch his children grow with one eye on the door and one hand on his sword, ever afraid. He will fear uprisings, he will fear rebellion, he will fear the night his slave comes seeking revenge for the defeat they suffered tonight. It might come in a year, or a hundred, but it will come. You have lived long enough to know this is the truth."

Rani thrust both swords into the sand. She buried them until they were half-blade-deep. Then she stepped back, holding out her hands to show she was defenceless. "And this is the other choice. Choose this and you will sleep peacefully. You will rest knowing the one you fought today guards you as you slumber. You will watch your children grow to joy, knowing that the man you once sought to kill will protect them as he would his own. Two choices. Follow the path of war. Or follow me."

The air did not stir; it was as if the world held its breath. No one moved. All eyes remained on Rani.

We're too different, rakshasa and human. How can there be common ground between us?

The hate ran too deep and for too long. There was barely peace between humans, and they were all but identical. Mankind made war upon itself over the smallest things: the colour of skin, the style of clothing, the way they worshipped. So how could there ever be peace between demon and human?

Then someone threw down their sword. The weapon struck a pebble and the sound rang out over the battlefield.

Another dropped their shield.

Ash searched the crowd, trying to find the one who'd done it, his heart racing with... hope. A small hope. Hope and trust. Trust that between the two armies there was something they both valued. He looked at the demons, watched the strands of webs drift overhead. He looked at the blade in his hand, the blood encrusted on the chipped metal. He let it fall.

The trickle became a stream, then a river, then a tidal wave as rakshasas and humans alike discarded their weapons. People stared around them in bewilderment, as if waking from a nightmare.

Ash let out a breath.

Rakshasas crossed the ground and bent down before Rani.

❖

They touched her feet, prostrating themselves in the bloody sands. They kissed her hands.

Ash blinked, wiping sweat (it was sweat, not tears) off his face. He was the Eternal Warrior; he'd been in countless battles. None had ended like this.

Parvati took his hand and looked at him. "Ash..."

The cliffs trembled. Rocks cracked and boulders shook free, bouncing down and crushing the rocks and the shanty towns beneath. The sands swirled, gaining a strange sort of life.

The waves rose and stirred with anger.

Ash had known it. He picked up his sword. There would never be peace. War was eternal.

Ashoka steadied himself as the ground shook. "What's going on?"

"He's here," said Ash.

Lights burst in the night sky. The air groaned, a deep sound that went down into the bones. People screamed.

The ships on the shore began to bend, to mutate. The gigantic structural beams twisted like rubber and rebuilt themselves into legs. The panels peeled themselves into new skins. The fields of spotlights tore free from their frames, blinked into life and reassembled themselves into immense unblinking eyes.

Ash had seen stone statues come to life, even one almost thirty metres high. But these towered over a hundred metres. The dozen dismantled ships merged together to create three monstrous, living automatons.

One was a spider, striding out of the sea on eight legs

the size of tower blocks. Cables swung from its body, and cogs and engines and gears screamed into life, controlling its movements. Its eyes were made of hundreds of spotlights and its gaze cast a field of brilliant white over the panicking crowds.

The second metal beast was a giant lion, its teeth over ten metres in length, its claws made of iron girders. It swiped one paw across the beach and bodies went flying.

Then the third strode out of the sea. An elephant. It trampled dozens of people under its massive feet, demolishing more with each swing of its tusks. It was the size of a cathedral, its trumpeting so loud the cliffs cracked. Electric sparks jumped from its body, rising around its legs and over the beast's gigantic frame, framing it with an azure haze.

A palanquin rested on its back. A mockery of a maharajah's silken seat, made of black iron. The canopy was ribbed steel and barbed wire. It was a dozen metres in diameter, with room for fifty people, but on it was only one. Stark white against the black sky he stood, a cane in his hand. The wind ruffled his long blonde locks.

The rakshasas charged. Some formed a wall around Rani, but in moments they were overwhelmed. Chaos reigned and the slaughter began again.

And Savage, high up on the imperial elephant, laughed.

Chapter Forty-six

Two eagle rakshasas swooped down towards Savage, shrieking with their talons thrust forward. Savage raised his tiger-headed cane, its ruby eyes flashed and the two raptors burst into flames and plummeted into the sea.

The elephant marched along the beach, destroying everything in its path. The lion roared and leaped among the army, human and demon, and the spider crawled over the cliffs, hunting. Hundreds of smaller spiders grew from its body and scuttled into the tunnels.

The human–rakshasa army might have won, but with Savage here, many of the demons, most of those infected by his chemicals and others awestruck by his presence, sided with him.

Savage was a disease – he infected everything about him.

A howl carried across the sky, fierce and filled with bloodlust and the joys of slaughter.

❖

Ash gasped. "Jackie..."

A beast leaped across the battlefield, huge as a house and packed with muscle.

What had Savage done?

Jackie threw back her head and roared with manic glee. Her mouth was red, and broken bodies hung from her massive fangs, each as long as Ash's arm. Her forearms rose like columns and were covered in gore. Spears, blades and bullets merely bounced off her thick tawny pelt.

Parvati stumbled up next to Ash, her own eyes wide in horror. "Savage has transformed her. He's filled her with too much power. Look at her."

The flesh mutated under Jackie's pelt and she shivered with pain. Her eyes were feverish and she grinned so tightly her lips bled. She snapped her jaws and swallowed three men whole.

Then she saw them.

"Go." Ash pushed Ashoka away. "Go after Savage."

"We'll fight her together," said Ashoka.

Jackie shook her mane as men crowded around her, stabbing and slashing with whatever they had. She barely noticed until, with one swipe of her forepaw, she turned them to red ruined smears. She licked her claws.

"No." Ash gritted his teeth. "You have to stop Savage. Leave her to me."

"You'll never beat her. Look at her!" said Ashoka.

"Then so be it." He turned to Ashoka. "Now go! Get Savage."

Parvati flicked out her urumi. "Ready?" Her fangs were extended and slick with venom.

❖

Ash picked up a discarded sword and moved it from one hand to the other until he got a comfortable grip. "Ready."

Jackie saw them and hunched down, her mane bristled with excitement and her claws dug into the ground. She giggled and her tail swished back and forth, flicking up huge clumps of blood-soaked sand.

She leaped.

The wind blast almost sent them both flying as the hulking mass sprang at them. When Jackie landed, the earth cracked, and suddenly Ash was airborne, spinning head over heels from the impact.

He hit the ground and rolled as a cloud of fetid breath blew down over him. Jackie's teeth snapped closed, centimetres from where his head had been.

Ash stabbed hard with the sword, but it didn't even scratch her. Jackie twitched her shoulder and Ash was knocked metres back.

Gritting his teeth, he forced himself back up. Jackie had to have a weak spot. Once, when he'd had all of Kali's gifts, he'd have seen them, perfect golden lights shining upon his target's body. Now all he could see was a mountain of muscle.

The urumi sang and Jackie snarled as the serpent sword cut four shallow lines across her face, a chaotic, hideous hybrid of a jackal's head and a woman's face.

Jackie turned angrily towards Parvati.

Parvati launched herself at the monstrous beast, Jackie snarling and snapping at the serpent princess. Fresh wounds from the urumi cut her pelt, but Parvati hissed with frustration as the weapon merely scratched the gigantic jackal

349

❖

rakshasa. Ash knew what she was trying to do — get close enough to bite. But Jackie kept her at bay.

Ash hauled himself up using a broken spear. He couldn't breathe without pain. He felt his lungs were being sliced. His chest was black with bruises and he spat out blood.

He stood, trembling with effort, among the dead. Nameless men littered the ground.

They died trying to help me and I didn't even know their names.

He should know them. He should have their names carved into his soul.

Jackie howled and a sea of fresh rakshasas answered her call. More and more piled across the battlefield, devouring all that stood in their way. Ash watched helplessly as Parvati was surrounded. Her urumi flashed like lightning and limbs and heads were parted from bodies, but second by second more encircled her. She screamed with rage, and she killed.

Jackie approached Ash, her mane soaked with blood, her eyes on fire with madness.

Parvati lashed left and right, but she couldn't get to him. "Run, Ash!"

Run? He could barely crawl.

Ash gripped the spear with both hands. "Come and get it, Jackie. Let me ram this down your throat."

Jackie broke it as if it was a matchstick.

She cuffed Ash backhanded and something in his chest cracked as he struck the ground and lay there, beaten.

He was human. He broke. He bled. His body could not support his will. He lay on the ground, and looked up.

❖

He'd done everything he could. But it was over. Now all that was left was to die. "I hope you choke," he snarled.

Jackie bore down upon him, opening her jaws.

"No!" Parvati's cry rang out across the battlefield.

A thunderbolt, a thunderbolt of gold, flew through the air, into the jackal demon's eye. It whispered in, then exploded through the back of her skull, hurling fur, skull, brain high into the sky. The force lifted her up into the air. She blazed with white fire, and as she rose, turning in midair, the flames multiplied and filled the night's battle with blistering light. A wind swept across the sands and Ash gasped as the heat almost overwhelmed him.

Jackie was obliterated before she hit the ground. She simply disintegrated into billions of particles that vanished in the trailing wind.

"No..." Ash whispered. He should be dead.

Aching, bleeding, ribs broken, he struggled but couldn't get up.

A figure stood over him. "Let me help."

"Ashoka, what have you done...?"

"I wasn't just going to stand by and watch you die."

Ashoka lifted Ash up. Ash groaned as he rested his arm over Ashoka's shoulder.

Ashoka held an empty bow in his hand. He'd shot the Kali-aastra at Jackie, killing her and saving Ash's life.

But dooming them all.

Chapter Forty-seven

"I'm going after Savage," said Ash.

Ashoka shook his head. "No. We'll both go. I'll distract him and you finish him off. You're the Kali-aastra."

Ash rubbed his thumb, out of habit. "There's only one Kali-aastra and you've just wasted it. You should have let me die."

"Forget it, Ash! That's not how it should be." Ashoka grabbed his arm and swung him round. "Look around you. Look."

Men fought demons. With swords, spears, stones, their bare hands. A boy sobbed, cradling a man in his arms. He rocked back and forth, wiping the man's face with a rag.

Two others lay dead, their bodies entwined, their fingers grasping each other's. High up on the cliffs the women wailed as the demons screamed. He watched one rakshasa drag another free from a melee, shielding the monster with his own body, then falling as the arrows pierced him.

"Aren't there enough deaths out there without adding your own?" said Ashoka.

Ash saw sons take up weapons to defend their fathers. He saw demons gathering up their dead, crying over fallen comrades. The carnage was endless, and so was the grief. Each life gone resonating across so many others.

A sharp stabbing pain shot up from Ash's thumb.

"It is a paradox," he whispered, "but I think I get it."

"What?"

Ash scratched his thumb. "I'm going after Savage."

"You've a plan?"

"I've a hope, Ashoka. Just a hope." He held out his hand. "Goodbye, brother." Ashoka didn't move. He met Ash's fierce gaze. Then he took Ash's hand and shook it. "May the gods go with you."

Ash ran towards the sea. It wasn't easy as he had to force each step out of his battered body, but he didn't look back.

The beach where the elephant stood was a quagmire as the sea and blood mixed to create a sucking bog.

The ground shook under its feet. In its wake lay hundreds. Savage stood above it all, summoning fire and lightning, revelling in his power, certain of his victory. Ash waded into the sea, the waves rising over him, as he approached a leg the size of a tower block. It was made of girders and beams and patched with steel panels. Cables ran within the exposed structure like veins and sinew.

Ash stared up as the elephant's body passed overhead.

❖

Cables dangled loose and he grabbed one, swinging himself up on to the leg. His joints screamed in pain as he reached out and wrapped an arm around a beam as the leg rose, water pouring from it. Up and up it went, stepping over the crowds clustered beneath it, the wind howling through its body.

Ash climbed.

Chapter Forty-eight

The elephant swayed and Ash struggled to steady himself. The wind roared this high up and he felt as if he was in another world, far from the death and destruction.

Savage had his back to him, but Ash had dropped his sword in the climb. Savage laughed and thrust with his cane and a wall of fire erupted along the beach. He wove it in this direction and that, the wall responded and rolled across the sands, consuming all in its path.

Ash stepped over the low steel wall of the palanquin. The floor was a network of steel, there was a carpet of barbed wire, but there were gaps, and one slip or misplaced step and he'd tumble a hundred metres, if he wasn't smashed upon the beams that comprised the elephant's body.

"It's even better than I imagined," said Savage. Slowly he turned. "Thank you, Ash."

❖

"You're proud of this?"

"Who will defy me after tonight?" said Savage. "I'll rebuild my factories, soon the RAVN-I will flow and within weeks I'll have it flying over a dozen cities. The world is mine. How can you deny it?"

"You've created a world of darkness. That's nothing to be proud of."

Savage scowled. "I've saved the world, but you're too small-minded to see it."

Ash made his way closer. Savage didn't try to stop him. With the Koh-i-noor embedded in his chest, he was invulnerable against any mortal weapon.

"Why are you here?" asked Savage. "You really think you can stop me?" He smoothed his hair from his face. "Do you want to try? Come on, Ash. Shall I show you how it's done?" He wedged his cane into the floor and pulled off his jacket, exposing the bare flesh beneath.

The ten skulls shone upon his chest, glowing with an eerie white light that looked almost radioactive. The skin seemed to glisten, as if his diamond heart had filled his veins with crystal.

"Are you ready?" said Savage, holding his fists up in a mocking gesture.

Ash screamed as his arms pulsed. He saw his bones flex, push and warp. Ash stared in horror as he watched them move under his skin. Bruises swelled, ugly and purple, as the blood vessels were torn by the moving bone.

Savage was mutating him.

"Hurts, doesn't it?" said Savage. "This is just a fraction

of what I suffered. I thought you should have a taste, before I kill you."

Ash gasped as his ribs twisted. Savage held him to stop him falling off their perch, but drew his fingers gently over Ash's chest. Flames licked his skin, bubbling the flesh. Ash cried out, barely able to stay conscious. But he needed to hang on.

"Why are you here?" asked Savage again. "To beg for your life? Those of your friends? Quite hopeless to even try, boy." He took hold of Ash and held him at the edge of the palanquin. "See that, Ash? See my new world? Isn't it glorious?"

Through mind-numbing pain, his vision dimming with creeping unconsciousness, Ash gazed over the battered cliffs and the carnage as thousands fought. He glimpsed flashes of light in the haze of the smoke and fire-filled darkness. He blinked. Golden lights blinked. Each one was a life.

All lives were great. So each and every passing of it was great. A Great Death. They were all around him.

Rishi had tried to tell him. So had Reggie – this was what the visions had been trying to say. Ash should have known from the very beginning. It was always about life. The Kali-aastra swelled with the power of lives you valued as great. Now Ash could see – all lives were great; all deaths. It didn't matter whose.

Ash had been seeing it through his human perspective. The lives that *he'd* valued – his uncle's and aunt's, Rishi's, his sister's and Gemma's. These were the lives that were important to him.

❖

But a god's perspective encompassed all of humanity. Kali rescuing the baby from the battlefield. A child that could be anyone, and everyone. All of us.

I understand.

He tingled as images snapped in his mind.

A young man who played the sitar. Ash felt the strings on his fingers. The hours he'd studied, night after night, to become a musician. He had played in small, cramped restaurants and in tiny temples down alleyways to a handful of people. But each listener had been touched by him, even if all they remembered was a single note. His life had been great.

Another life entered him. This was a builder, a maker of bricks, and each house he'd built had a part of him in it. Families sheltered and lived within the walls he'd raised. Another great life.

A woman's soul slipped into the Kali-aastra. A cook who'd worked decades on a roadside stall. Her chapattis had been thin as tissue, and her dhal watery and spicy, and there were coach drivers and passengers and other travellers who sought her out when they pulled in for their meal.

No kings died tonight. No great rulers or masters of the world. Just people. The people Ash had passed every day of his life without even noticing. Now he knew what each life had meant and realised they had all been great.

Demons too. Ancient and cruel, but loyal to their own cause and desperate to rebuild their nation and raise their people back to honour. They had had great lives too. How could they not?

Ally and enemy died out there and each life that passed entered Ash and he shed tears for each and every one, closing his eyes as the lives began to enter him. He felt them feed the Kali-aastra.

Chapter Forty-nine

*A*sh surged with power as all the deaths, all great, added their energies to him. Liquid fire flooded his arteries, shocking every nerve. The energies pulsed with his heartbeat and the heat spread through his bones, muscles and skin, reknotting wounds, resetting limbs, healing his injuries. The grotesque bruises faded to nothing.

"It's not... No, it can't happen," said Savage. He backed away. He snarled. "No!" He slammed his palms together.

An inferno consumed them. Jets of white-hot fire roared over the palanquin. The elephant shook and the steel frame around Ash buckled and melted, blasted with megatons of explosive force.

Ash bent before the hurricane of power. He should be atomised. The shock wave ended abruptly and though he stood in molten metal, Ash did still stand.

❖

I see it all.

Time. Life. Death. He could see the ribbons of destiny unweaving all around him. He could see the brightness of souls down below. He could see Savage.

The golden god was gone. This was Savage as he truly was. His body was monstrous, a wretched, withered thing with skeletal limbs and sunken eyes. The ten skulls smouldered with sickly light, but within Savage beat the bright, white crystalline heart. The Brahma-aastra. The source of all his power.

"It's over, Savage," said Ash. "You've lost."

"No," spat Savage. "I am the master of the ten sorceries. I cannot be beaten. I cannot lose."

Wave after wave of magic lashed out from Savage's fingertips. The ten skulls blazed upon his chest. Fire, ice, thunder and lightning. He brought them down upon Ash, but they fell from his shoulders without leaving a mark.

Savage grinned. "I'll go back. I'll go back and find you in your crib. I'll smother you on the day of your birth."

Ash shook his head. "Wherever you go, Savage, I'll be there. You cannot escape Kali."

Savage leered. "Just watch me."

Ash stepped forward. "No. Your time has come."

He punched Savage in the chest.

Flesh and bone tore under his fingers and Ash snapped hold of Savage's heart and ripped it out.

Savage gasped, clutching the bloody hole in his chest. The ten skulls blazed brighter. "What...?" He groaned, bent double, but, through insane will, did not fall.

❖

Ash opened his fist. A bloody stone rested in his palm. The stone was a diamond. Light burned from within it — a dazzling myriad of colours, fractured by the numberless planes and faces, shone out, growing brighter and brighter, flooding the night with their brilliance.

Chapter Fifty

S avage's body warped. The skin melted and the bones bent, twisting his limbs at unnatural angles. He strained his neck as his spine stretched, tearing itself out from his back.

All that magic — he can't contain it any longer.

Ravana had built himself a body of gold to withstand the vast magic coursing through him. No mortal flesh could survive the ten sorceries. Only the Koh-i-noor had kept Savage whole.

Savage clawed at the hole in his chest, but even as he tugged, his fingers mutated, turning back on themselves, bones fusing together. He cried out, and it was a terrible, inhuman screech.

The ten skulls glowed fiercely as Savage tried to use his magic to save himself. But it only accelerated the deformations.

Then, one by one, the skulls dimmed. They sank into his chest, each one's mark fading from his skin.

Their power transferring to Ash.

Savage's life force, all three centuries of it, all he'd been and learned and done, began to enter Ash. His atoms trembled. His chest burned. It was pure agony, as if someone had pressed an iron against him. He felt as if the heat was going straight through him.

Kali was a greedy goddess, the Kali-aastra for ever hungry. The more death that surrounded it, the more it fed. Ash was taking it all.

Savage as a young soldier, his first battle in India. Standing with his sabre in one hand, his flintlock pistol in the other.

Savage in the court of the maharajah of Lahore. Meeting Parvati for the first time. Stealing her father's scrolls.

Savage in a temple, his fingers around the throat of a monk. The first brand of magic upon his chest.

Savage gazing at a mirror, seeing the corruption growing on his face, the cancerous lumps and flaking, the bleeding skin. Savage smashing the mirror with his tiger-headed cane.

Savage's life passed before Ash's eyes. He moaned as the burning pain multiplied on his chest.

Savage writhed on the floor. His body was nothing human, not any more. A face could still be seen in the pulsing, fleshy mass, a pair of eyes, a hole of a nose and a wretched, grinning mouth. The tongue flapped grotesquely, splashing red spittle. The limbs were spindly and reversed upon themselves. The eyes, night-black, rolled wildly within their sockets.

❖

Ash got up. He clutched his aching chest as he stood over the writhing monstrosity.

So this was Savage. Stripped of all his power.

Ash felt no triumph, not even relief. Just... pity. Even for Savage.

Death would be a relief.

Their eyes met.

Ash tightened his hands around the Koh-i-noor. "Let me finish this."

Savage nodded, then closed his eyes.

Ash squeezed. He saw the minute patterns of golden lights over the stone, the fracture points and the weaknesses and he pressed against them.

The diamond splintered. Then it burst into a million sparkling motes of crystal that were blown away across the battlefield and sea.

And Savage died. Once and for ever.

Chapter Fifty-one

Ash lowered himself to the floor. The elephant rocked, but that was the waves crashing against its now immobile body. It had no life of its own any more. Over the cliffs the giant spider too had frozen and the lion stood, its mouth open in a silent snarl.

The Carnivals of Flesh fell apart. The thousands of bodies that formed each broke free. People crawled, bewildered and terrified, out of the pulsing mass of writhing flesh.

He'd awoken the Kali-aastra within him. He'd slain Savage. Then why was he so exhausted?

He heard the rattle of bones. The jangle of skulls.

He heard her footsteps.

He should have realised. She came for the greatest of deaths. She'd come for them all.

Ash closed his eyes and prepared to greet Kali.

❖

Chapter Fifty-two

*F*ifty miles up, Kali's head is crowned by storm clouds. Her arms fan from her body in their hundreds. A necklace of skulls hangs from her neck and her skirt is made of severed arms.

The waves crash around her ankles and she raises her swords, her long red tongue hanging hungrily from her fanged mouth.

Her body is shiny and as black as oil. Her chest heaves with passion as her eyes blaze over the battlefield. Her hands, each tipped with long, curved nails, sweep the souls from the ground.

Time stops. Kali is the goddess of death, destruction and Time. Ash, a mote in her awesome shadow, slowly stands. "Kali..."

She gazes down at him.

He shivers all over. Her eyes stare deep into his soul, seeing Ash bare and naked, and seeing what he is.

The Eternal Warrior.

One of so many that have come and will follow.

❖

Ash glimpses eternity in the blackness of Kali's eyes. Whole galaxies lie within them. Her arms could encompass the universe. Wherever you go, whichever direction you take, however far, Kali lies at the end of it.

She holds out her palm. The red nails unfurl as she offers her hand to Ash.

Take it.

He wants to. He is the Kali-aastra. He is part of her.

Kali is ultimate destruction, utter annihilation.

End it all. Be at peace.

The Eternal Warrior would end. It all ends in Kali's arms.

No more reincarnations. His soul would be freed after so many thousands of years.

He could rest.

Ash looks down at the battle, frozen in the moment of Kali's coming. His friends are down there, somewhere.

Elsewhere, in another timeline, his family searches for him.

All lives are great, and Ash is not done with his quite yet.

Kali withdraws her hand.

Remain then. Remain and fight. For ever.

Ash nods. "Thank you."

Chapter Fifty-three

Ashoka climbed the inanimate elephant, following Parvati. Rani was a little way behind him.

The battle was over. Savage's magic was gone, the automatons were frozen, the rakshasas had surrendered. No one knew what to do, what should happen next.

Ashoka hung on to the elephant, high over the city. He closed his eyes and waited for the dizziness to pass.

"Wait up, Parvati," he said. She didn't.

Rani clambered up beside him. "What's wrong?"

"Can't you see? I'm hanging on for dear life."

"You've just fought against a demon army. How can you be scared now?"

Not just scared, petrified. But why? She was right. Compared to what he'd done this was nothing.

Nothing to a hero like Rama, but a big deal to an overweight fourteen-year-old boy from south London.

He'd felt it the moment he'd let go of the bowstring. Rama had disappeared that same instant. The bow felt odd, awkward. He wasn't familiar with it.

The past lives had all vanished. They'd been there to help him, to steel his nerve and to fill him with courage, skill and strength. But the battle had been won and Ashoka was just Ashoka now. Frightened and hanging on to the leg of a steel elephant.

"Why didn't Savage build a lift into this?" he asked.

"Look, there's a handhold just above you. Come on."

Ashoka opened his eyes and Rani was right beside him. She gave him a lopsided smile. "You did great."

"I didn't. It was the past lives."

"It was all you." She shook her head. "When this is over, let me tell you about Dumbo and that feather."

He followed her up. What did she mean by that? He'd known things he shouldn't have, like how to fight like a god, how to make bows and arrows, how to hit impossible targets.

But they were all from lives buried within him. He'd learned to summon them as and when he needed them. They were as much him as the air he breathed in and out of his lungs, giving him substance, bringing him life, but never staying.

Rama, Spartacus, Ashoka the emperor. They'd all come to aid him.

It took longer than he would have liked, but Ashoka got to the top. "Wow, this is epic."

The metal palanquin was molten slag, deformed into rivers

❖

of steel and dripping iron. Patches still steamed and glowed red. This high up above the city there was an eerie silence. The acrid smell of burnt flesh stung his nostrils and collected in the back of his throat.

A shape lay dissolving on the twisted frame, pink and raw. "Is that... Savage?"

Rani looked down at it, her eyes cold. "What's left of him."

She bent down and picked up something. It was a cane with a tiger-headed top made of silver. Its eyes were rubies.

"Where's Ash?" said Ashoka, suddenly panicked.

"Shh," said Rani, pointing to the rear of the palanquin.

There was Ash. And Parvati. In his arms.

Ashoka smiled. How long should he wait before interrupting?

Right, that's long enough.

"Ahem," said Ashoka. "If you've quite finished..."

"Ashoka," said Ash.

"You did it," said Ashoka.

"Savage is dead, once and for all."

Ash's clothes were burnt and his body smeared with smoke and blood. Ashoka saw something bright burning on his chest. "What's that?"

A skull brand glowed there, just over his heart. Ash touched it. "Some of Savage's power has passed to me. It's one of his masteries."

Parvati spoke. "Time."

Ashoka stared. He knew what that meant. "You're leaving?"

Ash nodded.

"But how will you be sure? What if you end up in yet another timeline?"

"I'm the Kali-aastra, brother. Kali is the mistress of Time. She will guide me."

Ash nodded to Rani, and she nodded back, smiling.

Parvati looked Ashoka up and down. "Turned out quite the hero after all."

"Thanks to you," he replied, trying not to blush.

"No, thanks to you, for saving our lives," she replied, with a bow.

Ash's brand glowed brighter. He and Parvati looked at each other, and held hands. "Are you ready?"

Parvati nodded.

And then they were gone.

Chapter Fifty-four

Waves lapped against the legs of the elephant.

The battle, the war, was over. Below them stood demon and human, and scattered over the sands, in the water and upon the rocks, were the slain.

"The only thing as terrible as defeat on a battlefield is victory," said Ashoka. Rani nodded.

A hundred thousand weary faces looked up at them. Even the vulture rakshasas and other carrion birds that had settled upon the bloody sands, silent and watchful, left their feeding to stare up at them.

Not me, thought Ashoka. *Her.*

Rani looked out towards the vast waiting army. Smoke rolled across the city from a thousand fires, and burning ashes swooped in the wind, rising up and up into the night sky as if each were a soul bound for heaven. Ashoka watched her flex her fingers, testing them to see if they had the strength to grasp what was being offered. The greatest weight in the world.

The crown.

Her father had worn it and all but destroyed his race, and had made the rakshasa a vagabond hated and cursed throughout history. Savage had sought to turn them into tyrants over humanity. Ashoka, even from here, could see the bitterness and distrust, see how fingers locked around spears, swords and axes, and how claws, fangs, talons flexed and glistened in the moonlight.

Rani, her armour drenched in blood, her swords loose in her fist, spoke. "This is as much your victory as mine, Ashoka."

"No." Ashoka looked at the mess that was Savage. "I'm retiring from the hero business."

"What will you do instead?"

What indeed? Somehow school wasn't going to feel the same now he'd saved the world. He'd been terrified but excited. He'd faced horrors, and come out the other side, alive if not unmarked. He touched the long scar over his face. Life was going to be pretty boring after all this.

Well, maybe not that boring...

Ashoka smiled. "I'm going on a date."

Ashoka took Rani's hand. They turned to face the survivors. He raised it aloft. "I give you your queen! Your rani!"

They cheered. In ragged hoarse groups. They let their weapons fall and this time for good. People embraced each other. They sobbed with relief and joy and sadness. The rakshasas added their voices so the cliffs thundered with howls and roars and the high-pitched cawing of the crows and ravens and eagles as they rose into the sky and revelled in their freedom. It was a victory. Victory for mankind and demon nations.

A chant built. Feet stamped and hands clapped. Shields were beaten and swords rang together. Voices joined together, chanting, shouting a single name.

Rani. Rani. *RANI!*

Chapter Fifty-five

$\mathcal{A}$sh holds Parvati tightly. She smells of blood and war, but he doesn't care. It's over.

How quiet it is. He feels on top of the world. Fires glow below him and the air is heavy with burning smells and thick smoke. But all he cares about is Parvati, warm against him. "We did it."

The sea that was lapping against the legs of the elephant is frozen. Droplets, lit red by the fires on the beach, sparkle like rubies suspended in the air. The wind does not move. The shadows are still.

The world waits at Ash's command.

It's so easy. Ash sees Kampani, now, before, to come. He sees the bare beach, the palm trees and the crawling turtles that once made this place their home. He sees the huts being built, the fishermen assembling their nets on the land before rowing out into the blue, empty sea.

Houses go up. Kampani grows. The Union Jack flutters over the government house. Elegant mansions grow from the vanishing jungle.

❖

The years are layered upon each other and Ash can see them all simultaneously. He sees the ships come and go. He watches a new city start, frame by frame. Towers go up, the streets shine and the sea turns from oily black to green then crystalline blue. Jungle overwhelms ruins. The turtles return.

Time is all at once. He needs just to step this side or that, and let go. A century, a minute. It's all the same.

Ash looks at Parvati. "Repeat after me..."

"What?"

"There's no place like home."

Chapter Fifty-six

Ash stood in front of his house, a hand resting on the gate. Snow fell heavily, clutching his eyelashes and blurring his view. There was a car in the drive. Ashoka's dad had driven a Range Rover. With personalised number plates. It wasn't that.

It was a dented old Ford C-Max. Dad had buckled the boot when he'd reversed into a tree. He'd sworn the tree hadn't been there when he'd parked.

Ash pushed the gate open and walked up to the door, his footsteps crunching on the fresh snow.

He fished out his keys and entered the hall. This was it. Was he home?

There were Lucky's wellies, but no riding boots. Her school hat hung on the radiator, but he couldn't spot any riding helmet.

❖

So far, so good. That didn't slow his heart down any.

The kettle rattled and he heard the toaster pop. Lucks shook cereal into a bowl and he heard his dad ask what had happened to his watch.

Ash opened the kitchen door.

Mum looked at him, and sighed. "You're dripping snow everywhere, Ash."

"Why are you calling me Ash?"

She glanced at Dad, then back at Ash. "Because that's your name?"

Ash. Not Ashoka. Ash grinned. "That's totally right."

"There it is," said Dad as he collected his watch, his scratched and familiar Seiko, off the top of the fridge and clipped it on. "Late already."

A portrait hung on the wall. It showed an Indian couple. The man stared most seriously at the camera, his hair thick and slick and combed with a razor-sharp side parting, his tie knotted tightly and his shirt spotless white. Next to him was a woman in a sari, a *puja* mark on her forehead and a large gold nose ring, the traditional wedding jewellery.

A fresh marigold garland hung over the picture.

Dad stood beside Ash and put an arm over his shoulder so they looked at the picture together. "I still miss them."

"Me too," said Ash.

They were here. His mum, his dad and his sister. Ash hugged his dad, squeezing him. He'd thought he'd lost them for ever. He felt reborn.

"What's up, son?" said Dad.

❖

Ash grinned. "There really is no place like home."

"Get ready, Ash," said Mum. "You've got ten minutes."

Ash jumped three stairs at a time. He pulled off his running top and chucked it down. He would clean up afterwards. Honest. Out came one of his T-shirts.

He stopped. There was the faint outline of a skull upon his heart and a long, thin scar ran down his chest, from just above the solar plexus almost to his belly button. Then he put the T-shirt on. It fitted like a second skin.

He was home! He wanted to shout out and tell the world. Instead Ash did a little dance on the spot.

"You look exceedingly pleased with yourself," said Parvati.

Now his grin almost split his face in two. "I wondered when you'd turn up."

She wore a heavy coat and scarf and big boots. A pile of melting snow lay beneath the window where she'd crept in. She unbuttoned the coat and tossed it over the bed, adjusting the cuffs of her dark green shirt and smoothing out her long hair. Then she looked around his room. "It's even messier than last time."

"Well, I have been busy. With other stuff."

"So it's all back to normal?" she said.

"Sure is."

"And what about Ashoka? What'll happen to him?"

Ash paused. "Oh, he'll settle down and live a long and happy life. With Gemma. They call their first daughter Parvati."

"You're joking." She looked at Ash oddly. "Aren't you?"

"I am a master of Time now. Past, present and future and all that." He smirked. It wasn't often he could surprise Parvati. But she recovered her composure almost instantly, with a huff.

"Hmm, there were moments I preferred the other version," Parvati said. "At least he had some humility."

"Sorry, but I did just repair Time. This qualifies as a Pretty Big Deal in anyone's book."

Parvati shook her head. "I'm never going to hear the end of this, am I?"

"Nope. Not for any of my future incarnations. No matter how many Eternal Warriors come after me, I seriously doubt any will top this."

"Glad to see you'll remain your usual modest self."

"But you'll love me anyway, won't you?"

She gasped. And Ash discovered demons could blush. "I have no idea what you're talking about."

"I'm pretty sure you do."

"Honestly, you're so utterly full of yourself, Ash Mistry."

"Don't you mean, 'Ash Mistry, saviour of the universe'?"

Parvati smoothed her hair and brushed her coat again, composing herself. "I have better things to hear than you blowing your own trumpet. Goodbye."

"Wait. When will I see you again?"

"Hopefully never. At least not in this lifetime."

Ash grabbed her and kissed her. Well, he planted his lips firmly on hers and held her for a second or two while she squirmed. Then Parvati pushed herself off. "Honestly. You and your hormones."

❖

"I'd do anything for you, Parvati. You know that. We've been side by side for thousands of years, but never together. Let's fix that."

"Ash!" shouted his mum. "You'll be late!"

Ash gestured to the door. "Come downstairs and meet my parents."

"I cannot believe I'm doing this," said Parvati.

"We could hold hands, if you want." He held his out.

"Shut up, Ash. Just shut up."

THE END

Acknowledgements

I started Ash almost twenty years ago. That was when I first visited an old maharajah's palace in Varanasi. Even then I knew I'd come back to it.

So there are a lot of people I'd like to thank for keeping the faith on this long, long journey.

Sarah Davies, my agent at the Greenhouse Literary Agency, has been an epic supporter of all things Ash from the moment I pitched it to her. Her wisdom has taken Ash to heights I'd never have managed on my own. Needless to say, Sarah rocks.

Nick Lake at HarperCollins is way too talented for his own good and I was very lucky to land him as my editor. He and Lily Morgan have flooded me with the most excellent advice, and if there is any real depth or meaning to this trilogy, it's down to them. I'm actually very shallow.

And a mighty HUZZAH to the rest of the HarperCollins

❖

team. I'll mention Ann-Janine, Rachel, Mary and Hannah, but there are plenty more and you are all on my Christmas-card list.

Huge thanks to the team at Foyles Bookshop: Jen, Sam, Neil and Jo. They've patiently listened to Ash exploits and guided him (and me) all the way from first drafts to the shelf.

Jane, my office manager. To John, my harshest and best critic. To Kristian and to all the friends I've made along the way at schools, libraries and bookshops. Ash couldn't have done it without you.

My parents opened my eyes to what was out there, and my sisters have been companions along the way. And finally, my thanks to my wife and children. You are my greatest inspiration.